The Death Factory

Also by Joe Domenici

Bringing Back the Dead

THE DEATH FACTORY

A NOVEL

JOE DOMENICI

THOMAS DUNNE BOOKS
ST. MARTIN'S PRESS NEW YORK

This is a work of fiction. All of the characters, organizations, and events portrayed in this novel are either products of the author's imagination or are used fictitiously.

THOMAS DUNNE BOOKS.
An imprint of St. Martin's Press.

Printed in the United States of America. For information, address St. Martin's Press, 175 Fifth Avenue, New York, N.Y. 10010.

www.thomasdunnebooks.com
www.stmartins.com

Library of Congress Cataloging-in-Publication Data

Domenici, Joe.
The death factory / Joe Domenici.—1st ed.
p. cm.
ISBN 978-0-312-57030-9
1. Undercover operations—Fiction. 2. Egypt—Fiction. I. Title.
PS3604.O455D43 2011
813'.6—dc22

2011009349

First Edition: August 2011

10 9 8 7 6 5 4 3 2 1

To my mother and father.

I am who I am thanks to them.

ACKNOWLEDGMENTS

JIM SIMPSON DESERVES THANKS FOR ALLOWING the use of his and his family's names. The same thanks again to Fred Custer, Dave Hargis, and Neci Marr. Fred Custer deserves special praise for his encouragement and for selling *Bringing Back the Dead* from San Diego to Las Vegas and for only requesting his character get a wheelchair with a weapons platform.

Thanks to Andrea for translating the German. Jim Riggs and the Calvinist ghost of Larry Yoder earned thanks for reading early draft material. Thanks to Shameek the devious for providing the onion trick and turning me on to the CheyTac.

Special thanks to Trevor Paglen, who allowed me the use of

material from the amazing book *Torture Taxi*. Anyone seeking the real story behind the CIA extraordinary rendition transportation methods need look no further than that book.

Big thanks to John Paver of CheyTac USA for reading the material I wrote on their rifles and correcting early errors. Truly, an amazing rifle system.

Henry Schaffer deserves thanks for trying to help me understand big money matters and assisting in the German translations.

"Tee" deserves a big thanks for helping me understand Africa better. Thanks also to Matthias Fluckiger of Switzerland for making some needed corrections.

Sherry Evans deserves special praise for doing her mojo magic grammar-correcting and proofing the manuscript. Hercules had an easier task cleaning out the Augean stables.

My ever-growing thanks to my editor, Tom Dunne, John Schoenfelder, Kat Brzozowski, and Marcia Markland at St. Martin's Press. Everyone there and at Macmillan Publishing deserves deep thanks. Without all of their efforts we authors would be an unsung lot.

Of course, big thanks to the women at the post office—Sandra, Cindy, and Marisa, my biggest fans.

As always, any errors are to be blamed on the author.

There are those who may survive the field of fire unscathed.
There are those who may suffer wounds and illnesses.
There are those who may fight in the arena of the
prisoner-of-war camp . . .
Let it be said, "They fought their battle with honor."

—FM 21-78 Prisoner-of-War Resistance, December 1981

The only concern we had was getting the best security for our people. If we thought Martians could provide it, I guess we would have gone after them.

—A. B. "Buzzy" Krongard, August 2006

The war will be won in large measure by forces you do not know about, in actions you will not see and in ways you may not want to know about, but we will prevail.

—A. B. "Buzzy" Krongard, October 2001

CAPTURE

CHAPTER 1

Article II. I will never surrender of my own free will.

—FM 21-78 Prisoner-of-War Resistance, December 1981

JIM SIMPSON NOW KNEW HE WAS a man marked for death. If he hadn't already been working on the procedures for the last week, there was no way that he could have gotten almost everything done. He had laid down most of the needed groundwork during that week. That work had exposed him. It was only his overhearing the order to grab him alive at all costs that had sent him running to the com room.

Jim Simpson looked average. Average height and weight—a few extra pounds starting to stay on since his recent duties were more deskbound, far away from his previous active duty service as a U.S. Army Ranger. Dark hair, cut short for the desert heat of

Iraq. In spite of that heat he sported a thick beard and mustache. His eyes, a deep hazel, took in everything around them. Most people seeing him on the street would label him your average American.

He had left the break room of Protective Integrated Services after drinking a cup of coffee when he had come close to the major's office. As he approached the open door, he heard his name and froze. The major was briefing his paid men to grab Simpson. They didn't think he was in the building. That was a mistake.

Simpson knew he was trapped then. He could make it back to the front door, but the guard there might now be alerted. He couldn't take the chance. He decided to get the messages out. With his office now out of reach, the only place he knew he could do that was behind the locked steel door of the com room. That was in the back of the building, on the other side of the major's open door and then through the massive warehouse where the hundreds of cases of weapons, ammo, explosives, and other military supplies were piled high in crates. He knew he had to try. If he could get past the major's door, he might get to the com room.

Walk or run? Words his father had long drilled into him ran through his mind: *He who hesitates is lost.*

Simpson decided to walk past the door and run if he had to. Maybe they wouldn't see him. Taking a deep breath, he crossed the hallway in front of the major's door. He almost made it.

"There he is!" the major barked, looking up from behind his desk.

Simpson didn't hear the rest. He was off and running like a fox dodging the hounds. He was glad he had his Nike running shoes on as he took off. He put all he had into escape.

The men chasing him yelled at him to stop. He just kept going.

Boom!

A round slammed into the wall beside him. These men coming for him knew how to shoot. Whoever fired that round hadn't been set and must have just let a round fly on the run. Simpson had thought he was running as fast as he could. He found a new speed.

"No guns!" the major's voice boomed through the hall. "Take him alive."

The chase was on. Simpson slammed the release bar downward, opening the door to the warehouse, and ran into the large space. He veered left just in case the major's order not to shoot hadn't been heard by all. Now, if he could make it to the com room and lock the steel door, he might get done what he needed to do.

The heavy thuds from the leather boot soles of the men chasing him seemed to be getting closer and closer. With his chest aching already, he knew he couldn't outdistance these men for long. They were generally much younger and in far better shape then he was. Too much time behind the computer during the last few months. With his life on the line, he found still another speed, a still faster gear.

One man chasing him broke ahead of the pack. He was some sort of super sprinter. The others were a good thirty or forty feet back, but this one, he was gaining. Simpson imagined the super sprinter's breath on the back of his neck. He would never make it, the way the man was gaining on him. He had to do something and do it fast.

Simpson saw his chance. Just ahead, leaning against one of the large wooden crates, was a four-foot crowbar used for prying the crates open. He knew he would only get one shot. He had to stop the super sprinter.

As he approached the crowbar, he reached down and grabbed it on the fly. He didn't hesitate. Taking the dark steel in both fists, he turned and swung with everything he had. He was amazed at how slowly everything seemed to move at that point, how totally he was in control of everything. His mind didn't miss a detail.

The sprinter wasn't expecting an attack, but he still reacted quickly. He leaned away from the attack and threw his left arm up to block the blow. Had Simpson's strike been aimed at the man's upper body, it would not have worked. The man was too fast and well trained for that. But Simpson hadn't aimed for the man's upper body.

With every ounce of force and rage within him, Jim Simpson sent the steel downward toward the man's legs. The man's feet were already committed. He couldn't dodge the blow.

Simpson heard the snap of breaking bone as the crowbar smashed against the sprinter's knee. The man went down in a heap of screaming pain. Simpson didn't wait around. He was off and running again before the rest of the men chasing him even caught up to the wounded man.

Simpson turned past the last row of crates and saw the com room door. His lungs were aching. His calves felt like Jell-O. He ignored those pains.

He flung open the com room door and knew he would make it. Taking a quick glance back, he smiled at those chasing him. He slammed the door shut and threw the two solid steel bolts home. He was safe for a few moments. He hoped he would have enough time to do what needed to be done.

He paused a few seconds, leaning against the door, before he sat down in front of the bank of computers. He knew he didn't have much time. When he reached up to log on to the system, he found that he was still holding the crowbar in a white-knuckled death grip. He dropped it, and it clanged onto the cement floor. He turned to the keyboard and started typing.

He was still waiting for his password to be accepted when the hammering on the door began. From the sound of it, they must have found something heavy to use as a battering ram. Every thud against the door pushed a dent into it. It was only a matter of time until the very determined men on the outside of that door forced their way in.

Ignoring the hammering on the door, Simpson kept typing. He needed to send out two e-mails. The only question in his mind was whether he would have enough time to get the two e-mails off. Would the steel door hold long enough? If he failed, he would certainly be killed. If he got them sent, he had a chance to live.

Another thud from the battering ram dented the door. It would be close.

The fiber-optic Internet lines ran through heavy steel piping buried deep underground. His pursuers couldn't break that connection without a massive explosion somewhere on the base. Even they wouldn't risk that. Not here. Not in the Green Zone of Baghdad, Iraq. Even they couldn't do that on the massive U.S.-military-controlled base.

He knew which e-mail to send first. Quickly, he typed his father's Pentagon e-mail address and triple-tabbed to the body section of the e-mail. He typed only one word—"DELTA"—and hit SEND. At least his father was now alerted.

The latest blow against the door caused some weakening of the steel. Simpson heard the metal bend and give, an earsplitting shriek of metal being slowly rent apart. He ignored the attack and started typing his second e-mail. This one could not be short. It had to be correct the first time.

Even with the threat of life and death, Simpson remained calm under the pressure. His e-mail was professional, detailed, and complete.

What he didn't know was that the major was a very determined man. He wanted to stop Simpson from doing anything, and he was using every tool available to him. The men under his command were all highly trained ex-military men with years of hard combat experience behind them—the sharp edge of the sword.

The major ordered one of them to go grab some C-4 explosive and some blasting caps. The battering ram was taking too long. If applied correctly the explosives would blow through the steel door, ripping out the locks. The major and his men knew just how much of the plastic explosive to use and where to place the charges.

Simpson was typing his name into the e-mail, considering if he had time to proofread it, when the concussion from the explosion slammed his head against the table. Dazed, his right ear bleeding from the blast, he lost track of time. Everything moved into an even slower motion for him.

He remembered looking back toward the door and seeing two men forcing it aside, using the steel pipe as a battering ram. Once they were in, two more men quickly, professionally flowed into the room. They came at Simpson.

They were fast. Even in his slow-motion haze they seemed to flow like demon-possessed specters coming at him. All he could think of was sending the second e-mail. He turned back toward the computer bank and watched his hand slowly go toward the ENTER button, which would send the e-mail.

He remembered seeing his index finger just a couple of millimeters from that button when he felt a hard fist slamming against the side of his face. Then a pair of hands grabbed his shoulders and yanked Simpson back. The chair crashed to the floor with him in it. The back of his head slammed hard against the gray concrete floor.

Jim Simpson blacked out not knowing if he had sent the second e-mail.

CHAPTER 2

Do everything you can to turn the tables on the enemy.

—FM 21-78 Prisoner-of-War Resistance, December 1981

AFTER NAVIGATING THE MAZE OF HALLWAYS that is the Pentagon, Major Charles Simpson walked through his outer office door, greeted his aide, then walked through an inner door into his office. He sank into the thick brown leather chair behind his desk. He was an older version of his son without the beard, and his hair was more gray than dark these days.

The chair was one of the few luxuries Charles Simpson afforded himself. He was not drawn to extravagance in either thought or deed. Material things held no appeal for the veteran of two wars and nearly thirty years with the United States Army. The expensive chair had been a gift from his wife, Nora, after he had left line duty and moved into the Pentagon. Knowing he wouldn't buy something like that for himself, she had bought it and then arranged to get it moved into his Pentagon office.

At first Charles Simpson hadn't wanted to use the chair. He hadn't thought it was like him. Soon, though, he had seen the wisdom in using his wife's gift. His duties for General Morrell often kept him working late, and sometimes his old back injury from a parachute jump acted up. For those and other reasons, he now welcomed the comfortable chair.

He swiveled around and punched the red button on his coffeemaker, starting the hot water through the system. Turning back around, he faced his computer and brought it awake, typing in his passwords for the programs he would need.

As the earthy aroma of hot water flowing over fresh coffee beans filled the air, Major Simpson read through the in-box of snail mail and memos on his desk while waiting for his computer to come fully awake.

With his computer fully purring, the first thing he went to, like most people, was his e-mail. He scanned the header lines of the new e-mails and saw nothing that looked like it needed immediate attention. He scrolled down further, bringing more new e-mails to the screen.

It was then that he saw the e-mail from his son Jim. His eyes widened with concern. It had no header. Quickly, Jim Simpson's father double-clicked, opening the e-mail.

He was proud of his son. He had thought that Jim would remain in the military after spending eight years as a Ranger, but he wasn't totally surprised when his son mustered out and went to work for one of the many private contractors the U.S. military relied upon these days.

At first it had seemed like a dream job for the ex-Ranger. He was making five times what he had made in the army. That gave Jim Simpson's wife, Jan, and their son, Alex, the freedom most military families do not have. But after two years, Jim had started to have doubts. Not doubts about why he was in Iraq but doubts about the company he worked for. On his last trip back to the States, during Christmas, he had quietly confided his concerns to his father. Not everything. Not the complete details, but enough to worry his father. They agreed on some procedures for communication.

In one of his letters to his father's home, mailed from the safety of Italy while on vacation, Jim had confided more. He had also told his father that if he felt he was in danger he would send a one word warning: "DELTA."

It was the only word Charles Simpson's wakening eyes saw. Something was wrong. Terribly wrong.

Forgetting his coffee and his other duties, Major Simpson leaned forward and picked up his phone. He buzzed his aide in the outer office.

"No calls. No interruptions," he ordered.

Major Charles Simpson leaned back in his chair, the wood legs creaking as he did so, and he began to think. What would he do now? He would make official inquires, of course. Quietly, through contacts he had in Iraq. Working by the side of a Pentagon general gave him some access, but that might not be enough. Not when dealing with Protective Integrated Services, the company his son worked for. What could Charles Simpson do? His eyes lit up as he remembered some recent rumors about a former colleague in the Pentagon.

A man in a wheelchair.

CHAPTER 3

A member of the Armed Forces has the duty to support the interests of the United States and oppose the enemies of the United States regardless of the circumstances.

—FM 21-78 Prisoner-of-War Resistance, December 1981

IT WAS A SUNNY, CLEAR DAY in Vero Beach, Florida. Fred Custer was sitting on the patio of his beachfront home, his eyes wrinkled in concentration behind gold-rimmed glasses, as he tied saltwater flies. His wife, Geri, slid open the sliding glass door, popped her head out, and told him he had a phone call. She handed him their portable phone.

"Hello," he said into the phone.

"Fred, Charles Simpson."

"Charlie, nice to hear from you." Fred smiled. He and Simpson had worked together in the Pentagon. They and their wives had also socialized as couples, finding they shared much in common and enjoyed each other's company. As he had with many other people, Custer had stayed in touch with Charlie over the years.

"How's D.C.? How's Nora and Jim?"

"Nora's fine. Jim is . . ." There was a pause. "Jim started smoking again."

Custer sat up in his wheelchair and concentrated. The two old warriors had worked out a warning system while they were in the Pentagon—phrases and catchwords that warned the other of trouble. When someone was "smoking," there was a problem. If Custer and Simpson were in a meeting together, or perhaps by way of a Post-it note on a memo, one would use the word to warn the other to beware, something is up, come talk to me privately.

"I'm sorry to hear that," Custer replied.

"So am I, Fred. It's not a problem I am good at dealing with. I was hoping you might have some ideas."

"Well, I would have to know more details," the wheelchair warrior replied.

"It's not something I want to discuss on the phone," Simpson stated. "Is there any chance you'd have some time if I came down?"

"How about I come up there?" Custer questioned. "It's been too long since we all got together. Geri has been bothering me to go somewhere. D.C. is always nice."

Like all who knew Fred Custer, Charles Simpson was aware of the man's wealth. He knew that the man could afford such things as a trip to Washington, D.C., more easily than Simpson could afford a trip to Florida.

"Sure," Simpson replied. "That would be nice. I'll let Nora know. When can we expect you two?"

"I'll hop online and grab some plane tickets out of Orlando tomorrow. I'll call you at home and let you know what plane we're coming in on and what hotel we'll be staying at."

"Hotel? Nonsense," Simpson said, almost insulted. "You'll stay with us. Nora would beat me if I didn't make you. I wouldn't hear the end of it for months. With Jim gone we have more than enough room. We'll have more time to catch up on old times and discuss this problem."

"That sounds good," Custer said. "I mean Nora beating you."

For the first time that day, Charles Simpson laughed. Custer always could deliver, even under pressure.

"I'll call Nora, and she'll get the guest room ready for Geri," Simpson said, delivering his counterthrust. "We have a cot in the basement you can sleep on."

Custer laughed. "It's settled, then. I'll call your home when we find out what plane we're on."

Both men said their good-byes and hung up. Custer sat on his beachfront porch and contemplated the call for a few moments. What was up with Charles Simpson's son?

He rolled himself into his home and told Geri to pack. They were going to D.C.

CHAPTER 4

The interrogator should appear to be the one who controls all aspects of the interrogation to include lighting, heating, and configuration of the interrogation room, as well as the food, shelter, and clothing given to the source.

—FM 34-52 Intelligence Interrogation, May 1987

AS CHARLES SIMPSON AND FRED CUSTER were speaking on the phone, Jim Simpson was unconscious on the other side of the globe. Still out after being hit, he was restrained and under lock and key in a small storage closet in the warehouse of Protective Integrated Services.

Protective Integrated Services was the brainchild of Major Arnold Hataway, U.S. Army, Retired. After finishing West Point in 1970, Hataway had punched his ticket in Vietnam. Like many needing that combat badge for advancement but certainly not wanting to be in actual combat, he had desk-jockeyed his way through his tour in 'Nam. The closest he ever got to seeing bullets fired in anger was when a VC sapper had exploded a bomb in a Saigon club the major was about to enter for his nightly rounds of rum and Coke. He had milked a tiny scratch from a shattered window into a Purple Heart and finished his one-year tour in the land where bad things happened.

After 'Nam, Hataway carefully groomed himself for advancement. He dreamed of stars on his shoulders and being the commander of a mighty combat division. The problem was that after Vietnam there were no large wars for quite a while. Hataway waited and improved his paper résumé. Leavenworth for more schooling, in charge of weather at a minor base, command of the mess hall at another base waiting to be closed. Frustrated but still hopeful, Hataway continued advancing up the ranks—perhaps a bit slower than his contemporaries, but it was still advancement.

Then Ronald Reagan got elected. Hataway's hopes rose. Surely this president would end his desk-jockey career. Finally, by virtue of his skills and merits, he would be recognized for the future general he knew in his heart he was.

Grenada bolstered his fantasy, but it was too small and quick an operation for him to get in on. After Reagan's tenure he got wind of a possible attack in Panama. He tried to get in on it, pulling all the strings he had. There were no responses to his calls or letters. It was when the little puppet Noriega was in chains and the troops returned home that Hataway knew he had missed that train.

His final opportunity came during Desert Storm, the first Gulf War. Everyone knew that one was coming. It promised to be a mighty sirocco flowing over Saddam Hussein and his troops. Again Hataway tried getting released from his current duty—a posting as commander of a motor pool—to finally get to show his stuff to the top brass in the Pentagon.

He was mentally crushed when no release from his current posting arrived. Depressed beyond redemption, he sat night after night in his single-room base home watching on CNN as the finest forces the United States had assembled since Vietnam utterly destroyed the Iraqi Army. He watched, anger and depression growing each night. His only consolation came from the bottles of Captain Morgan that he drained.

By the time the U.S. Army obliterated what was left of Hussein's forces on the Highway of Death, Hataway was swallowing three-quarters of a bottle a night until he passed out in his easy chair.

He knew that was it; his final chance. The U.S. Army would never promote one of its finest strategic and tactical commanders—at least in his mind—into a battlefield command. Bitter, angry, and resentful, he retired after twenty-five years in the army and took a job with one of the many military contractors.

The thing was, he should have been satisfied with his military career. Not all who serve see combat. The tasks he had been assigned to over the years were important ones. Someone has to make sure that there is toilet paper and that the motor pool is efficient. Mess halls are necessary parts of running any army. Major Hataway did an above-average job at his tasks. He was a good organizer. He just thought he should have been a battlefield general by now.

Instead he was in charge of toilet paper, paper towels, and other such sundry procurements when Operation Enduring Freedom began in Afghanistan. Rushing home at night, he watched again on CNN, but this time without the glass of rum in his fist. Then came the second attack and invasion against Iraq, Operation Iraqi Freedom. Major Arnold Hataway, U.S. Army, Retired, watched as that began and as Baghdad was conquered.

He used his resources at his job and what few contacts he still retained in the army to keep abreast of the situation. He watched as the rules changed on procurement and fulfillment for the U.S. military. No longer was the military handling its own needs. The new administration, driven by Donald Rumsfeld, was rewriting the book. They needed every soldier on the front lines, so the support roles, once filled by active-duty men and women, were now being subcontracted to private industry. True, the costs rose, but it freed up troops to be carrying rifles instead of wrenches or stew pots.

Hataway began to see potential in these new systems and operating procedures. Then came Blackwater.

Blackwater saw the opportunity in the new methods of private contracting, and they leaped at it, filling the void. Soon they swelled and were the predominant private contractor providing security, training, and support for the U.S. military, as well as for many law enforcement agencies in the USA. If there was a mission, they were more than happy to jump in taking the jobs. With their ever-growing role, their profit margins and bank accounts grew, too. Grew to gargantuan proportions. Blackwater had soon billed the U.S. government for billions—and they weren't even on the list of top ten contractors in billing.

But there was just too much work for even them, KBR, and the other big players. From the start of the war in Iraq to when Hataway formed PIS, there was a trillion dollars on the table waiting to be scooped up. Try as they did, firms like Blackwater and KBR just couldn't grab double handfuls of money off the table fast enough. So other men with the right contacts saw opportunity and started forming other companies that also feasted from that bountiful table. Men like Major Arnold Hataway, U.S. Army, Retired.

That's how Major Arnold Hataway, U.S. Army, Retired, came to be in Iraq. Using contacts with businessmen he knew, he started Protective Integrated Services. His organizational skills and his business and Pentagon contacts helped him build the small company from a minor player into a medium-sized supplier of all things the military needed in a war zone.

Already providing uniforms, laundry services, and toilet paper, Hataway started exploring the needs of bullets for the units stationed overseas. It turned out there was quite a niche market to be found in supplying the many special forces with ammo for their unique weapons. Most special forces soldiers use personal weapons. These are often odd calibers and makes that require specialized fulfillment by a small firm.

The problem wasn't finding contracts to fill. The government seemed to have an endless list of former military occupations and tasks waiting to be filled by civilians. The problem was finding qualified ex-military personnel to fill the slots. There are only so many ex-SEALs, Delta, Green Berets, Force Recon, and other service special-ops-trained personnel to go around. By the time the smaller firms were staring up, the first companies in, like Blackwater, had already hired away the best with huge paychecks. Companies like PIS started scrambling for the second- and third-tier ex-military personnel.

Hataway saw his business grow. Within two years of arriving in Iraq he had PIS dealing in small-arms ammo—pistol, rifle, assault rifle, grenades, explosives, light and heavy machine-gun ammo, and even the occasional light artillery rounds. Hataway saw the need for more and more security personnel, and soon PIS was supplying bodyguard services to any unit or company that would pay. As the wars in Afghanistan and Iraq continued to grow, so did the small company's profits. There was just too much money to be made. Hataway scooped fistfuls from the table. By the time PIS had moved into supplying contract security personnel in 2004, the company profits were rising faster than a river's crest during a flood.

Besides the security personnel he had on payroll, Hataway needed an accountant. By then the company had amassed over $100 million in profits. He did some searching and dropped the word into the ears of a couple of people he knew stateside, and one of them told Jim Simpson about the job.

After mustering out of the military, Simpson, needing to support his family, took accounting courses and passed the CPA exam. While he wasn't thrilled with the idea of being away from his family, the job with PIS offered a lot of money. Much more than the entry-level accounting positions he was finding stateside. Besides, Simpson figured, he would be with the good guys, on the team again. He would be helping the troops in their war against terror. Jim Simpson went to Iraq for the right reasons.

That is how Jim Simpson ended up in Iraq in 2006. Before his disillusionment. Before his waking up. After those events, Simpson had ended up being held captive by his employer.

Confinement

CHAPTER 5

Article V. When questioned, should I become a prisoner of war, I am required to give name, rank, service number, and date of birth. I will evade answering further questions to the utmost of my ability. I will make no oral or written statement disloyal to my country and its allies or harmful to their cause.

—FM 21-78 Prisoner-of-War Resistance, December 1981

JIM SIMPSON WOKE UP WITH WHAT seemed to be a jackhammer drilling into the side of his head. The right side of his head was throbbing from the bomb concussion as well as the fist he had taken. In addition to that ebb-and-flow-pain, the back of his head felt as if a sledgehammer had landed there. It was the concrete floor his head had slammed onto that brought that pain along.

He was laid out on an old steel army cot. A bare lightbulb mounted into the ceiling gave off a dim light. Simpson tried to sit up. This effort was stopped by thick ropes around each of his wrists and ankles. The knots weren't tight enough to cut off circulation, but they were certainly tight enough to keep him restrained.

He turned his head to the right and stared at the ropes around his right wrist. Standard military half-inch rope. He tugged it up as far as it would go. Four inches. Examining the rope, he saw that the knots were well tied. Still, given time he might find a way to free himself.

Simpson figured that he was in one of the many small storage rooms of the Protective Integrated Services warehouse in Baghdad. He stared around the room into the gloom, trying to see everything. Not much here. His cot, a wooden chair against the far wall, the single bulb in the ceiling. Nothing else.

He tugged on each of the restraints holding him and found them quite secure. The rounded metal tubing of the cot frame offered him nothing sharp to rub the ropes against. Simpson was thinking of what to do when he heard the door being unlocked. Quickly, he laid his head back down and closed his eyes, pretending to still be out.

The brighter lights from the warehouse outside filled the little storage room as John Lowsley opened the door and looked in. Lowsley had joined PIS after being forced out of the army because of a questionable incident during the first Gulf War. It wasn't the death of some of Hussein's soldiers that had bothered the military, but the two women—a young mother and her grandmother—he had gunned down in the same attack had been an issue. He had always claimed that he had not seen them, but other witnesses countered his story.

An international news crew had been there. Two reporters stated that after killing the soldiers Lowsley had seen the women, turned his weapon ninety degrees, and opened up again for reasons no one could fathom. If those reporters had not been there and threatened to report the incident, Lowsley might well have finished his military career. As it was, Allied Command in Riyadh had gotten the reporters to quash the story with the promise that they would get an exclusive on another issue and that something serious would be done to Lowsley. He was forced out after Desert Storm was over.

Gone from the military, Lowsley had drifted back in the States. One too many bar fights had gotten him thrown into prison for a short stretch. It was only eighteen months, but it was enough to disqualify him for the A-Teams like Blackwater in the early days of Gulf War II. When PIS came knocking, Lowsley was more than happy to sign up, no questions, for $60,000 a year plus bonuses.

He walked over to Simpson and stared down at him. The major wanted to know if the prisoner was awake yet. Lowsley was bored with guard duty. He took his thumb and forefinger and squeezed Simpson's nostrils shut. Simpson had no choice but to open his mouth to breathe. He opened his eyes and stared up at the man.

"Yeah, I thought so," Lowsley said, letting go of Simpson's nose, turning and walking away. "I'll let the major know you're wide awake," he commented before heading back out into the warehouse.

Jim Simpson wondered what was next.

CHAPTER 6

Article VI. I will never forget that I am an American fighting man, responsible for my actions and dedicated to the principles that made my country free. I will trust in my God and in the United States of America.

—FM 21-78 Prisoner-of-War Resistance, December 1981

FRED CUSTER ROLLED HIS WHEELCHAIR OUT onto the deck behind the Simpson home in Alexandria, Virginia. Charles Simpson settled into a large, comfortable patio chair on the other side of a wooden table. It was late on a Saturday afternoon, and the sun was beginning to wane in the sky. The two men stared silently out past the well-manicured lawn and into the tangle of woods just beyond the property.

With a pitcher of iced tea and an ashtray on the wooden patio table between them, they settled in to talk. Geri had taken Nora out shopping to get her mind off her missing son. Of course, there was no way the mother in her could completely stop thinking about her son's fate. Having the Custers there helped, though.

Custer accepted a cigar from Simpson. He cut the end, pulled out his old, battered 82nd Airborne Zippo, and sparked the fine tobacco to life. Simpson lit his own cigar. The silence sat between them like a brick wall. Custer could only imagine the thoughts flowing through his friend's mind. Custer flanked the silence with a sneak attack.

"Horticulture had departed," he quietly said, "nature had returned."

"Huh?" the major replied after a few seconds. "Sorry, my mind was elsewhere."

"Of course it is, Charlie," Custer remarked. "I was quoting Hugo's *Les Misérables*. Those woods beyond your yard"—he pointed—"remind me of a passage from the book."

Charles Simpson sat and contemplated the trees and wild overgrowth just beyond the spaces where his lawn mower and clippers kept nature in check. "Yes, the woods. One of the reasons we bought this house. There's a small river out there about a hundred yards. Protected. No one will develop that land and put houses there."

The two old soldiers sat in the growing dusk puffing cigars for a few moments. Custer decided to wait out his old friend. Soon the major was talking.

"I don't know what to do, Fred," he opened. "Something has happened to Jim. Something's terribly wrong."

It flowed from there. As if a dam had broken, the story came out for the next thirty minutes. Custer said nothing, holding any questions until he had heard the story up to that moment.

Charles Simpson held nothing back. He knew Custer could be trusted. He spoke of the slow disillusionment of his son. The hints and suspicions. The code warning they had agreed upon. How, after receiving the last e-mail, Charles Simpson had tried calling his son in Iraq. Whoever had answered the phone at PIS had told him that his son had gone on R&R for two weeks and they didn't know where he was.

"Bullshit," the elder Simpson emphasized. "He would have called me. At minimum he would call Jan and Alex if that was true."

As a major working for General Morrell in the Pentagon, Simpson had tried the official channels that a two-star general's aide can bring to bear. He had called around to some fellow warriors in Iraq, commanders at various levels he knew.

"They all told me the same thing. The contractors are private industry, and officially the U.S. military doesn't have anything to do with them unless a specific unit is ordering from them or using their mercenaries."

They sat in silence, the dark closing in around them.

"Plus I got this. A letter to his wife, Jan." Simpson handed over a letter to Custer.

Custer read it in amazement.

"What do you want me to do, Charlie?" Custer finally asked.

"I'm not sure, Fred," Simpson replied. "I guess I called you for two reasons. One, your mind. You always were good with problems. Two . . ." He paused. "There were rumors I heard."

Custer sat up a bit straighter in his wheelchair.

"Rumors?" he asked. "What kind of rumors?"

"Off-the-record stuff. Between the lines." Charles Simpson turned toward his old friend. "Something last year in South Florida. An incident."

Custer was more than surprised. He and his men had done everything not to let that operation be known.

"What did you hear?"

"Nothing specific, Fred. But we're not all dummies at the Pentagon. There were some mighty fine coincidences last year. Too many former Vietnam Special Forces men who had served together being at the same place when things went boom."

Custer was quiet.

"You know every former Special Forces soldier is mildly kept track of. I was questioned because I knew you. It's how I found out."

"Sure." Custer replied, "but not heavily watched."

"True, but like I said, Fred, too many in one place with a lot of explosions. Investigations were made. Nothing could be proven, but . . ." Simpson let that hang in the air.

"Well, Charles," Custer came back, "if something happened like what you describe, why wasn't I questioned?"

"The word for the few who saw the material, and it was only a handful, Fred, was to bury it. It seems that a former soldier of yours went missing under suspicious circumstances. Reading his record, he looked to have been a good man."

"Yoder was."

"Well, it seems no one else has gone missing down there after whatever happened."

Custer thought it out quickly. Yes, he could trust Charles Simpson. So Fred Custer briefed him on what had happened to Larry Yoder and what he had done about it. The stars were filling the night by the time he finished the story. Now it was Charles Simpson's turn to be quiet and think. He decided on a rare second cigar and sparked it to life, its orange tip burning a bright hole into the fabric of the night.

He finally spoke. "Well, like I said, the incident was looked upon as something not to investigate any further. It was deemed just. Some of us still see in black-and-white, Fred. Some of us still know why we do what we do."

"So you called me," Custer said.

"Yes. I called you because I didn't know what else to do. My wife and I need help, Fred. My daughter-in-law and my grandchild need help. Most of all, my son needs help. Do you think you can help us?"

Fred Custer took another cigar and lit it. He felt the warm metal of the old Zippo in his hand after lighting the cigar. He watched as fireflies began to fill the woods—they reminded him of tracer fire from a place far away and long ago. Tracer fire from the night he took that piece of shrapnel in his spine. He let that memory drift away. He was here now, for a reason.

"I can try, Charlie," Custer finally said. "I can sure as hell try my best."

CHAPTER 7

HAVE A ROUTINE. Every PW must have a daily routine.

—FM 21-78 Prisoner-of-War Resistance, December 1981

HICKEY WAS IN LAS CRUCES, NEW Mexico, when Custer called him. Six foot three and still the lean 210 pounds of his Vietnam days because of his daily five-mile runs, only his hair seemed to have changed. He kept it in a crew cut, but it was now white instead of the blond of his youth.

He was there taking part in Appleseed Project training. It was the closest spot to his home in Arizona where the group had an event. He had heard about them and liked the concept. Training people to be sharpshooters while educating them on Lexington and Concord was a good idea. Their Revolutionary War idealistic roots appealed to him. He went to participate to see if they were real or camo-clad nuts. If they were real, he was thinking about getting the training going back near his home.

They were real and they were interesting.

After being on the firing range all day popping off rounds from his .223 Ruger Mini-14, he had shared dinner with the others around the campsite before retiring to his tent. Hickey still liked roughing it. He was surprised when his cell phone rang and it was Custer calling him. They traded hellos, and then Hickey listened. He didn't hesitate.

"I could fly there Monday," the old warrior stated. "I'm committed to something, and we won't finish until tomorrow afternoon. Then I have to drive home, pack, and get to the airport."

Hickey listened again.

"I'm in Las Cruces, New Mexico," he replied.

More listening. "Sure, I could do that. If it's that important." More listening. "OK, I'll look for your chartered plane tomorrow after six P.M. at the Las Cruces airport. See you at Ronald Reagan Airport between ten and midnight."

Hickey disconnected the call and sat in his tent, wondering what Custer had going this time.

ANOTHER MAN TOOK A CALL from Fred Custer that night. Like Hickey, the quiet man named Van Zandt didn't question Fred Custer much. He just asked when he should be where.

Both men knew that when Fred Custer asked, you came. Fred Custer wouldn't ask if there wasn't a damn good reason.

Unlike Custer, Van Zandt was available immediately. As soon as he hung up with Custer, he grabbed an overnight bag he had packed for times like this and headed to the Orlando airport.

Custer's third call of the evening was to an Orlando charter plane company. A jet was waiting for Van Zandt when he got to the airport. He was in D.C. by 11:00 P.M. and checked into the Hilton Crystal City next to Reagan Airport by midnight.

Just like Charles Simpson, Van Zandt had met Custer while working in the Pentagon. He had other talents on his long résumé that made him a valuable man to know. He was asleep by 1:00 A.M. and would meet with Custer the next day to get his marching orders.

SUNDAY WAS A BUSY DAY for Fred Custer. He woke up early and did his daily exercises. He showered and shaved next and found Geri was up and moving by then. They planned their day. While Geri bathed, Custer went to find some breakfast. He found Simpson and his wife already at the kitchen table, sipping coffee over the remains of their breakfast dishes. Nora Simpson asked Fred what he wanted and began to fix it after planting a large mug of black coffee in front of him.

Except for her question about Custer's choice of food, Nora had been quiet around the house. She was worried about Jim, wondering where he was right then, wondering how he was. She decided to call her son's wife and her grandchild after she made breakfast for her guests. As she silently decided what to do, Custer and the elder Simpson planned out their day.

"I have two friends to help us. One arrived last night, and the other comes in later today," Custer explained. "We'll brief them, and I have some tasks for both. They might need your help. Can they call you at the Pentagon?"

"Absolutely," Charles Simpson said.

"One of them is named Hickey," Custer continued.

"I read about him in the Florida data," Simpson cut in. "He served with you in Vietnam, as I recall."

"Yes. Good man to have on your side."

"So do you have a plan yet, Fred?"

"I have a seed of a plan, Charlie. I want to send Hickey to Iraq. He's not that far out of the army. He might know some of the Special Forces men there. He might be able to ask around the stone walls you ran into. I need eyes on the ground. See what he can rustle up. We also need to get your daughter-in-law and grandson off of the grid."

Charles Simpson just sat and listened. Custer wanted to engage Simpson and his wife in the entire process, not only to help his friend relieve the tension of his missing son by doing something toward freeing him but also because of his Pentagon contacts. Those might become very valuable for what Custer had in mind. He needed a legitimate reason to get people into Iraq.

"Charlie, how difficult is it to secure a contract over there?" the wheelchair warrior asked.

Simpson took a sip of coffee before answering.

"It's not impossible. There are, of course, forms to fill out. You have to get on the approved list of contractors. Then the firm bids on a contract and, in theory, the low bidder wins."

"Any exceptions?"

"There are exceptions for something that is needed quickly. I can certainly push the required paperwork through."

"That's what I need, Charlie," Simpson stated. "I need to bend the rules, cut corners—and fast. Can you do that?"

"I work for a general. I think we can find a shortcut through the maze."

"I need to blow a hole straight through the maze," Custer explained. "I want to form a contracting company selling something—anything—and get Hickey and maybe a couple more men over there. I need you to find me that 'something' that someone over there needs and needs now."

Charles Simpson thought of his son. He looked over at his wife as she prepared food. He saw the sadness in the woman he had known and loved for over forty years. She had been with him through it all and had rewarded him with a son. Charles Simpson knew he would find something in that maze. The tool Custer and his men would need. He owed it to his wife, and he owed it to his son.

"Fred." Simpson looked his old friend square in the eyes. "I'll blow a damn hole through that maze big enough for a battalion to march through."

Fred Custer smiled.

VAN ZANDT WAS SITTING IN his room at the Hilton staring out of the window when his room phone rang. Slowly he walked over and picked it up. It was Custer on a cell phone. He and his wife were within five minutes of arriving. Van Zandt gave Custer his room number and hung up. He sat down, staring out of the window again, waiting. He never had a problem waiting. He was a very patient man. He had a long history of waiting and observing.

Soon the knock at the door interrupted his thoughts. He stood up and opened the door, greeting Custer and his wife. They all settled down around a small table by the window and started talking. Custer explained the situation and described what he needed quickly.

"Passports," Custer exclaimed. "I'm going to want at least ten of them. I want plenty of them. I suspect we'll need to get blanks for creating identities quickly. Do you know where we can get those?"

As Van Zandt thought, Custer watched the quiet man. Since he had met him while working in the Pentagon in the eighties, Custer had found him a person with amazing abilities to get things done. Others came up with ideas, but it was Van Zandt who made them happen.

"I think I know where we can get some," Van Zandt replied. "They'll be authentic but not registered on the system. They are real passports, but if anyone dug deep they wouldn't be on the State Department database."

It was Custer's turn to think now. He replied after a moment.

"That should be fine for our purposes," he concluded aloud. "For now, anyway. If we need to make them real on that database, maybe we can do that down the line. But for now what you describe will work."

Custer looked over and nodded at his wife. She reached into her purse and took out a thick envelope and a cell phone. She handed them to the quiet man from Orlando. He opened the envelope and looked inside.

"Ten thousand in cash," Custer informed him. "Out of my home safe. Clean money. Twenties and fifties mostly. That should get you started. If you need more, just call me."

Van Zandt nodded his approval.

Custer gave more orders. "My cell number is programmed into the phone. Both are new phones. No one else knows your number. Get the passports and call me. How long do you think that will take?"

"If we're lucky, a day or two. My contact is in New York City. I can leave as soon as we're done here."

"Good. Get them and call. I'm off to Delaware later today. I'll be busy there for a couple of days. We'll be setting up a new company. After that I'll need you to go to the Cayman Islands to set up a bank account or two. Geri and Mrs. Simpson are flying out to the West Coast to get the wife and grandson under cover until this is taken care of."

Custer took a pad and pen from the table and scribbled something. He ripped the top piece of paper off and handed it over to Van Zandt.

"This is my banker's number there. He'll handle anything we need. After that is all done, I'll probably have other tasks for you."

Van Zandt nodded again.

"Good." Custer smiled.

He put his hand out. He and Van Zandt shook hands.

"Until we meet again," Custer said.

"*Se Dio vuole,*" the mysterious Van Zandt replied.

CHAPTER 8

Generally, the enemy does not want to kill PWs for one major reason, among others: A DEAD PW CANNOT BE EXPLOITED.

—FM 21-78 Prisoner-of-War Resistance, December 1981

As Charles Simpson and Custer were talking at breakfast, half a world away Jim Simpson was strapped into a metal chair in Iraq, screaming. The chair had been bolted into the cement floor. Simpson had been carefully moved from his bed to the chair in another room by three of the PIS personal. A soundproofed room with thick foam on all of the walls.

Lowsley and two other men had moved Simpson. All three were big men. Lowsley stayed back with a Taser in case he needed it. The other two knew their work. First Simpson's hands were freed from the bed and retied behind his back before bonds on his feet were cut loose. He was walked to another room, where the chair waited, and strapped in by the reverse process—legs bound tight, then hands cut loose—and his wrists were restrained under thick leather straps around the chair arms and legs. His clothes were then cut away from his body.

The men then attached thin wires from a hand-cranked field generator to Simpson's body. The wires connected to Simpson's testicles and nipples. From his military training Simpson knew better than to talk to his captors.

Then the major entered the room and shut the door behind him. Simpson knew why he was there. He knew why he was still alive. Money.

He was still alive because of what he had done the last week before being taken captive. Simpson now knew that his two e-mails had made it out and done what he planned for them to do.

JIM SIMPSON WAS CONTENT WHEN he started working for Protective Integrated Services. While it wasn't being in the army, it seemed to be the next best thing. The company was helping to supply the troops in Iran and Afghanistan. Someone had to fill those orders for the brave warriors fighting on the streets of an unfriendly nation. Plus, as one of his fellow ex-Rangers had said, "You'll be with the good guys."

It was with his slow realization that PIS was hardly "the good guys" that Simpson's disillusionment came. As the company's accountant, he saw the double, triple, and even much higher billings. He stared at spreadsheets full of massive overcharging for everything from toilet paper to bullets. It wasn't just those things that began Simpson's change of heart; it was the deep greed he saw in Major Hataway's eyes whenever he spoke of the profitmaking abilities of PIS. There was something wrong there. The man was getting even or something.

His first years with the company, 2006 and 2007, were busy

ones. He spent most of his time just bringing long overdue accounts up to date. By the time that was done, well into his second year in Iraq, he began to sense the outright greed involved in the billings by the private contractor. That's when he started studying all of the records in detail. He went through the entire history of the PIS accounts. What he saw staggered him.

By the time of Simpson's capture, Protective Integrated Services had amassed well over $330 million in profits. As a former line combat soldier, Simpson became disgusted. He was appalled that this private firm should so profit from the life and death, blood and toil, of the average grunt serving in Iraq and Afghanistan. Simpson wondered what to do.

PIS was hardly the worst of the offenders. Simpson didn't work for the other contractors, though. He worked for PIS. If he could do something, he would, but it could be only against the firm which he worked for. He thought about whistle-blowing, but that didn't look like a successful path. Congress didn't seem to care. If Blackwater had been before Congress and nothing had happened, what chance did Simpson have exposing PIS?

As a contract employee in a war zone, he got frequent vacation breaks. They were mandatory, as a matter of fact. Four a year. Simpson used them carefully. He divided the time between seeing his family and doing research.

He was still unsure of what to do when he went to Rome for his last vacation. It was there, as he stared marveling under the twelve thousand square feet Michelangelo had painted at the Sistine Chapel, that an epiphany came to him.

The next day he rented a car and took a trip to Zurich. Using $1,000 of his own money, he opened an account at a very small, discreet bank off the main streets of the old Swiss city. When he got back to Iraq, he studied the Bahama Islands bank accounts of PIS. He found what he needed.

Major Hataway was new to money. The cash had rolled in so

fast that it just piled up, Hataway failed to properly secure those accounts, much less move them around in reinvestment. Simpson had control of all the PIS accounts.

Simpson was a signatory on all of their accounts. He had to be to pay the bills and move the money. What these greedy men within PIS management had failed to see was that they had opened up their system to a man who didn't like the duplicity, dishonesty, and greed he had found himself swimming in. Major Hataway and the other owners of PIS had trusted Simpson because he was an honest man. It never occurred to them that his moral code would allow him to betray his employers.

Simpson had made the right inquiries and set up the correct procedures with the bank in the Bahamas. He was planning on taking another vacation, draining the accounts to his Swiss bank, and disappearing from Iraq. Free of the constraints of being in a war zone, he could figure out what to do next. He would grab his wife and son and hide away somewhere until he did. He snail-mailed his wife instructions and details of what he had done. Somehow he would figure out a way to return the obscene profits to the United States government. He hadn't done what he did for personal gain.

He was setting this all up during the week he was grabbed.

The only reason the major had gotten wind of Simpson's plan was that he had called the bank on his own personal account. The major was planning a gambling and whoring trip to Dubai City. Located on the tip of the United Arab Emirates on the beautiful Persian Gulf, Dubai is the playground for the Middle East countries where strict Islamic law forbids such vices as drinking and prostitution.

The head of the Bahamian bank had mentioned certain inquiries by Jim Simpson to the major when they were on the phone. It was then that the major had become suspicious. If he had been a smart man, he would have sealed off Simpson's access to the accounts right then. But he was unsure. He decided to talk to Simpson first. That was the day they had ended up grabbing Jim Simpson.

Simpson had had to go back into the PIS offices to set up some final details. He wanted to make copies of his hard drive as proof. That was when he had overheard the major briefing his men. That was when the chase had happened and Simpson had locked himself into the room and sent his e-mails.

The second e-mail was to the Bahamian bank. With it Jim Simpson instructed them to transfer the accounts to which he had access. They were to send all of the money—except one hundred dollars in each account, to keep them open—to the account Simpson had opened in his name in Switzerland.

Jim Simpson had drained a little over $330 million of PIS's money and hidden it away. Slipped it into a bank account that only he had the keys to unlock.

As often happened, the grifters had been grifted.

SIMPSON SCREAMED AGAIN AS THE crank was twisted by Lowsley. Lowsley's face lit up with some perverse joy as he inflicted the electrical pain throughout his prisoner's body. He was in another place, some dark world away from humanity.

Major Hataway waved, and the electricity ceased. They stared at Simpson, naked and sweating, bound before them. The smell of burning flesh, sweat, and urine filled the room.

"Now, Jim," the major cooed, "all you need to tell us is where the money is and how to get it back."

Simpson stared back at them with determination.

"Simpson, James. Sergeant, United States Rangers, 18120590" was his only reply.

The major waved at Lowsley. The pain came again at higher levels. Simpson gritted his teeth together and held in the pain as long as he could. He screamed finally, letting the pain free.

When the pain stopped again there was silence in the room.

"Jim," the major said, attempting to persuade him, "this will go on until you talk. All we want is the information to get our money back. Once we have that, we'll clean you up and send you back home."

Simpson knew that was a lie. If he told them, he was signing his death warrant. Life was cheap in Iraq.

"Simpson, James. Sergeant, United States Rangers—"

The rest was cut off by the growing flow of electricity through his body. Eventually it stopped. Simpson felt as if his heart were beating as fast as a hummingbird's. His chest heaved up and down from his deep breaths.

"We have nothing but time," the major commented.

"So do I," Simpson gasped back.

The major waved again. The juice came again and again in waves.

Simpson dug back to his Catholic roots. Once a Catholic, always a Catholic. He began to pray.

"Our Father, who art in heaven, hallowed be thy name. Thy kingdom come, thy will be done, on earth as it is in heaven—"

A massive jolt of electricity flowed through his body.

Jim Simpson passed out.

CHAPTER 9

A good way to keep your interrogator/indoctrinator from getting military information or otherwise accomplishing his mission is to ask him questions, in a calm, quiet, serious manner.

—FM 21-78 Prisoner-of-War Resistance, December 1981

HICKEY FINISHED READING THE LETTER JIM Simpson had mailed his wife. He took another sip of coffee as he thought about it. The remains of his breakfast lay on the room service cart. Custer had explained the situation to him before handing him the letter.

Hickey looked up. "So what's the plan?" he asked.

Custer explained. "As soon as I leave here, I am off to Delaware. I'm setting up a new corporation there. Soon I'll have a Cayman Islands bank account to go with it. It will be some sort of company to contract out goods in Iraq. Charlie is going to find us something to hang that all on. That should all be done within a couple of days. I want you in Iraq as quickly as possible. Do you have a passport?"

"Not here."

"We can get an emergency second copy done. You're my eyes and ears on the ground, Ted. We know what you're looking for, Jim Simpson. We know where he was last week when he sent the e-mail to Charlie. If possible I need you to see if he's still there." Custer paused, thinking. "How are your contacts over there?"

"I don't know." Hickey rubbed his chin while thinking. "I still have contacts at Bragg. I can check to see who's over there."

"Good." Custer pulled a thick envelope from between his thigh and the wheelchair. He handed it to the former Special Forces trooper. From inside his jacket pocket he removed a cell phone and handed it over as well.

"There's ten thousand in cash. Should be more than enough to start. The phone is set up for international calling. I have no idea what the ability is in Baghdad. If it doesn't work, buy a satellite phone. Those work anywhere."

Custer then explained how Charles Simpson came to call him. How the Belle Glade operation wasn't as invisible as they had thought it had been.

"I thought we covered our tracks," Hickey commented.

"So did I. We'll have to do even better this time. I want zero signs."

"That's almost impossible," Hickey said. "Especially if I am going over there under my own name."

"Well, be as discreet as possible, then."

"Will do."

"I'm working on getting us clean passports that we can fill in as needed. If we locate Simpson, then a team will have to go in to free him."

"That might mean using force," Hickey finally said.

"It might," Custer agreed. "Are you up for that again, Ted?"

Hickey was silent for a moment.

"That depends," he said. "From what you have told me, I see no problems. But it depends on what I see when I get there. I won't go against regular army, Fred. Not even for you."

"Neither would I. That's not what we're facing here."

"Maybe, maybe not. But you can be sure that company is located within the confines of the U.S. military's control in Iraq. In the Green Zone, I suspect."

"You'll go see, though?" Custer asked.

"Yes," Hickey said with no hesitation. "That I'll do."

"Ted, I don't know if or even how you could, but if you can get a message to Jim Simpson, do it. Let him know the cavalry is on the way."

"If I can. I'll want Charles Simpson's number, by the way. I don't know what all I'll need to get into Iraq on short notice, but if there are any obstacles, I want help getting by them fast."

"It's programmed into your cell phone."

"Always prepared, aren't you, Fred?"

"Fail to plan—plan to fail." Custer smiled.

THE MEN PARTED. WHILE CUSTER was driving to Delaware, Hickey used the hotel phone and Internet service to find out what he would need to get to Iraq. He checked the State Department Web site, where he found that "Iraq remains dangerous, volatile, and unpredictable." He would need a passport, of course. He found that he could get an emergency replacement of his within twenty-four hours.

He wouldn't need a visa if he was a contract worker for the military. Just a CAC—a Common Access Card. If Custer's company could get set up in time, and Charles Simpson could get the paperwork done for the Department of Defense, he would get a CAC. Failing that, he could buy a visa for eighty dollars.

Royal Jordanian Airlines was running two flights a day into Baghdad International Airport. After that, all he would need was a hotel room. They were available. The Sheraton Ishtar, right across from the Green Zone, was where many international journalists and businessmen hung their hats. After it had been attacked with rockets targeted by truck bombers, the security had been beefed up. It was as safe as anyplace he could find on short notice.

Once he knew what he had to do, Hickey called Charles Simpson. Simpson pulled strings where he could. By noon, Hickey had been to the State Department in D.C., filing for his emergency passport. It would be ready the next day. He would meet up with Simpson later that night and get his CAC. Back at the hotel he booked flights on RJA from D.C. to New York City direct to Amman, Jordan, and from there to Baghdad.

His final call was to Fort Bragg, home of the Green Berets. His name was still fresh enough there with the right soldiers. Hickey found out what Army Special Forces were currently stationed in Baghdad and who was there that he knew. He got a couple of names. Good men. Men he had worked with before.

After settling all of that, he went shopping. He spent over $3,000 on a good camera and telephoto lens, a Nikon D300 with an F-mount lens system. He might need the digital tools once on the ground in Iraq. He added a NIKKOR 300mm telephoto lens and a good tripod to his purchase. He paid by credit card, wanting all his cash for Iraq.

It was all coming together.

AS HICKEY WAS CHASING DOWN what he would need for the trip, Van Zandt was stepping out of a cab in Chinatown in New York City. Being a man of experience, he had many contacts with people of worth. One of them was an ancient man named Li Ang. Li Ang had escaped China in 1950 when the Communists took over. One of the followers of Chiang Kai-shek, he knew his chances under the Communists were thin at best. After getting to Taiwan, he immigrated to New York City, where his sister had been sent early in World War II. They opened a little restaurant in Chinatown. It did well.

He also began selling documents to his fellow Chinese who needed paperwork to escape the Communists. To Li Ang it wasn't a question of legality as much as it was a mission of mercy—mercy for those needing to get out from under the repressive regime that had taken over China. He wasn't concerned with the legal question of whether the documents he produced were valid. His opinion was that if they passed being scrutinized they were good papers. He produced good papers.

It was after the Vietnam War that Van Zandt met the forger. Van Zandt needed good documents to help a new generation of Asians escape yet another Communist regime. Now in his eighties, Li Ang still dabbled in passports from time to time.

As he sat behind the cash register of the restaurant and saw the quiet man from Orlando enter, he knew why he was visiting. Smiling at his long-absent visitor, Li Ang waved a grandson over to run the register. It was past lunchtime, and the business was slow. He rose and beckoned Van Zandt to a corner booth. A granddaughter came to the table, and Li Ang ordered hot green tea for the two and told her that they were not to be disturbed.

The two men traded pleasantries until the tea had arrived and the granddaughter was gone. It was time for business.

"So, old friend," Li Ang opened, "what can I do for you?"

"U.S. passports. Ten. Clean as you can get." Van Zandt always spoke in a minimum of words.

Li Ang was quiet as he thought. He sipped some tea.

As a matter of fact, he did have a supply of very good U.S. passports. They came out of Thailand. The Thais had some notorious gangs dealing in real and fake passports. The real ones were good. They were stolen or bought off of tourists who needed some quick cash. The fakes were even better.

Those were blanks with every page valid and authentic RFID chips embedded into the back cover. When the State Department started mandating RFID chips be buried within the back cover of U.S. passports, they found no firm in the United States could do the work. For reasons only to be marveled at and welcomed by those in the black market, the USA outsourced the manufacturing of these security papers. The covers were chipped in Europe and then shipped, quite insecurely, to Thailand, where a tiny antenna was attached to the RFID chip. Thailand was well known for being a place where forgers prospered, buying and selling state documents from all over the world. That the Americans handed them authentic blanks amazed these criminals. They didn't bother to question their good fortune. They just prospered from it.

The resourceful Thai forgers simply printed good copies or sometimes made a few hundred of the authentic passports disappear. It was some of those that ended up in the office safe of Li Ang.

Yes, he had twice the number of passports Van Zandt was looking for. Of course, that would eat up half his current supply.

"One thousand each," the Chinese man said. "That's a friend's price."

Van Zandt sipped his tea. Then he reminded Li Ang of a cousin. Van Zandt had gone into China and helped get the woman out. They settled on $600 each. Though they only cost Li Ang $250 each, in his mind he was practically giving them away to Van Zandt. Still, debts have to be paid.

"Cash," Li Ang said, saving face.

"Always," came the reply.

Van Zandt reached into his jacket, pulling out the envelope Custer had given him. He started counting off $6,000 as Li Ang went to his office and moved ten of the passports into a large to-go food container and slid that into a plain paper sack. When he returned to the table, he handed the bag to Van Zandt and took the cash. Both men smiled and nodded at each other.

Van Zandt didn't even check the contents of the bag. He had known Li Ang too long. The man was honest in transactions. Li Ang would never consider cheating the quiet man from Orlando. He knew the man's abilities and had seen the results of crossing him.

Business done, the two men sat and talked until the tea was finished. Thanking his friend, Van Zandt then departed. Outside he called Custer.

"I have those ten Yankees tickets you asked for."

"Great," Custer replied. "I'll be in Dover, Delaware, by tonight. The Hilton Garden Inn."

"I'll get there," Van Zandt said before he disconnected the call.

THE TWO MEN MET THAT night in Custer's hotel room. Custer took possession of nine of the passports, leaving Van Zandt one. Custer was feeling his organizational powers coming fully to life as he held the ten blue booklets in his hand.

"I've booked you a flight tomorrow afternoon to the Cayman Islands," Custer ordered. "I'll need you down there to deal with the bank. When I form a corporation here, I'll call you. I'll need at least one account down there for that firm. Tomorrow morning we'll find a lawyer and get you a power of attorney for me. You'll have total access to my accounts there."

Custer was in no way worried about handing the quiet Van Zandt such authority. He had known the man for a long time. He knew the man's worth and merit. Fred Custer was also one of the few people on the planet Van Zandt had told his full life story to.

Custer knew he could trust Van Zandt with his bank accounts, his life, and then some. There were no worries there.

"Draw what cash you think you'll need. I might be sending you to Europe after the Caymans."

That would be no problem. Van Zandt had seen all of Europe in his time. He knew it well.

"Any questions?" Custer asked.

The quiet man from Orlando shook his head no.

"Let's go find some dinner, then."

Custer led the way.

CHAPTER 10

Article III. If I am captured I will continue

to resist by all means available.

—FM 21-78 Prisoner-of-War Resistance, December 1981

JIM SIMPSON WOKE UP AND FOUND he was again strapped to the metal frame of the bed. He was dressed in some sort of one-piece jumpsuit. His body was still singed from his earlier torture. There was nothing he could do about that.

He didn't know what time it was or what day it was. Was it daytime or nighttime? Trapped in the sealed storage room within the warehouse, he had no idea. He tried his bonds and felt their secure bindings. He tugged at them anyway, trying anything to cut them. Anything to try to free himself and perhaps escape. The smooth, round metal of the bed frame still offered nothing against which to cut the rope.

Simpson tried moving the bed by shifting his entire body around. The effort took all his energy. Even after sleeping, he was wasted after the torture. Nothing. The bed frame must be bolted to the floor.

Unable to move or escape, Simpson did what he could. He closed his eyes, prayed, and then tried to sleep again. From his Ranger training he knew to rest while he had the chance. Somehow he fell back asleep.

HE WAS AWAKENED BY THE sounds of a key turning a lock, then a metal bolt being pulled back. The door opened. Simpson feigned sleeping. He listened. He heard a man stepping forward, then a scrape across the cold concrete floor.

Step, scrape . . . step, scrape.

Simpson wondered who this was and what that scraping noise was. The noises stopped as whoever it was reached the bedside. Simpson wanted to open his eyes—the instinct rode through his brain at a million miles a second—but he didn't.

He heard a soft and familiar sound. What was it? The next thing he heard was the sound of metal on metal right at his ear. A voice joined the sound to invade his ears.

"The major says he'll pay a hundred thousand cash to anyone who gets you to talk," the voice calmly stated. "I'm going to earn that money."

The scraping stopped. Something hard and cold pressed a dimple into the skin under his neck. Simpson knew what that soft sound had been—a knife being drawn from a leather sheath. The sound in his ear was the knife edge being sharpened on a piece of steel.

"Wake up," the voice teased. "Talk to Scott."

Simpson opened his eyes, staring at his captor. The man's face instantly came back to him. This was the super sprinter from the warehouse chase. The man Simpson had sent down with the crowbar.

The man's name was Scott Rose. Former 101st Airborne, he had mustered out after the first Gulf War after an injury to his knee. He had surgery on his knee and functioned fine, but not well enough for Airborne standards. Back in civilian life, he just never could find a job that measured up to the adrenaline high of jumping out of an airplane and then taking on an enemy. His knee healed well enough over the years.

When the second Gulf War started, he was disappointed that he couldn't be there. Then, like most other elite troopers, he heard about Blackwater. He tried but wasn't chosen. He fumed until he heard about PIS. He got hired and was soon in Iraq doing security duties on supply convoys. He loved it. He was back in his element, war. Better than that, there seemed to be no rules of engagement other than what they made up day to day. More than once Rose and his teammates had opened up on an Iraqi car or group of men not knowing for sure if they were enemy combatants or just civilians in the wrong place at the wrong time.

Had there been proper investigations of Rose's shootings, at least three of them would have been found questionable and one downright wrong. An Iraqi man driving his wife and infant in the backseat had paid with his life just for being on the wrong stretch of highway on the wrong day.

The man could barely make ends meet as it was, much less maintain his car in perfect running condition. He was taking his wife and son to her cousin's wedding when the car's water hose blew. Being a resourceful man, he had duct tape in the trunk. He was leaning over the engine—deep under the hood in the brick-oven-like summer Iraqi heat—wrapping the hose when he died.

Rose was in the lead Humvee, manning an M-60 machine gun, when he saw the stalled car through his Oakley sunglasses. He didn't hesitate. There was no way that some car bomber was going to kill him. He opened up on the vehicle without warning. The .30-06 rounds ripped through the thin metal of the car. The woman was wounded in the shoulder, but her husband took three rounds high in his chest. He slumped forward over the hot engine, dead, his blood mixing with the water from the burst hose on the pavement below.

The convoy just rolled on by.

The widow tried to get justice, but it was impossible in those days. Scott Rose never lost one minute of sleep over the incident. "One less hajji," he told anyone who cared to listen.

Jim Simpson didn't know any of this. All he knew was that a man was holding a very sharp knife at his throat.

"Now, you ruined my knee the other day," Rose informed him. "I can't work now, and that hundred grand will see me through until I'm fit again."

Simpson stared over at the knees of the man. There was a heavy brace on the left one. The knee Simpson had shattered with the crowbar. That was the scraping noise he heard when Rose had entered the room; the man was dragging his wounded foot behind him as he walked. Rose pulled the knife away from Simpson's throat and moved the tip to the side of his knee. In his hand he held a hammer.

"Now, this is just where that crowbar hit my knee." Rose pressed the point onto the spot on Simpson's knee. "I figure if I start tapping the top of this knife here with this hammer, you'll tell me what the major wants to know."

"The major doesn't know you're doing this," Simpson said.

"He won't care, when you talk."

"I'm not talking."

"We'll see," Rose stated. Then he used his weight and his good leg to pin Simpson's leg down tight. Simpson tried squirming, but it did no good. He felt the tip of the blade being pressed against the side of his knee.

"What's the stuff the major wants to know?" Rose demanded.

"Go to hell," Simpson replied.

Simpson heard the tap of the hammer on the top of the knife. The tip cut into his skin. He felt the pain shooting through his body, fire in his knee. Simpson bit his lip so as not to scream.

"Tough guy, eh?" Rose tapped again.

The blade cut deeper. Simpson thrashed now and almost threw Rose off of him with that energy, but the man just put more weight down, pinning Simpson.

"Talk," came the demand.

Simpson held his lips tight.

"OK," Rose calmly stated.

Another tap. Simpson felt the blade carve deeper into his knee. This one was too much. He screamed. He looked up and saw only a demonic glow in Rose's eyes.

Rose barely twisted the knife. It was enough. The fire in Simpson's knee grew to volcano levels. He screamed louder.

Rose was saying something, but Simpson couldn't make it out. He stared and watched the demon's face come fully alive, eyes lit up, lips grinning. Simpson screamed again.

Simpson was right about one thing. In no way had the major authorized this torture session. Rose had thought it up alone. Not only to get the information and the money but for payback for his ruined knee.

Simpson's screams carried through the warehouse. Other PIS employees came running. When they got to the holding room and saw Rose, they shouted for him to stop. The major had left strict orders. Only if he was in the room was the prisoner to be tortured. Every man working at the warehouse was promised a fat bonus when the information was extracted from Simpson. Greed overcame what little scruples the men there had.

Two men rushed Rose to pull him off of the prisoner. Because his body blocked their view, they had no idea what he was doing.

Looking over his shoulder and knowing he wouldn't get another chance, Scott Rose lifted the hammer and brought it down one final, vicious time. He brought it down hard and fast.

The knife cut deep under Jim Simpson's kneecap. He felt the sinews and cartilage being cut. He felt his kneecap being shifted out of place. That sent a blinding hot shaft of pain from his knee to his brain.

Once again he passed out from the pain.

CHAPTER 11

Weigh the danger of refusal against the price of compliance.

—FM 21-78 Prisoner-of-War Resistance, December 1981

WHILE JIM SIMPSON WAS LAPSING BACK into unconsciousness, the body's response to such trauma, Fred Custer and Van Zandt were in a lawyer's office in Dover, Delaware. They were signing a power of attorney for the quiet man from Orlando. They then began forming a Delaware corporation.

There are many advantages to a Delaware corporation. The chief advantage is that the shareholders have limited liability. Shareholders can be held accountable only to the extent of their investment in the stock of the corporation. Any liabilities are also generally subject only to Delaware law. Delaware's Chancery Court system has a long history of writing clean law in defense of the state's corporate charters. The system delivered large amounts of business to the small state each year. Custer figured that if the IRS, Federal Reserve, and CIA had thought Delaware the best state to incorporate within when they chartered themselves, it was good enough for him.

Gilgamesh Services LLC was born. Custer liked using the name of the Babylonian king as his corporate name. That king had ruled and built his myths in Sumeria, which was modern-day Iraq. It seemed proper.

Custer became president, Van Zandt vice president, and for an extra fee, two of the lawyer's staff became corporate officers. Now all Gilgamesh Services needed was something to sell.

With the paperwork all done, Van Zandt and Custer left the offices. Their first stop was the airport; from there, Van Zandt would make his way to the Cayman Islands. Custer drove back to Alexandria.

AS THOSE TWO WERE COMPLETING their tasks, Hickey was picking up his emergency passport. He bought some clothes, boots, toiletries, and a carry-on bag to stuff them all into. With everything he needed, he headed to the airport and began his trip to Baghdad.

CHARLES SIMPSON HAD NOT BEEN any less productive in following his orders. Back within the thick walls of the Pentagon, he searched for something a unit needed in Iraq and needed imminently.

He called coworkers, chided and prodded them. If there was a stall, he called in debt chits. It took him most of the morning to find exactly what he needed. He got the contract transferred to his office. The fellow officer who sent it over was more than happy to send it along. He didn't want to bother with it. The contract was too small for what he usually dealt with. Just a few rifles, some scopes, and a few thousand rounds of special ammo. For him, it was a drop in the ocean of materials he usually requisitioned for the army in Iraq.

When Charles Simpson read the actual request from the field, he smiled. *This will do,* he thought. *This should do quite nicely.*

He called Custer's cell phone to let him know the news.

"Will that work?" he asked Custer.

Custer thought a moment. Indeed, it would. It was perfect for what he needed.

"Yes," Custer replied. "Beautifully. In fact, I have just the man for that contract."

After hanging up with Simpson, Custer dialed his phone. He called Beaumont, Texas.

Dave Hargis screened all of his calls. It was after he heard Custer's voice that he grabbed the phone, interrupting the recorded message.

"Yeah, I'm here," he said to his former commander.

"Dave, how are you?" Custer greeted the old sniper from Texas.

Custer then explained why he was calling and what he needed Dave Hargis for. Hargis was grinning as he listened more.

"Hell, yes," he finally said, beaming. "Count me in. When and where?"

Custer had him book a flight out of Houston to Reagan Airport. Custer would pick him up when the flight came in.

GERALDINE CUSTER AND NORA SIMPSON were just as busy as the men. They were jetting across the continent to the Seattle area, where Jim Simpson's wife and son lived. As long as he was missing, they were not safe. The last thing Custer and his people needed was a threat or attack upon innocents.

Custer wanted the wife and son hidden away. He didn't even want to know where his wife was going to perform the task. He just wanted to know that they were off the field of fire if anything came down.

Geraldine Custer understood completely. No one else knew Fred Custer and his ways as well as she did. Like the men who followed the former Special Forces major, she knew there was always a method to his madness.

She would get the job done.

CHAPTER 12

EAT THE FOOD AVAILABLE. You will get less, worse, and stranger food than you ever had.

—FM 21-78 Prisoner-of-War Resistance, December 1981

JIM SIMPSON SAT ON THE BUNK in his improvised cell. They hadn't tied him down after Rose cut his knee. Simpson didn't know what happened to Rose, but he never saw him again.

The major had been almost human toward Simpson after the cutting. There was no torture. He was getting decent meals three times a day, and a portable chemical toilet had been placed in the corner of his room. They had treated his wounded knee as best they could. Simpson was stuck with a serious limp for now. Other than meals, he was left alone in the cell.

What he needed to do was buy some time. He knew that his father was aware that something was up. Jim wanted to give him some time to do something. Jim wasn't sure what his father would do, but he was sure there would be some attempt. He knew the major's kindness would be limited. Eventually he would try to force the information on the bank account from Simpson again. He thought of how he could steal some time. After thinking it out, he came upon an idea. The inspiration was born from his son.

When Lowsley came into the cell to feed him, Simpson asked if he could have a whole onion cut in halves with his next meal.

"A what?" Lowsley asked.

"A whole onion," Simpson repeated. "I like raw onion."

Lowsley looked at him with disgust. Simpson thought that for a man who cranked handles on field generators to torture people, it was an odd reaction. He kept that thought to himself.

"I'll see," Lowsley said, leaving the cell.

Sure enough, when his next meal arrived Simpson found two halves of an onion on top of the tray. The thin plastic spoon and fork offered him nothing useful. The plastic tray—well, other than hitting someone with it, it was useless. Two men always came to serve him lunch. One entered the room, and the other remained at the door with a Taser in hand in case Simpson tried anything.

Even with his gimp knee they weren't taking any chances with Simpson. Simpson wasn't worried. He had his weapon.

After eating the food, he choked down a few bites from one of the onion halves. He wanted it to look good. It tasted awful, but he did it. Then he lay down and waited.

They checked on him every four hours. Two men unlocked the door, peeked in, making sure he was OK, and then relocked the door. Simpson waited two hours, stuffed the untouched half onion under his armpit, then lay down and waited.

He had discovered this trick when his son kept getting a fever on some school days. Simpson noticed that these were the days when his son had English tests. The fevers were real, once hitting 101 degrees Fahrenheit.

One day when his son complained of not feeling well, Simpson went to get a thermometer. When he returned to his son's bedroom, he saw the boy cramming something under his pillow. As the boy lay there, thermometer in mouth, Simpson dug to see what the boy had hidden. He found half an onion. He looked into Alex's eyes and saw the child's guilt at being caught.

Jim finished taking his son's temperature (100 degrees that morning), told Alex that he could stay home, called Alex's school, and then went to investigate the mystery. A short search on the Internet found the answer to his son's sudden test-day ailments on a blog by a junior high kid. He researched and found the claim was true.

For whatever reasons, half an onion pressed under the armpit for a couple of hours will give the person a fever. The fever is quite real and lasts three to four hours. Alex's days of missing English tests were finished. Simpson was now grateful for the duplicity.

After two hours he felt his fever rising. It had worked. When he heard the locks being opened for the four-hour check, he quickly removed the onion and threw it under his bunk. By the time the door was opened, he was lying still in bed.

As one of the PIS workers looked in, Simpson attacked.

"What did you feed me?" he asked. "I'm sick as a dog."

The man didn't come check Simpson. He stared at him for a bit, then wordlessly exited the room and relocked the door. He then went and informed the major of the complaint. After the Rose incident, the major had given strict orders that he was to be informed if there was any problem, day or night. Wake him if necessary. "If I'm talking to the president you interrupt. Am I clear?" he had firmly directed his men.

Simpson soon heard the door unlocked again. The major came in and examined him.

"Hum" was all the major said as he left the room, ordering the men to remain at the door, keeping Simpson on his cot. The major was quickly back with a first aid kit. He opened it, removed a thermometer, and checked Simpson's temperature. It was a hot 101 degrees. The last thing the major needed was Simpson getting seriously ill.

"I'm going to get a doctor to examine you," the major stated. "When he examines you, don't say anything. I'll be in the room. If I even think you're trying something, I'll kill the doctor. If I have to, I'll have your wife and son killed. Understand me?"

Simpson thought for a moment. He didn't know if the threat was real, if the major could pull that off. Simpson decided he couldn't take the chance. He looked back at the major with hate in his eyes.

"I understand," he coldly replied. "But if anything happens to my wife or son, even a scratch, you better make sure I'm dead first. Do *you* understand *me*?"

The major didn't reply. He left to go find a doctor. Once the door was closed and locked again, Simpson dug the half onion from under his bed. He would wait a bit and bury it under his armpit again.

The trick had worked. Simpson figured he had bought at least one day's time.

THE MAJOR ARRANGED FOR A doctor. While he waited, he thought. He came to one basic conclusion. He and his team were not trained in getting the information the major needed within the short period of time they had. Eventually someone would come looking for the missing Simpson. The major didn't think the two-week-leave story would hold with Simpson's wife and parents. No, the clock was ticking for the major.

Hataway realized that neither he nor his men had the necessary skill set to force the information from Jim Simpson, but the major thought he knew who did. Through PIS, some specialized items were ordered by a unique man. A man working in one of the secret prisons run by the United States. The major had heard rumors of the purpose of the unique supplies.

Although the supplies for the prison were ordered and transported out of Iraq, it was not in that country. It was in Egypt. Deep in the desert, far away from civilization, the prison was run by both the CIA and the Egyptian police and security forces. It was used for "extracting time-sensitive intelligence from known enemy combatants who are reticent to reveal said intelligence."

The prison was nicknamed "the Death Factory" by those who were sent there.

CHAPTER 13

THE ENEMY'S THE BOSS. Unless you take steps to counter your captor, everything you get—food, drink, clothing, shelter, etc.—depends on him.

—FM 21-78 Prisoner-of-War Resistance, December 1981

HICKEY'S TRIP INTO BAGHDAD WAS UNEVENTFUL. He was surprised at how "by the book" it went. There was at least some form of stability returning to Iraq. Once he had arrived and cleared customs at Baghdad International Airport, he pulled out his cell and found it delivered a signal. That was something good. He had brought along phone cards just in case, but the cell phone worked for now.

He called his hotel, the Sheraton Ishtar. In spite of its name, the hotel had nothing to do with the worldwide Sheraton Hotel chain. Saddam had seized the hotel after the first Gulf War. It had reopened in 1992 and kept the name, much to the annoyance of the former owners. Located in the Sadoun, or downtown, district, on Firdos Square, across from the fortified Green Zone, the hotel is among the tallest buildings in Baghdad. Only the Baghdad Tower is taller.

Hickey confirmed his reservation and asked about ground transportation. The desk clerk suggested he take a taxi. There were plenty waiting to make a buck, and Hickey soon found himself at the hotel. After a slight delay he was checked in and was in his room.

He had requested a room facing the Green Zone. An extra fifty slid across the counter to the clerk had assured him a high-floor room facing the U.S.-military-controlled area. Hickey wasn't sure where the PIS building was located, but he wanted to be able to spy on it if possible. He would have to locate some good binoculars, and another tripod. Once he found the enemy's stronghold he could study it, study them. Look for patterns and weaknesses.

His second call was to Shameek Chakrabarti, a Green Beret Hickey had met in his final couple of years of active duty. Shameek was part of the new post-9/11 army. He had moved from India to the United States in 1996 to study computer engineering at the University of Texas at Austin. His IIT entrance exam test scores allowed him to go to any university he wanted. With a million-plus Indian students taking the exam every year, Shameek had scored in the mid-three-hundreds in final numbers.

He finished his degree just after 9/11. He loved America as much as anyone, so he wanted to go fight for his new country. His knowledge of four languages, including Arabic, didn't hurt his chances of getting into the military. The FBI did check his background, though. First, they found a grandfather who had flown dangerous missions for the British RAF in World War II as a tail gunner and survived. Then there was Shameek's father. He was still in the Indian Army training their antiterrorist squads. There was no question as to the young immigrant's history. Still, the FBI questioned him.

They found a man who knew more about the USA than most people born there. His favorites pastimes were reading and sports.

He loved watching any MLB, NFL, or NBA game. He knew more about the three sports than most team rooters. He could name a team's record, player's stats, and other intimate details as few fans could. Peyton Manning was his favorite athlete and the Houston Rockets his favorite team. Shameek was known, among other things, for his love of beer, his hatred of anything related to the Dallas Cowboys, and an inability to speak for long without cussing.

Beyond that, the pair of FBI agents who interviewed him found a hungry young man. A young man who ached to earn his U.S. citizenship more than anything else in his life. He was accepted into the army with the promise that he would get his citizenship when his tour was up. Shameek leaped at the opportunity.

Once in the army, he excelled and was welcomed by the Green Berets. He had earned their beret and then some. His Special Forces training and language skills assured that he was sent to Iraq. He was on his third tour there.

"Yeah, who the hell is it?" Shameek demanded when he answered his cell phone. The caller ID on his cell phone didn't register that it was either his mother or father calling. Hickey grinned.

"It's Hickey, you wog," Hickey replied.

"Hickey? The old dude? The jackass hillbilly?" the Indian shot back. "Man, you were dead by now, I figured."

"That's Major Jackass to you," Hickey chided, "and I'm not dead yet."

"So where are you at these days?"

"Baghdad," Hickey informed the young Green Beret.

"You're shitting me, right?"

"Nope. I'm sitting in my hotel room across the river from the Green Zone."

"No way. This is unreal," Shameek said. "You're joking with me, right?"

"I'm at the Sheraton Ishtar."

"You're crazy. Only a crazy man comes to Baghdad."

"Then call me nuts," Hickey replied. "Can we meet?"

"You're serious. You are here." Shameek paused. "Sure, sure. We can get together. Not now. We have a patrol soon. Won't be back for hours. Can I call you when I get back in?"

"Roger that," Hickey replied and gave the man his room number.

"OK. OK, I'll call later."

"Can you clear me to enter the Green Zone now?"

"Sure, sure," Shameek answered. "I'll get you cleared to visit me. It will be done before I leave. And Hickey . . ."

"Yes?"

"Dude, you really are nuts if you came here."

Hickey laughed again, said good-bye, and disconnected.

With time to kill, he went to find food. He would look for a serious pair of binoculars after that. They might be useful. When he finished those tasks, he would call Custer and check in.

AS HICKEY AND SHAMEEK WERE talking, another Special Forces trooper was walking into the Protective Integrated Services warehouse. His name was Brad Borden. He had been sent to look at Simpson. PIS did lots of business with the Green Berets, supplying their varied, odd-caliber weapons, so the major called a Special Forces commander he knew. Borden was well qualified as a field medic. All Green Berets were. The man didn't mind the request. Everyone had to team up to keep things going in Iraq.

He was glad to get out of the blast-furnace heat of the Iraqi sun and into the cooler space of the warehouse. Even on the short walk from his bivouac he had sweated heavily. That sweat was drying as he walked down the hall and met the major. The major told him that one of his men had fallen sick with a high temperature. Briefed, Borden followed the major into the warehouse and back to where Simpson was being held.

He noticed that two armed men followed them. It wasn't until he had examined Simpson that Borden knew something wasn't right. He didn't know what was bothering him, but he kept his thoughts to himself. As he took Simpson's temperature, using an electronic ear thermometer, he asked when this had happened.

"After we fed him lunch," the major answered. Simpson had been warned not to talk unless he absolutely had to. "He just got sick."

Borden didn't say anything. He looked down and saw Simpson's heavily bandaged knee.

"What happened there?" he asked, pointing.

There was silence in the room. Too much of it.

"He hurt that when a crate fell on him," the major finally lied.

"Mind if I look?" Borden asked. He was quick and had his scissors out and was cutting the rough bandage the PIS soldiers had put over the handiwork of Rose. What could the major say? He had to allow this.

"I was more worried about the fever," the major said, trying to ward off the examination. "Food poisoning, maybe?"

"Maybe," Borden mumbled as he fully exposed the ruined knee.

It was a mess, a nightmare. Anyone looking at it could tell that the wound needed a doctor's examination and treatment, and soon. The area around the cut—and Borden knew a deep cut when he saw one—had swelled to twice its normal size. Infection was settling in. If untreated, the wound might turn gangrenous.

Borden looked directly into Simpson's eyes.

"How did this happen?" he asked.

Simpson thought about his wife and son. He thought of the Special Forces soldier in front of him. He repeated the major's lie.

"A big crate fell on my knee."

Borden was quiet for a bit.

"Yeah, I can see that happening. What's your name?"

"Jim Simpson."

"Jim." Borden played it cool. "You allergic to anything?"

"Not that I know of," Simpson said. "When I was in the Rangers there was never anything given that I couldn't take."

Borden caught the message: fellow warrior. He stood and dug into the medical kit he had brought. He pulled out some penicillin tablets.

"Take these. It should cut your fever and help with the knee's infection." Then he handed Simpson some more pills. "Painkillers if that knee hurts."

Borden turned to face the major. "That fever is the least of his problems," he informed him. "That knee needs attention—and quickly, or he might lose it."

The major was silent.

Borden couldn't believe what he was seeing. Something was definitely wrong here. He didn't know what, but he needed to get away from the warehouse to do anything about it. He smiled at the major.

"Yeah, get him to a real medical facility and get that knee treated and he'll be fine. They can check out the fever also. Anything else I can do?" Borden asked. He was playing it just right under the circumstances.

"No," the major said. "We'll get him to a hospital. Thanks. If there's anything you need, just let me know. We sure appreciate this."

I'll bet you do. Borden kept it to himself as he smiled. "Great. Well, I'm off, then. Our unit is off on patrol soon. I can just make it. They're expecting me."

"Thanks for coming."

"Glad I could help," Borden said, following the major from the makeshift cell. As he reached the door, he turned and faced Simpson again. No one else could see Borden's face.

"Oh yeah, those pills, take two of the penicillin every four hours and the painkillers only if you need them. No more than one of those every eight hours. Sorry I couldn't do more."

Then he winked at Simpson. The major walked him to the front of the PIS warehouse. When Borden had made it back outside the building, he turned and faced the major.

"I'd get him to the Ibn Sina Hospital for that knee," he said. "I'd do that today if I were you. Like I said, I'm going on patrol soon, but when I get back I'll check in and see if he was treated. We all have to work together here to make sure the right things happen."

Borden wasn't sure if it was hate in the major's eyes, but it was something. Borden walked away. Yes, he would definitely check when he got back from patrol. No falling crate could do what had been done to that knee. That knee was cut.

CHAPTER 14

Make him aware that though he may be in solitary confinement, he is not alone—is never alone.

—FM 21-78 Prisoner-of-War Resistance, December 1981

After lunch Hickey had managed to find a decent pair of binoculars and another tripod to mount them on. He also found a good map of Baghdad, with the back side showing mainly the downtown and Green Zone areas.

When he retuned to his hotel room he set up the camera and binoculars so that they faced the Green Zone. He scoped things out and found that he had a decent view of most of the area. A 300 mm lens goes a long way. He would have to find out where the PIS building was and see if he had a clear field of view on it.

Baghdad, like much of Iraq, is flat as a pancake. This feature is what allowed General Norman Schwarzkopf's plans to become a deadly reality during the first Gulf War. The country was a natural for tank warfare.

Generally the tallest buildings in Baghdad reach three stories at most. The Sheraton Ishtar's extra floors allowed Hickey a fine view of what he needed to see. He took a red Sharpie marker and made some notes on the map. He took special notice of what looked to be an event being prepared for in the middle of the Green Zone. A large platform was being set up with speakers and a light grid around and above a stage.

Done for now, he packed the camera and binoculars up and stored them. The last thing he needed was some maid thinking he was with the CIA or al Qaeda. Neither would be good. *The world sure is getting paranoid,* Hickey thought.

Hickey sank onto the hotel room bed and dialed Custer. It was time to report in and see what the leader of this operation was up to.

Custer had just picked up Hargis at the airport, and they were settling into the rented car when his cell phone rang. He saw it was Hickey calling and pressed the call alive.

"Ted," he said in greeting, "good to hear from you. How go things?"

"So far so good," Hickey replied. "I'm in the hotel on the ground. I'm meeting up with a friend later, and hopefully he can take me to the company we want to deal with. Doing a little recon work."

"Great," Custer said. "I formed the new company. Gilgamesh Services. I'll have a contract in hand soon and bank accounts set up. It should cover anything we need to do business over there."

"Sounds good," Hickey replied.

"Anything you need over there?"

Hickey thought for a moment.

"Can you send me a picture of Jim?" he asked. "It might be useful. And I would like some cash on tap."

"I'll talk to Charlie on the picture. The cash, I'll set something up. A wire transfer to a bank or the hotel if necessary. Where are you staying?"

Hickey told him.

"And they have Internet services there?"

"Yes. Half the press people live here. The hotel keeps that running."

"What's your e-mail address?"

"HickeySOF at aol.com," Hickey told him.

"Got it," Custer said. "Anything else?"

"Not that I can think of."

"Good," Custer said. "Here, talk to an old friend."

Custer handed the cell over to Hargis. Dave Hargis's long hair in a ponytail rode down his back over his favorite Hawaiian shirt; jeans and cowboy boots finished his outfit out. His skin was bronzed from the South Texas sun. Over the past year he had spent a lot of time in that sun on the gun range playing with his custom-made Barrett .50 caliber rifle. He beamed as he spoke to Hickey, the two men catching up on things.

"Hear I might be working with you again," Hargis drawled in his Texas accent.

"That's mighty fine," Hickey replied.

"Yeah," said Hargis. "Custer found me a new toy to play with."

"What's that?" Hickey questioned.

"You might just see," came the reply. "I have to go to Idaho first. Then I should be jetting my way to you."

"Well, it would be good to see you," Hickey replied.

They finished the conversation, and Hargis disconnected the call. The two old troopers headed back to Charles Simpson's house to see what hook he had found to hang things on.

THE HOOK CHARLES SIMPSON HAD found was a new sniper rifle system.

In the 1990s, Professor John D. Taylor saw the need to improve the over-eighty-year-old technology of the .50 caliber round. He put together a small group of extremely talented people, and they formed a company called CheyTac Associates. That team developed a new round: the .408 caliber. This wasn't chance, it was done by science.

Designed as an antimateriel weapon—intended to penetrate armored vehicles or fortifications instead of shooting enemy personnel—the .408 round was more effective than even the .50 caliber at ranges above 700 yards, the realistic engagement range for antimateriel rifles.

While the .50 caliber starts out with more punch—11,200 feet per second leaving the barrel verses the CheyTac's 7,700 fps—after 700 yards the .408 bullet keeps more remaining kinetic energy. The .408 proved better at penetrating armor and laminated glass. Its speed to the target was faster—a full second quicker at long ranges. It also delivered a flatter and more stable flight to the target. There was no doubt that the round was superior. Not even the .50 caliber Raufoss round did better when tested. The CNC-turned rounds made from a hard copper/nickel alloy penetrated Level IIIA body armor at 2,000 yards. They ripped through a half inch of cold-rolled steel at 850 yards.

But that was only the cartridge and bullet. The next step for John Taylor and his team was to build a rifle to shoot it. The CheyTac Intervention was born. Bolt action, holding seven rounds in a detachable clip, fully able to be broken down and reassembled without losing its zero. The team had a winner.

It still wasn't fully what they wanted. They wanted the best.

Day- and night-vision scopes were added. If needed, the night vision has an infrared laser option, developed by B. E. Myers. A Leica Vector IV laser rangefinder was added as well. The shooter straps on a Suunto X6 wrist computer, which collects environmental data as well as temperature and slant angles. There is also a Kestrel 4000 sensor package to collect wind, air temperature, and air pressure, plus relative humidity, wind chill, and dewpoint.

All of that raw data is fed into the unique IT-70 tactical computer. This is what really sets the CheyTac system above the rest. The system digitizes all of the relevant data a sniper needs and factors it at computer speed. The scope's crosshairs are automatically adjusted. All the sniper has to do is get the crosshairs on his target and pull the trigger.

In the hands of a trained shooter the CheyTac system can easily hit a man-sized target at 1.5 miles. Shots at 2,500 yards have been recorded. Further testing showed that on the open desert floors of Idaho a shooter without camouflage could not be seen at 2,000 yards.

Not anyone can just grab the rifle and achieve these results. It takes some training to compose one's shot with all of these systems and the rifle. Dave Hargis was well trained in sniping. He also had years with the Barrett .50 caliber rifles. He quickly learned what he needed to know about how to use the amazing CheyTac system to its fullest effect.

Charles Simpson had found a small contract from an army sniping unit in Iraq. They wanted four of the CheyTac rifles and systems. Under the eternal, seemingly conflicting, rules of war, the rifles would save lives by taking lives.

Custer now had the contract to fill for his little company, the reason for his team to get into Iraq and, more important, inside the well-protected Green Zone where PIS lived. Custer ordered five complete rifle systems directly from the small Idaho company. They checked the contract at the Pentagon and found it to be quite real. Their weapons wouldn't be getting into the wrong hands.

One complete rifle system was a little over $25,000. That included 5,000 rounds of standard ammo and 500 rounds of armor-piercing ammo. Custer wired their bank $140,000 to make sure nothing would slow the deal down. Next he sent Hargis to go get the rifles and train on the system if he could.

Hargis flew a charter jet to Idaho Falls, rented a car, and settled into a hotel in the small town of Arco, where CheyTac was located.

He had thought he could learn what he needed in one day. It took two. With the expert assistance of the staff and John Paver doing the bulk of the hands-on training, he mastered the weapon.

Hargis then arranged for the shipment of four of the rifles with accessories and most of the ammo to Iraq. Custer would find a bonded warehouse to accept the materials. The army would get their four rifles more quickly than if they were procured through normal channels.

Hargis took the fifth rifle with him. He also carried a hundred rounds of standard ammo and fifty of the armor-piercing rounds. Before the sniper headed off to Iraq to join Hickey, he flew back to D.C. to see if Custer needed anything else.

If that ain't enough ammo, then I don't deserve to be shooting anything, he thought.

DURING THE TIME THAT HARGIS was training in Idaho, Geraldine Custer and Nora Simpson had arrived in Seattle, where Jim Simpson's wife and son lived. Like the rest of Custer's soldiers, they were under strict orders. Get Jan and Alex Simpson out of Seattle. Out of Washington State, as a matter of fact.

Buy a good used car off of Craigslist and pay cash. Don't get it titled in your name. Stall the seller somehow. Travel somewhere; anywhere. Do what you want. Only use cash. Never use any credit or debit card. Get pay-per-use cell phones. Don't tell anyone where you are going.

Over three days Geraldine had drawn $20,000 in cash from their accounts. She toted a Smith & Wesson small-frame model 442 chambered in .38 caliber. She knew how to use it. She wasn't worried.

The women knew what to do. They went first to San Francisco. If you're going to be on the run, it might as well be in someplace nice.

* * *

WHILE HICKEY WAS WAITING FOR Shameek to call, he checked his e-mail at a row of computers the hotel had set up. He had two clear pictures of Jim Simpson waiting. Charles Simpson had scanned one family photo that sat on his desk, as well as his son's official army photo from his file. The weight of a general's aide makes things happen fast when necessary. Hickey set off to the Green Zone.

True to his word, the Indian Green Beret had left instructions to let Hickey in. His CAC as a contractor helped make it real. The guards at the gate between the seventeen-foot walls took only ten minutes of calling around until they spoke to the Special Forces unit Shameek was with. Yes, a Hickey was authorized to enter the Green Zone. The guards wished him a good day as they opened the gate. Hickey got directions to the area where the Green Berets were living. He also asked where Protective Integrated Services was located.

"Got a friend working there. Haven't seen him in years," he told them to keep the front up.

The guards didn't care why he wanted to know. One of them pulled out a rough copy of a map of the Green Zone that the post kept to hand out. The guard clearly circled the areas where the Green Berets were, where PIS was, and, finally, the spot where Hickey was now. It made navigating easy. Hickey asked for another copy of the map, one with no markings on it. The guard handed another over. Hickey set off.

His first stop was the warehouse where PIS was. He didn't even act like he was interested as he walked by it. He just went forward, eyes straight ahead. He went well past the building. A couple of minutes away from the PIS building, Hickey found the stage he had seen earlier. It looked to be set up for a musician to play. Hickey walked over toward that area and studied it. After five minutes he did a 180 and walked back from where he had come, map in hand. He tried to put a confused look on his face.

Hickey walked past the front entrance of PIS and turned down the side of the building. He walked as far as he could before hitting a barbed-wire fence protecting the loading dock area in the rear. He folded the marked map up and slid it into his back pocket. He walked back to the front of the structure. He held out the unmarked map.

Now to see how far he could get into the building. He stopped in front of the main glass door entrance and stared at his map. He didn't know if there were cameras or if he was being watched. Looking bewildered, he turned the map upside down and stared around the area, trying to appear lost. Then Hickey went to the front door and grabbed the handle. He walked in.

There was a small foyer area in front with a standard military-issue steel desk. Scott Rose sat behind the desk guarding the door behind him, which led into the hall where Jim Simpson had started his sprint. Rose had been put on guard duty as punishment. He looked up at the visitor. Not many came through the front door. Rose didn't say a thing.

"Hi," salesman Hickey opened. "Hope you can help me. I seem to be lost. I'm trying to find the CPA mess hall. Have to meet someone there, and I'm late."

Rose looked bored. He didn't care where this stranger had to be or when.

Hickey spread the map out on the desktop. "First time in here. Not even sure where I'm at," he said.

Rose bent over to stare at the map. Hickey used the moment to study the small foyer. He saw no cameras.

"You're here"—Rose pointed—"and you want to go here."

"Have a pen?" Hickey asked, patting his empty shirt pocket.

Rose looked up at him and grimaced. He wasn't happy being stuck out behind this desk all day. The major pretty much had him on permanent guard duty, only letting him go off to sleep before having to return. *It's not like anyone is going to break in or attack the place,* Rose thought. *We're in the middle of the Green Zone.*

Wordlessly, Rose opened the desk drawers and rooted around until he found a pen.

"You're here," Rose repeated, circling the PIS building, "and here's the CPA mess hall."

Rose drew lines and arrows from the two points in hopes that the stranger would go away and never return. He slid the map back at Hickey.

"What do you all do here?" Hickey asked.

Rose was silent.

"Top secret, I guess," Hickey said. Seeing that he couldn't get farther into the building, Hickey took the map, studied it, and smiled. "Thanks."

"Yeah, sure," Rose replied.

Hickey exited the building. He walked back toward the music area. There were some men setting up speakers and running wires. Hickey walked around until he found a roadie working behind a sound board. Hickey approached the man.

"When's the show?" he asked.

The soundman looked up. "Eight o'clock tonight."

"Who's singing?"

"Chely Wright."

"That will be great," Hickey said. "Someone I know said he wanted to come to the show."

"That right?" the soundman said, not really caring. "Well, she puts on a great show. He'll like it."

"That's the problem," Hickey spun a tale. "He can't make it. Guard duty."

The soundman twisted some knobs and adjusted sound levels.

"But he's close. He can hear it, I bet," Hickey said.

"That's nice." More knobs adjusted.

"But I would like to make sure he hears it. Especially one part." Hickey reached into his pocket and pulled a hundred-dollar bill off of a wad he carried. He dropped it on the sound board where the soundman couldn't miss it. "Think maybe you can help me?"

The knob turning stopped. The man looked up at Hickey. Hickey dropped another hundred on top of the first.

"Maybe," the soundman said. "Depends on what you want done."

Hickey added a third Franklin. He had the soundman's full attention.

"It's my nephew," Hickey lied. "He's a big fan. Has all her CDs. I swear it's all he listens to. I want to do something special for him since he can't make it."

The soundman stared at the three hundred dollars in front of him.

Hickey explained what he wanted.

The soundman just stared at Hickey, down at the stack again, then back at Hickey.

Hickey added two more bills.

"Yeah, sure." The soundman scooped up the bills and slid them into his pocket. "I think we can do that. Anything for the troops, right? What's his name?"

"Jim Simpson," Hickey said.

"She'll start at nine or so. Listen for it."

"I'll be here." Hickey smiled.

CHAPTER 15

The use of force, mental torture, threats, insults, or exposure to unpleasant and inhumane treatment of any kind is prohibited by law and not authorized nor condoned by the US Government.

—FM 34-52 Intelligence Interrogation, May 1987

MAJOR HATAWAY WAS NOT HAPPY. HE had no choice but to get Simpson to the Green Zone hospital. The Green Beret medic had left him no option. He would go with Lowsley and Simpson to the hospital and get the knee taken care of. With $330 million on the line, he didn't want any more screwups. The situation was getting out of hand.

The major would warn Simpson again about his family and get him in and out of the hospital as fast as he could. Once that was done, Major Hataway would make a call to Egypt and talk to the man who ordered odd items, the man who ran the Death Factory. The major would travel with Simpson to the faraway Egyptian desert and be there for every session until the much-needed passwords were forced out of Jim Simpson.

From what he heard, the man in Egypt was very good at obtaining information from uncooperative prisoners.

AS THE MAJOR THOUGHT OUT his next moves, Scott Rose was still in the front foyer doing guard duty.

From outside, the sounds of some country music band leaked through the thin walls of the PIS building. Rose had heard about the free concert. Some country singer was doing a show. Not that Rose cared. He hated country music. Rose stared at his watch. It was twenty to nine. He wondered when the major would let him go to sleep tonight.

WHILE ROSE WAS STEWING IN his punishment duty, Hickey was very close to the PIS building. He had come back to the music stage to wait to see if his plan would be pulled off as he had paid for.

Hickey stood listening to some backup band kick off the show at 8:00 P.M. They played forty-five minutes. Hickey wandered the area until he was close to where the soundman was. They eventually made eye contact. The man behind the board smiled, winked, and threw a thumbs-up at Hickey. Hickey gave him a return thumbs-up and waited.

At 9:05, Chely Wright came onto the stage. The crowd of soldiers and others cheered the pretty country singer as she said hello and started her show. The soundman did what he had been paid for. After a brief introduction the singer spoke into the microphone.

"This first song goes out for one of you soldiers out there. A Ranger."

There were cheers and catcalls from some Rangers in the audience. They yelled, "*Hoohah!* Rangers all the way!" at the mention of the oldest United States military fighting force.

The soundman earned his five hundred dollars. He lowered the sound on the front speakers and upped the volume to an ear-splitting shriek on the speakers in the rear. The singer's words boomed out across the entire area.

"He can't be here tonight because he's on guard duty," the singer said, "so this song is for you, Jim Simpson! Your daddy says he's sending your uncle to you!"

With the message sent, the soundman returned the sound levels to where they should be and turned until he spotted Hickey. He shrugged his shoulders as a question. Hickey beamed a big smile and gave another thumbs-up. The soundman smiled back.

It had worked.

INSIDE THE PIS WAREHOUSE, LOCKED in his makeshift cell, Jim Simpson suddenly heard his name and the message from his father rumble through the thin tin walls. The noise was faint but he heard it.

The message swelled Simpson's heart and spirit. His dad had gotten his e-mail and acted upon it. Someone was doing something to find him. Bolstered for the first time since his capture, Jim Simpson lay down and went to sleep with a smile on his face.

THE MAJOR ALSO HEARD THE message thumping through the walls of the building. How many Jim Simpsons could there be in the Green Zone? The major assumed the worst and redoubled his resolve to get Simpson out of Iraq to the Death Factory.

He went to find Lowsley. They would get Simpson to the hospital that very moment.

* * *

HOPING HE HAD GOT THE message through to Simpson, Hickey walked over and found a secluded, dark spot where he could watch the front of the PIS building. He wanted to see if the message had caused a reaction. He watched for fifteen minutes. Nothing. His cell phone rang. He answered it quietly.

"Hello."

"Hickey, Shameek. We're back, man," the Indian Green Beret said. "Come pop a beer open with us."

"Be there in fifteen," Hickey replied and hung up. He waited five more minutes. Still no movement from the warehouse. He left to go meet Shameek. He had a little shopping list he hoped Shameek could help him with.

Hickey knew the drill as he approached the Special Forces compound deep inside the Green Zone. There was a guard at the gate of a barbed-wire perimeter as well as a tower. The man in the tower manned an M2HB .50 caliber heavy machine gun. Hickey knew that .50 was kept on him as he approached the guard.

No matter where in the world the Green Berets were stationed, they ran their own security 24/7. It was from hard lessons learned that this was done. Hickey would have done the same thing.

He announced himself to the guard and waited while the soldier radioed Shameek. Hickey had to stand there while the Indian came out to walk him into the compound. Shameek smiled broadly, and they shook hands. Then Shameek hugged him hard and patted his back.

"Good to see you, man!" Shameek said with an even bigger smile. "Man, I can't believe it's really you." Shameek turned to the guard. "He's cool, dude. He just retired after thirty years in the Berets. He started in Vietnam."

Hickey and Shameek entered the compound and settled into the rough area Shameek called home, a field cot sitting among twenty other cots in a small warehouse space. A cinder-block-and-boards bookcase was stuffed with Sherlock Holmes, Alistair MacLean, Frederick Forsyth, and Stephen Hunter books, among other thrillers. While growing up in India, Shameek had learned English by reading about Doyle's detective. As a teen, he discovered MacLean and Forsyth. He had read all of their titles at least ten times each.

Shameek found a wooden chair for Hickey, sat on his cot, and pulled an Igloo ice chest out from under the cot. He pulled out two ice-cold Miller Lite beers and handed one to Hickey. They caught up on old times.

"I thought Iraq was alcohol free," Hickey commented, taking a long drink from the cold can.

"Maybe," Shameek said, "but this building ain't Iraq. Far as I'm concerned, this is the USA."

They finished the beers before Hickey got down to business.

"I'm looking for some things," he stated. "I could use a little personal protection while I'm here."

Shameek sat and listened.

"A pistol would be nice. A .45 if possible. And a good knife. And if there's any way, a good rifle might come in handy."

Shameek looked around the room before replying. There was no one else close.

"Hickey, man, this is between you and me. I owe you some from when I started out in the Berets. That DI wanted me gone from the program. You saved my butt then and a couple more times. I didn't know anything, and you taught me. If it wasn't for you, I wouldn't have hacked it. But you're asking a lot, man."

"It's important, Shameek."

Shameek sat up, crushed his beer can, and threw it into a paper bag for trash. He pulled out another beer. "A rifle is easy. We got more AKs than we know what to do with. We keep finding them on patrols. Ammo might be a problem."

“I need three full clips max,” Hickey informed him. Shameek nodded.

“A .45 is another thing, but I think it could be done. But Hickey, I got to know why.”

“This stays between us,” Hickey stated.

“One hundred percent,” the Indian said.

So Hickey told Shameek why he was in Baghdad. The Green Beret sat silently listening until the story was told.

“No shit, man?” he finally asked.

“No shit.”

“Man, that’s messed up. No idea where this guy is now?”

“That’s why I’m here. To find out,” Hickey said.

“OK, I can do what I can do,” Shameek said.

He sat up and dragged a duffel bag from under his cot. He opened it and dug through it until he found what he was looking for. He handed a knife over to Hickey.

“That good?”

“Perfect,” Hickey said as he hefted the Gerber Mark II in his hand. The twelve inches of steel and edge felt good. He pulled his pants leg up and slipped the knife and leather sheath into his boot.

“That’s my knife, old man,” Shameek said. “I’ll want it back when you’re done. Pistol and rifle I’ll have to work on. You’re at the Sheraton, right?”

“Yes.”

“I’ll see what I can dig up and get it over to you. Bring it myself. They won’t be assigned pieces. Stuff we grabbed off of patrol. This is going to cost me some.”

“If you need money . . .” Hickey said.

“Not money, you crazy old man. This is the Green Berets. We take care of our own. But it will cost me paybacks down the line.”

“The way it’s always done.”

“Yeah, I pay you back by owing someone. I pay him back down the line. All good,” Shameek said. “That’s some serious shit you're involved in, Hickey. You realize Baghdad is like the Wild West. Not many rules here. Lot of strange stuff goes down."

"I can handle it."

Shameek looked at Hickey. "Yeah, I suppose you can. You're a tough old bird."

With business done, the two soldiers traded stories. Shameek told him how Iraq was. How the patrols were not easy—but then, what in war is?

"But if I wanted a boring job and a white-picket-fence house in suburbia, I wouldn't have joined the army," the Indian said.

They chewed the fat for a good hour. Hickey enjoyed being among his beloved Green Berets again. He almost wished he was still in, but what old soldier doesn't think that? Hickey was thinking it was time to leave when another young Special Forces man walked over.

"Beer me, beer man," he demanded.

Shameek dug a fresh can of Miller Lite out and tossed it to the man.

"Where you been?" he asked him.

"Went to the hospital," came the answer.

"Man," Shameek joked, "you get the clap again?"

Hickey and the other Beret laughed.

"No. I was checking on something. You want to hear some messed-up shit?" the man asked.

"Tell me," Shameek answered.

So Brad Borden told them why he went to the hospital. He told them of the cut knee. Shameek and Hickey sat up with interest.

"Did you get his name?" Hickey asked.

"Sure," Borden answered. "Jim Simpson."

"Dude, sit down," Shameek said. "We got to seriously talk."

Borden told them the full story.

"If I showed you a picture, you could identify the man?" Hickey asked.

"Yeah, sure," Borden replied.

"Let me go to my hotel and print a couple pictures off from my e-mail."

"OK. Or we could pull up your e-mail account on my cell phone and see the pictures now," Shameek said.

"You can do that?" Hickey asked. He wasn't that fluent in cell phone use.

"No wonder you guys lost Vietnam," Shameek said as he dug out his BlackBerry and brought it to life. "We'll win here, you know."

"Yes, but not in Afghanistan," Hickey said. "I'll pay five to one on bets."

"No shit. Five to one?" Shameek said as he punched buttons on his cell phone.

"Yeah. Three for the British, one for Russians, and one for Alexander the Great."

"OK, no bet," Shameek said quickly. He was also very well read in history. "Who's your e-mail provider?"

"AOL."

Shameek punched buttons and pressed the screen. "Screen name?"

"HickeySOF."

Shameek punched more buttons and handed the phone over. "Type in your password."

Hickey followed orders, then handed the cell phone back to Shameek. Shameek scanned through the e-mails.

"What was the header on the e-mail with the pictures?" he asked. Hickey told him. Shameek pressed a couple more buttons and handed the phone to Borden.

"That the man?" he asked.

"That's him," Borden said, staring at the photos of the man he had worked on. Borden handed the phone back to Shameek. The Indian was silent for a bit.

"Definitely SNAFU, Hickey," he finally said.

"At least I know where he is."

"Well, he's not at the hospital," Borden said. "They did take him in and get his knee fixed. But then they got him right out of there. The doctor said they told him that he was flying home tomorrow."

"If he's flying anywhere, it's not home," Hickey commented.

"Let's go see if we can fill your shopping list, old man," Shameek said, standing up, "and find you a bag to carry it all in."

THE TRIP TO THE HOSPITAL done, and with Simpson back in his cell, the major started making calls to people he knew. It was late, but he emphasized the importance of the task. He pushed buttons where they needed to be pushed.

He finally got through to the man in Egypt. He explained briefly what he wanted and what he was offering to pay for the information: $100,000 up front to any bank account the man wanted and $900,000 more upon the prisoner giving the valid information requested.

The major didn't explain it all. He didn't tell the man in Egypt how much money was at stake. All he told him was that he had a prisoner, he needed the prisoner to talk, and needed him to talk fast.

With the swinging carrot-on-a-stick of a cool million in cash to his Swiss bank account, the man from Egypt told the major to stay where he was until he was called back. The man in Egypt hung up and quickly dialed a number in Smithfield, North Carolina.

Not many people in the world had that telephone number. Not many needed it. The man in Egypt did. He also had the clout to make whoever was answering that phone do what needed to be done. The man from Egypt did a lot of work for the people who paid for that phone. He stressed the urgency of the situation. He was told that yes, there was a plane that could be in Baghdad soon. By 4:00 A.M. if necessary.

"It's very necessary," the man in Egypt informed the other end of the line.

"It will be there," he was told. "You know the procedure."

The man in Egypt hung up and called the major back. He told him to have the prisoner at the Baghdad airport at 3:00 A.M. and to expect the plane at 4:00.

The major smiled as he hung up. He knew he would soon get the information he needed. The man he had called was a professional. He was very good at what he did.

CHAPTER 16

PWs must be moved under humane

conditions and treated humanely.

—FM 21-78 Prisoner-of-War Resistance, December 1981

JIM SIMPSON AWAKENED TO THE SOUNDS of the lock on his door being turned and the door being opened. The light switch was flipped on, and the dull glare filled the room. Simpson's eyes tried to adjust.

The major led the way, followed by Lowsley pushing a wheelchair. A third man stood back holding a Taser ready if necessary. The last thing Simpson wanted was to feel those fifty thousand volts flowing through his body. He didn't know what was going on, but he knew he had to preserve all his strength in this battle. Jim Simpson knew he was in a war.

The last time he had been taken from the room was to go to

the hospital. Before they left the PIS building, Simpson had been reminded of the threat to his wife and son. Until Simpson knew they were safe, he wouldn't do anything to endanger their lives. But he could still fight as best he could. He could still resist.

At the hospital he had played along as the major wished. The doctor on duty just wanted to take care of the wound and get on to the next case on his busy roster of patients. The doctor checked the cut, dressed it, and gave Simpson antibiotics. He found a knee brace and put it on Simpson's wounded knee.

The major stood watching the entire time with two of his henchmen in tow. The doctor informed them that the knee needed surgery as soon as possible.

"Oh, he'll get that quick," the major lied. "He'll get the best care we can find. We just have to fly him out of Iraq tomorrow."

Placated, the doctor finished dressing the knee and went on his way to the next name on a chart. The major and his men quickly got Simpson out of the hospital.

So Jim Simpson wondered what the major was up to this time. He hopped over from the bed to the wheelchair.

"Where are we going?" Simpson asked.

"You'll see" was the major's cryptic reply.

Lowsley wheeled Simpson through the warehouse and out the front door. They passed Rose sitting at his punishment station as they exited. Out front was a van, its engine already running, the wide side door already opened.

It was the dead of night. Simpson knew it must be past midnight at least. He wondered what was happening.

"Are we out for a midnight snack?" he sarcastically asked.

His question was ignored. Simpson was manhandled into the middle seat. Lowsley slid in next to him after folding the wheelchair and placing it into the van. The third man with the Taser sat behind in a bench seat. His orders were clear: If Simpson tried anything, shock him until he was down.

The major slid the door shut, hopped into the passenger seat, and barked, "Let's go."

It was a little after 2:00 A.M. when the group began their drive to the airport. The major had planned to be at the airport at least fifteen minutes before his 3:00 A.M. mandate. He knew they would have to wait for the 4:00 A.M. rendezvous, but that was fine. As long as the major felt that he was making progress, he was happy.

Whoever the man in Egypt was, he carried clout.

At the airport, they were quickly routed toward a U.S.-military-only section. Once they passed through the gate, two Humvees full of men took control, one in front and one behind the PIS van. Each Humvee had one man sticking out of the hole in the roof on an M-60 machine gun. The Humvees led the van across the tarmac to a large hangar. As the convoy approached, the large double doors of the hangar opened.

When the three vehicles were inside, the two Humvees quickly drove away. Their job was done yet again. The hangar doors closed, leaving the van alone on the empty floor of the structure. Bright xenon arc lights filled the space with a clean white luminance.

Four men walked out of an office connected to the hangar interior. Even the major was shocked by their appearance. Dressed in matching black full-body coveralls and boots, and with black wool ski masks covering their heads, they looked like terrorists to the major. All one could see were their eyes, mouths, and hands.

Two armed with M-4A1 rifles stopped, rigid with arms at port, and stood ready in the background. The other two continued to the van. One of them circled his fingers in the air, motioning the major to lower his window. Once the window was down, the black-clad man spoke.

"Who's Major Hataway?" he asked.

"That's me," the major replied.

"Come with me, please, sir. Everyone else stay exactly where you are. Those two men's rifles are locked and loaded, and they will use whatever force they deem necessary," the man said, turning and heading back to the office. He didn't look back. He had done these procedures scores of times. He was used to being in control, and men either followed his instructions or . . . well, men eventually followed his instructions, no matter what.

The major got out of the van and walked toward the office with the second man behind him. The other two with their rifles stood like granite. They looked as if they could stand that way until the end of time.

Once inside the small office, the first man, the only man of the four anyone heard speak that night, explained the procedure. He quickly told the major what would happen to Jim Simpson to get him on the 4:00 A.M. plane and off to Egypt.

Briefed and a little shocked, the major asked, "Is that all really necessary?"

"That is the procedure, sir," came the reply.

The major didn't have any control here. He had entered the domain of the CIA's extraordinary rendition program. The four black-clad men didn't know who the major or Jim Simpson was. They didn't care. That wasn't their job. Their job was to professionally get the prisoners onto the CIA flights and off to wherever those prisoners were bound. What happened after that was not their concern.

"Just the prisoner and you are going aboard, correct?" the man asked.

"Yes, just us," the major replied.

The man looked at his watch. "Let's get to it."

Quickly, he exited the office with the major in tow and the second man in black behind them both. As they reached the van, the first man barked his next order.

"Bring out the prisoner."

Lowsley looked over at the major. The major quickly nodded an affirmation. Lowsley stepped out of the van and then pulled the wheelchair out.

"What's the wheelchair for?" the black-clad man asked. "I wasn't briefed on any medical condition." He wasn't used to surprises.

"It's his knee," the major replied. "He was injured. We just got back from the hospital a couple of hours ago. He's been treated."

The man turned and looked at the major. His eyes did not look friendly.

"Can he stand?" he asked.

"Yes, I think so," the major said, but with an uncertain quiver in his voice.

The black-clad man turned back toward Lowsley.

"Stand him up and we'll see."

Simpson was brought out of the van and left standing. He leaned his weight away from his wounded knee. He could stand. Barely, but he could stand.

"Spread your legs. Two feet apart," the man in charge ordered.

"What's going on?" Simpson demanded. "What are you doing with me?"

Questions. The man in black hated questions.

"Whatever I want," he coldly replied. "Now you're going on an airplane. You're going one way or another. Some do as they are told. I've sent some knocked out, but they all went."

Jim Simpson thought for a moment. No, this was not the time to fight. These men were not where he needed to use his energy. *Pick your battles. Buy time*, Simpson thought. The country singer's voice and the message she delivered flowed back through his mind. He spread his legs as far apart as he could without falling over.

"Good enough," the black-clad man said. "The van and your men can leave now."

Not realizing for a moment that he was being addressed, the major didn't speak at first. He eventually understood and ordered

Lowsley and the van away. "Yes," he said. "Hand me my bag and get back to the warehouse. Lowsley, you're in charge until you hear from me."

Shrugging, Lowsley got the major's travel bag from the back and handed it over. Then he slid the side door on the van closed, hopped into the passenger seat and looked at the major. "Yes, sir," he said with a half salute before slamming the door shut. The van circled around to leave. One of the rifle-armed men went over and pressed a button and the hangar doors slowly parted. Once the van was gone, he reversed the movement of the doors and they closed again. He then returned to his post.

The other two black-clad men walked over to a wall where a tall metal cabinet stood. Number one opened it and pulled out a large, sealed package. He headed back toward Simpson. Number two had grabbed a small two-foot-square folding metal table and a folding metal chair.

Number one set the package on the table. Stenciled across the top of the package was POW KIT 2R-3A. Number one pulled a folding knife out and cut the package open. A bright orange jumpsuit sat on top of the other things in the package.

Number one turned and faced number two. Using only a few hand signals, they began their work. They had worked together for almost three years now, had the procedure down pat. Number two also pulled out a sharp folding knife.

They walked over to Simpson and started cutting his clothes away.

"Hey!" Simpson protested.

Number one looked up at him. "Easy or hard?"

Simpson shut up.

He was soon almost completely naked. They had left the knee brace on. The two men thoroughly searched Simpson, even under the knee brace, in case he had any weapons on him. Suddenly one of the two guards with rifles walked up with a digital camera. Numbers one and two stood back.

"Stand up straight," one said. Simpson complied, but not without some bite.

"You guys ought to consider getting proper dates," Simpson threw out.

The black-clad men ignored him.

The pictures done, the guard went back to his post. Numbers one and two sorted through the package and grabbed what they would need next. Number two held Simpson's shoulders and leaned him forward. Simpson felt number one spreading his butt cheeks.

"Hey!" he protested again.

A suppository was slid inside his anus. Number two stood Simpson up again.

"Geez, buy a guy a drink first," Simpson spat out. "I bet you don't even give a reacharound."

Neither one nor two reacted.

Next, an adult diaper was slipped onto Simpson. They then forced him into the jumpsuit. Simpson looked over at the major.

"I hope you're enjoying this, Hataway." He looked the major straight in the eyes. "You're going to pay for this."

The major looked embarrassed. "I didn't know this would happen."

Simpson just glared at him. He was handcuffed behind his back. A chain shackle connected his ankles. Then earplugs were forced into his ears. Next he was blindfolded.

A thick cloth hood was then slipped over his head and secured around his neck. Finally, heavy sound-blocking earphones were slipped over the hood. Some sort of shoes were forced onto his feet.

"Wow," Simpson said in a loud voice, "you guys believe in overkill. Does your mom know what you do for a living?"

A flash of his mother's face flew into number one's mind. She had learned to stop asking, when he visited home, what he did in Iraq. He just became sullen and morose at the question. *I'll have to start gagging these bastards,* number one thought.

The POW kit emptied now, numbers one and two brought a chair over and sat Simpson down until the airplane arrived.

Simpson sat there, unable to see or hear, for almost half an hour before he felt himself being hustled aboard the plane. He was led up some short steps, then chained down in a harness. After a few more moments he felt the unmistakable sensations of an airplane taking off.

As his ears popped, he yelled out from under the hood, "Hey, do I get a drink? Some peanuts?"

CHAPTER 17

Achieving and maintaining the initiative is essential to a successful interrogation.

—FM 34-52 Intelligence Interrogation, May 1987

HICKEY AND SHAMEEK WORKED QUICKLY. WHEN it had to be done, it had to be done. Shameek rounded up an AK-47 and four full clips from a store of captured arms. One clip went into the rifle, and the other three went into a cloth bandolier.

Shameek couldn't locate a Colt .45 on short notice, but he handed over a 9mm FN GP-35 Hi-Power pistol to Hickey, along with a couple of loaded spare clips. The pistol had the crest of the Iraqi Army etched into the top of the frame. Everyone had sold guns to Saddam for decades, including the fine Belgium Fabrique

Nationale firm. Finally, Shameek found Hickey a canvas bag to stuff the rifle into.

"Don't get caught with that, old man," Shameek warned.

"I'll try not to, son," Hickey replied. "A couple more things. Have a roll of duct tape and some plastic handcuffs?"

"No problem." Shameek smiled. "Standard-issue stuff. Don't leave home without them."

Hickey added those to the canvas bag. He slipped the pistol behind his back, into the top of his pants, and beneath his shirt. The knife remained in his boot.

"Have any whiskey?" he asked. "I just need a mouthful."

Shameek went over to another trooper and returned with a fifth. They found a screw-top aspirin bottle, and Hickey dumped the pills and poured just enough of the booze for his idea.

"So what's the plan, dude?" Shameek asked.

"I'm going into PIS," Hickey said. "I might be able to grab Simpson and get him out."

"Now?"

"Now."

Shameek looked at his watch. "Yeah, it's oh three hundred. Right time."

"Hopefully, there won't be but one or two of their people there. They shouldn't be expecting an attack."

"Might work."

They both would have preferred a more organized plan. They had also both learned, through their Special Forces training and actual experience, that sometimes you had to take advantage of the moment. Sometimes a spur-of-the-moment attack worked best.

"We'll see," Hickey said. "If I haven't called you in an hour, you'll know it went bad. Call this number." Hickey wrote Custer's cell number on a piece of paper and handed it over. "Tell him everything."

“Hickey, if you don’t call me in an hour, me and a couple of the others here will come charging in, locked and loaded.”

Hickey grinned. “You’re all right for a wog.”

“Yeah, and you are OK for a hillbilly,” Shameek countered. To the Indian, most white Special Forces troopers were hillbillies. They liked guns, knew how to live off the land, and handled problems themselves whenever possible. It was an honor to earn hillbilly status from Shameek.

Hickey looked at his watch. “I have oh three twelve.”

Shameek adjusted his minute hand. Then he started a stopwatch built into his watch.

“You got sixty minutes to call, Hickey.”

Hickey stood up, saluted, and grabbed his canvas bag and took off. The trip from the Special Forces building to the PIS building took him ten minutes. The streets were empty. Hickey flowed alone through lights and shadows.

As he approached the front of the PIS warehouse, he slipped over to the side and dropped the canvas bag down against the tin wall. He then took the pill bottle and drained the whiskey into his mouth. He swished it around like mouthwash, then spat it out. Taking the 9 mm pistol out, he chambered a round and slid it back behind his back into his pants.

He walked to the front door and peered in. He saw Scott Rose still on guard duty but asleep, leaning back in his chair with his feet on the desktop. Hickey banged on the glass door. No reaction. Hickey banged again.

Rose’s dream was invaded by a rapping sound. It grew louder. Rose woke up and looked around. There was someone at the door. He looked at his watch. It was almost three thirty. Who was knocking at this time of the morning? Groggily, Rose stood up and walked to the door.

“We’re not open,” he protested. “Come back later.”

Hickey started banging louder. The glass started throbbing as if it would soon shatter. Rose studied the man pounding on the glass. It was the guy he had given directions to earlier.

"Not open!" Rose yelled through the thick glass.

Hickey pounded harder.

Rose unlocked the door and pulled it open just enough to talk to the man. Hickey stumbled forward until he was face-to-face with Rose. Rose smelled the whiskey on the man's breath. *Great, he's drunk,* Rose thought.

He wanted to tell the man that he needed to come back tomorrow. "We're not open," Scott Rose wanted to say. He just wanted the drunk to go away. Rose didn't care where. Anywhere but here. He just wanted to get back to his dreams.

"You need to come back—" he began.

Hickey seized the opportunity. Using all 210 pounds of his weight, he slammed the door open, forcing Rose back on his heels. Hickey struck like a cobra. His movements were lightning, his resolve absolute.

He lifted his left arm up to distract his opponent's gaze. His right went under his shirt behind his back, and he had the pistol out in a flash. He used the butt and slammed it hard into Rose's sternum, stunning the man. Hickey continued the offensive.

He pressed forward until Rose's legs hit the front of the desk. Hickey kept pressing ahead. Rose was quickly forced backward onto the top of the desk. Hickey wrapped his strong left hand around Rose's neck and squeezed, pinning the enemy to the desk. Hickey then placed the barrel of the pistol an inch from Rose's forehead.

"You even breathe wrong and you die," Hickey warned. "Clear?"

Rose croaked out from his strangled throat, "Yes."

"Roll over," Hickey commanded. He let up the pressure enough so Rose could do that. When the man was on his stomach, Hickey commanded, "Slowly, hands behind your back."

Rose did it. Hickey pulled out two of the snap-lock plastic handcuffs from his pocket and firmly ratcheted one around each wrist. He used a third to connect those together and pulled until there was no slack. Rose was secured.

"Don't move an inch," Hickey said. He quickly slipped out the door and grabbed his canvas bag. He was back inside before Rose realized the man had moved outside. Hickey pulled the duct tape out and wrapped Rose's wrists tightly four times. Hickey then wrapped Rose's ankles a foot apart with a sticky rope of the tape between them. He left enough slack so that Rose could do a slow penguin-like waddle. Hickey rolled Rose over onto his back and pressed the pistol against his temple.

"How many others are here?" Hickey demanded.

"No one," Rose said.

"Crap!" Hickey pulled the hammer on the pistol back. Rose heard the click.

"It's true. They all left. I'm here alone," Rose pleaded.

Hickey almost believed him. "Where's Simpson?"

"They took him. That's where they all went."

"Where to?"

"I'm not sure."

Hickey slammed the butt of the pistol at the same spot on Rose's chest. It took Rose a full thirty seconds to recover enough to talk.

"It's true," Rose whispered, unable to speak.

"Where to?"

Rose was silent too long. Another slam into the sternum, still harder. It took Rose almost a minute to get his breath back.

"Airport," he croaked in a weak voice.

"Where to?" Hickey demanded.

"I don't know." Rose looked up in pain.

Hickey raised the pistol again.

"I do not know!" Rose coughed out, desperate to stop the blows. "Someplace, but I wasn't told. The major said he was flying away with Simpson, but he didn't say where."

Hickey thought. He took a quick look at his watch. Thirty-five minutes to go.

"We'll see," Hickey finally said. "Up." He yanked Rose up by his shirtfront and turned him around.

"I ask questions now." He pressed the cold steel of the barrel against the base of Rose's spine. "One lie and I pull the trigger and you'll walk funny forever at best. I have no use for liars. Clear?"

"Yes," Rose replied, believing the man threatening him.

"If I see even one other person, I pull the trigger on you first. If I even think I hear someone else, you die. Clear?" Hickey spat like a cobra. "Now, again, is anyone else in this building?"

"Not that I know of." Rose hoped no one else was here. He hoped the van had not returned. He knew this man was serious.

"What's behind that door?" Hickey asked.

"A hallway." Rose's voice was returning.

"Then what?" Hickey pressed the cold steel harder into Rose's skin.

"Coffee room. Three offices, then the warehouse."

"Where was Simpson kept?"

"In a storage room in the back of the warehouse."

Hickey thought again. He couldn't leave Rose here. Someone might see him through the glass.

"We walk now. You do your best." Hickey prodded him with the pistol.

With Hickey forcing him, Rose wobbled along as best he could toward the door leading to the hallway. Hickey barely opened it and peered down the hall. Empty. He fully opened it and forced Rose along. They entered the coffee room, and Hickey sat Rose in a chair. He wrapped the prisoner's chest three times in the thick, sticky duct tape, trapping him in the chair, then taped his calves to the chair legs.

"Anything else you want to tell me?" Hickey asked.

Rose could think of nothing. "No."

"If I get any surprises, you better hope I don't get back to this room," Hickey warned. He then taped Rose's mouth shut and placed the canvas bag on the table in the middle of the room. He pulled the AK out and slid the bolt back, making sure there was a live round in the chamber. He slung the bandolier over his neck and across his chest so he could easily reach the spare clips.

"I'll see you in a few minutes." He smiled at Rose and took off down the hall.

Hickey was careful. He paused just before each office door and listened. He heard nothing. Slowly he checked each room before closing the door and proceeding forward. He was soon at the door that opened into the warehouse. He checked his watch.

Hickey quickly entered the warehouse in a crouch. He moved behind the first row of crates and waited. No human sounds. Nothing but the hum of the xenon lamps above. He stuck his eye out past the edge of the stacked crates and peered down a long row of more crates. He pulled back and closed his eyes to listen. Nothing. Hickey moved back to the other side of his cover and repeated the movements to see down another long row. Still nothing but stacked crates. No movements. No new sounds.

Hickey stood up, AK-47 pointed forward, and walked around the side of the crates he was behind. He started walking through the warehouse, waiting for any sound, any warning. If he had heard anything, he would have ducked down and found cover.

Hickey began to believe what Rose had told him. There was no one else there.

He moved quickly down the long rows to the back of the warehouse. Again he paused and listened before fully exposing himself. Again, nothing.

By the time Hickey found the room that had been Jim Simpson's cell, he had twenty minutes left before Shameek would come running. Hickey studied the room. What Borden and Rose had told him was true. Simpson was gone. Gone on an airplane to who knew where. He noticed dried blood on the floor and frowned, but moved on. Nothing he could do here.

Hickey then found the room where Simpson had been tortured. A sick stench still remained. The chair bolted to the floor and the field generator with long wires attached to it left no doubt in Hickey's mind as to what had gone on in the room. His iron resolve doubled.

Hickey stood in the small room considering what to do next. He was about to call Shameek when he heard sounds. He flattened himself against the wall and slowly moved deeper into the room so that no one could see him.

The sounds Hickey heard were from a back door being opened. A man entered the warehouse and started pulling the chain that slowly opened a large steel door by the back loading dock. Hickey heard the van being driven into the warehouse and its engine being shut down. The big door was lowered again. Hickey heard the talk of the three men who had just returned from delivering Simpson to the airport. Their voices echoed through the open spaces of the warehouse.

"Let's find that beer!" someone boomed.

"Yeah, with the major gone we can relax some," another said.

Hickey looked at his watch. The sands of time were running out on him. These men might find Rose. Shameek and his men might be wounded or killed in a confrontation with them. Hickey had to act now. He had surprise on his side.

He dropped to the floor and moved until he was just barely peeking out of the door into the warehouse. He saw the van. Two men stood by the open side door. A third sat in the driver's seat. Hickey saw the spark of a lighter and one of the standing men lighting something. He took a long hit.

"Don't bogart that joint," one said. "Pass it on."

The first man laughed and took another deep drag before passing the joint on.

"Hand me that and go find some beer," the driver said.

It's time, Hickey thought. *Can't let them split up.* Hickey stood up and stepped out and started calmly walking toward the van, the AK-47 pointed forward, his grip upon it steady and true. He watched as the driver took the joint and smoked it.

Hickey was silent as he moved forward. He was twenty yards away from the van before any of the three noticed him.

All of the PIS hired guns had been soldiers. All had been in combat. Every one of them knew that a stranger with an AK-47 was a threat. One just stood there gawking. The other two men knew what to do.

Lowsley was standing by the van when he saw Hickey. He dove into the van and went for his rifle. The driver grabbed the sawed-off shotgun he kept under his seat and rolled out of the van door, attempting to get a bead on the stranger.

Hickey saw the movements and opened up. He fired below the driver's door. The rounds ripped through the driver's legs before he had cleared the door. The driver went down howling in pain. Hickey sent another burst into the man's body. The driver stopped moving. Hickey readjusted his aim to the open side door into which the second man had disappeared. For whatever reasons, the third man just stood there. Hickey kept him covered as he slowly improved his angle of fire on the interior of the van.

"You," Hickey barked. "On the floor facedown."

The standing man didn't seem to register the words. He wasn't sure if they were spoken at him. He was still standing there as Lowsley came out of the van. Hickey saw the barrel of Lowsley's rifle emerge first. Hickey sent a long burst at the van as he moved away from the side door to the front of the van for better cover, cover where he was in control. He emptied the clip at the van. He saw the standing man fall to the ground, hit by the burst Hickey had fired.

Lowsley stuck his rifle out of the side door and ripped off a quick burst. Hickey had already shifted to where the arc of fire couldn't reach him. Hickey dumped his empty clip—not hearing it clang to the floor, he was so focused—and grabbed a fresh one and slammed it in. He brought the AK to his shoulder, taking a quick look at the downed driver. He sent a short burst into the man's head. He didn't need anyone behind him.

Then he carefully sent more short bursts into the van as he walked down the side of it. The bullets ripped through the thin metal, leaving little puckered holes where they went in. Hickey kept moving around the opposite side of the van from where the side door was. He carefully watched for the man inside trying to leave the van. Hickey would see if his boots hit the ground. He kept firing until he finished off the second clip. He was now behind the van, five yards away from it. He loaded the third clip.

Lowsley had no choice. He had dropped to the floor between the front and second row of seats when the shooter had started firing at the van. He was pinned now. He couldn't see anything. He had to get out of the van. He made his move.

Hickey saw the man's feet hit the ground as he jumped out of the van. He stepped sideways so he had a full field of fire and let loose with the AK. Having expected the move, he led the enemy's movements.

Lowsley took three rounds in his side and slid to a stop. Hickey carefully kept the two men under watch. The one who had just stood there wasn't moving. Hickey didn't assume he was dead. If there was movement he would shoot again.

Lowsley moved slowly but not offensively. His back to Hickey, he was just crawling, a trail of blood staining the concrete floor of the warehouse. He had left his rifle behind him after he was hit. Hickey kept moving around the van and back a bit until he could cover the side door in case there were any others coming out.

"Anyone else?" Hickey asked. Wounded men often don't think clearly. He got no answer.

He moved to the man who had been standing still when the bullets flew and kicked him. No reaction. Hickey rolled him over onto his back, using his boot. There were three holes in his chest. The man was dead, but Hickey made sure. He sent a short burst into the man's head. The body twitched, then stopped.

Hickey now had just the wounded man to deal with. He carefully approached him with the muzzle pointed at his chest while he kept a quick eye on the van lest any surprises appear from inside.

"You." Hickey spoke to Lowsley. "Anyone else here?"

Lowsley stared up at the stranger, pink blood bubbling from his mouth. Lung shot, Hickey figured. He wouldn't last long.

"What?" Lowsley asked from his death daze.

"Anyone else in that van?"

Lowsley laughed and then coughed up more blood. "No. Who the hell are you?"

"Friend of Jim Simpson's," Hickey informed him.

Lowsley thought a moment. "OK. OK. That makes sense."

"Where is he?" Hickey demanded.

Lowsley's mind was starting to wander. He heard words, but he was losing his ability to understand them or to speak them back.

"Where" resounded through the fog in his mind.

"Went with the major," Lowsley said. "Far away."

"Where to?" Hickey asked.

"Don't know. Major wouldn't tell us. Someplace strange, I bet," Lowsley said. "That hangar was weird, man. Dark men there."

"Where?" Hickey repeated. "Where are they flying Simpson?"

"Same place I'm going." Lowsley laughed again. "Same as you. Hell."

The last word came out with a final cough of blood, and John Lowsley died.

Hickey made sure the man was gone. Then he made sure the van was empty. He looked at his watch. He got his cell phone out and dialed Shameek. The call was answered before the first ring finished.

"Hickey?" came the Indian's voice.

"Yeah, it's me."

"Everything good?"

Hickey stared down at the bodies. "Yes, everything is fine."

"We were about to come there," Shameek said.

"It's OK, Shameek. No need."

"What are you going to do now?"

Good question, Hickey thought. "I'll be here a few more minutes, and then I am off to the hotel."

"OK, call me when you get there."

"Roger that," Hickey replied and hung up.

Hickey thought a moment. He had just missed Simpson. *Bad break*, he thought.

He stared around the warehouse of arms and decided to inflict a little more pain on PIS. He went through the crates until he found what he needed. He placed plastic explosives in key munitions crates, fused them, and set timers. The fireworks would go off in one hour. The warehouse would explode and burn at 0500. Early enough for the streets around the warehouse to be empty. Someone would know something had gone on here. He left the AK and the pistol on a crate where they would be destroyed.

Then he moved back though the warehouse into the hallway. He checked the offices until he found the major's. Hickey quickly found the major's computer, unplugged the cables, and grabbed the box only. He would take it with him in the canvas bag and ship it to Custer. Then he went back to the coffee break room.

Rose looked up at him with fear in his eyes. He had heard the shots from the warehouse. Hickey walked over and ripped the tape off of Rose's mouth. He studied the man's face. He saw the fear.

"Tell me about Jim Simpson. Everything you know."

So it flowed. Rose let it go, even what he had done to Simpson's knee. Hickey sat and listened, his face unresponsive as a professional poker player's. When the story was over and Hickey knew that Rose could offer him nothing else, he decided what to do.

"I'm moving you into the warehouse," Hickey told him. "You'll be safe there until I am gone. Some people will be here in about an hour. They should find you."

Hickey grabbed the back of the chair and dragged Scott Rose through the hall into the warehouse. He pulled the chair up next to a crate of M-16 ammo in which he had set plastic explosives.

If Rose hadn't told Hickey about the kneecap he would have lived. Hickey was not one to kill indiscriminately. He would have let the man go, scaring him enough so that he didn't talk. As soon as Hickey had heard what Rose had done to Simpson's knee, he knew he had to do something. So he did what he did. He felt no remorse. It was a just action.

As Hickey exited the front door, he saw movement across the street. Shameek appeared from the shadows. He was in full battle armor with his M-249 SAW rifle in his hands. He nodded at Hickey. Another figure emerged, Borden toting his Mark II Mod O rifle. A third Special Forces soldier stepped forward holding an MP-5A machine gun.

Hickey nodded at the men. He walked over, handed Shameek his knife, and looked the young soldier in his eyes.

"Thanks," Hickey said.

"Nothing to it," said Shameek. "Just covering you, hillbilly."

"See you around, wog." Hickey smiled. He walked away. After a few steps he turned back. "Oh, I wouldn't be in this vicinity at zero five hundred."

All the men melted away into the night, going their separate ways.

Hickey was back in his hotel room watching through the binoculars when the Protective Integrated Services warehouse went up in a fireball.

After watching the building burn and the live ammo pop off for an hour, Hickey went to sleep.

* * *

WHEN HE WOKE UP A little after noon, the first thing Hickey did was call Custer. With his corporation set up and his men on the move, Custer had the most hated task of any field commander, waiting. He quickly answered when he saw it was Hickey calling.

"Fred here."

"Hickey" was the reply.

"Where are you?"

Hickey had moved over to the hotel room window. He stared down at the still-smoldering wreckage that had been the PIS warehouse. The Iraqi police and U.S. Army were keeping everyone well back, as an occasional round still cooked off from the area.

"I'm watching a fire," Hickey finally said. "Some warehouse went up last night. Someplace called Protective Integrated Services."

Custer was a bit surprised but not completely. "Probably insurgents striking," he said.

"Yeah, that makes sense," Hickey replied. "I'm sure that's what CNN will say."

"I'll have to tune in," Custer mused. "Protective Integrated Services, eh? I'll have to check with a friend. His son worked there."

"He's gone," Hickey informed his commander. "Flew out last night with some major. I spoke to his coworkers."

"Flew out? Where to?"

"They didn't know. I thought you could find out."

"I can try," Custer said. "I'll get someone looking. So where are you off to now?"

"I'm not sure," Hickey responded. "I could come back there. You have any ideas?"

Custer thought a moment. "Stay there another day. I'll call you back later."

"Roger that," Hickey replied. "My computer is down, by the way. I'll ship it to you today for repairs. What address?"

Custer gave him Charles Simpson's address. "Anything else?" he asked.

"Can't think of anything right now," Hickey said.

"OK, thanks for the update. I'll call you later."

Hickey ended the call and went down to get some lunch. Later he would watch the worldwide CNN and Fox news feeds. Indeed, it appeared that Iraqi insurgent enemies had somehow penetrated the Green Zone and blown up a U.S. supply warehouse. The lies were carried in the newspapers from London to New York, Los Angeles to Sydney and Hong Kong, within a day.

CUSTER WAS UNSURE WHAT TO do next. Simpson had been taken out of Iraq by Major Hataway, but where? *It's a big old world out there,* Custer thought. He needed someone to do some research. He needed someone who could track the truth through the knee-high muck of lies and deceptions. Custer dialed Miami, Florida.

Judy Wainscott was in her garden battling weeds when her husband, Cy, came out telling her there was a call for her. Happily retired from the *Miami Herald,* she still freelanced from time to time to bring in some cash. Health insurance was expensive these days.

When she heard Fred Custer's voice in her ear, memories of the previous year flooded her mind. Memories of what had happened in a little town called Belle Glade. While Judy didn't like the killing of people, she had to admit that only the right people had died there last year. After reading in the local papers and watching the TV news about what had happened to that little town, she had strong suspicions about who was behind the explosive events there. She didn't try to find out if she was correct. What had happened there had been for the good. Very good. She liked the man.

"Mr. Custer," she answered. "How nice to hear your voice."

"Please," Custer said, "it's Fred. I might have some work for you. Are you available?"

"Perhaps," the careful former newspaperwoman replied. "What do you have?"

"It would be best if I spoke to you face-to-face," Custer replied. "Can you come to D.C.? All expenses paid, of course."

Wainscott remembered the solid fees the man from Vero Beach had paid her for her work. She also remembered the reasons. "I could do that."

"Great. Tell me when, and there'll be a private jet waiting at the Miami airport."

"Make it Fort Lauderdale," Wainscott said. "It's much easier to get in and out of and is about the same distance from my home."

They agreed on a time and hung up.

Now that he was working to find out where Jim Simpson had gone, the ever-planning Custer thought out what his next move would be. Like a master chess player working moves ahead of an opponent, Fred Custer knew how to analyze a problem far ahead and put in place everything he might need to resolve the issue.

When they found Simpson, he would still be a prisoner. Those holding him would not want to hand him over. Custer and his men would have to make them. Custer started assembling his team.

He already had Hickey. Hargis was on his way back from Idaho. The mysterious Van Zandt had finished his work on the Cayman Islands and was still available. With himself that was four. Not enough.

Custer called Atlanta and located Jeff Winkler. The warrior trained by Apaches was happy to hear Custer's voice.

"Sure!" Winkler said enthusiastically. "Yeah, I can come up to D.C. Business is slow. Not a lot of remodeling going down right now. I could use a break from all the worrying."

Custer called Seattle and found that Dan Hadad was not available for anything extended. If Custer had anything the engineer could do in the Northwest, he would help, but an open-ended affair was impossible right now. Custer said he understood. Since Hadad was in Seattle, Custer put in the back of his mind that maybe he could assist his wife and her traveling gang as they stayed out of harm's way.

Custer thought. He had five. That might be enough. If it wasn't, he would find others.

MOVEMENT

CHAPTER 18

The number of approaches used is limited only by the interrogator's imagination and skill.

—FM 34-52 Intelligence Interrogation, May 1987

THE MAN IN EGYPT WAS WAITING in the restricted area at the Cairo airport. He stood ramrod straight in the Egyptian sun, in front of a special van with two men sitting in it. The men were well trained in their tasks. The van had no windows save the front windshield. There was a partition just behind the front seats so that anyone in the back of the van could not see out.

The man's name was Manuel Kramer. Like his parents' marriage, his name was a mixture of European and South American. Manuel's father had been an SS doctor in the camps during World War II, where he had begun his craft. Seeing what would happen to his beloved Nazi Germany and, more important, what was happening to any SS officer captured, Dr. Hans Kramer had fled Germany to Argentina using the ODESSA organization. With a new name and enough money to start, he rebuilt his life.

He found the leaders of Argentina, Juan and Eva Perón, quite warm to the arriving Nazi refugees. Men like Dr. Kramer were not only welcomed but put to work by the repressive regime. Their skills at repression, torture, and dealing out death were fully utilized by the Peróns in their quest to remain in power. Dr. Kramer was a busy man until the coup of 1955 threw Perón out of power and sent the dictator fleeing. The new leaders left the Nazis alone, and by then Dr. Kramer had a résumé and other clients in South and Central America to fill his bank accounts. From the fifties well into the seventies, men like Dr. Kramer were kept quite busy and were well paid for their services.

Het met Gloria Cordova, the upper-class daughter of an owner of numerous plantations, at a state ball in 1959. They were wed a year later. When their son was born in 1960, Gloria insisted that he retain her grandfather's first name. Hans Kramer didn't complain. It was a form of the Germanic name. As long as his son was a Kramer he was happy. Gloria Kramer didn't want to know what her husband did. As long as she could attend the balls and high social events she was a very happy woman.

Sheltered from the civil unrest of the country, Manuel Kramer grew up not knowing what his father did for a living. All he knew was that his father was often away for weeks or months at a time in other countries. Upon his father's return from these trips, the child would ask him where he had been. "Protecting our family and race" was the eternal answer the boy received before being given the new toy or gift his father had acquired while away.

Later he would tell his son, "Only God gives and takes life. But God is busy elsewhere, and so I must undertake this task in Argentina."

Between his parents, Manuel learned to speak Spanish, Portuguese, and German. His expensive private schools added French and English to his vocabulary. He was quite an intelligent student. He might have gone on to university and become a serious scholar if it hadn't been for the elections of 1973. A stand-in for Juan Perón, Dr. Héctor Cámpora, was elected president. He took control on May 25. On June 20, Juan Perón returned to Argentina to be met by a crowd of two million at the airport. Dr. Kramer, his wife, and young Manuel were in that crowd.

As Perón spoke from a platform, undercover agents and soldiers of José Rega's Triple A—the Argentine Anticommunist Alliance—opened fire on the crowd. Thirteen died and over three hundred were wounded. This became known as the Ezeiza Massacre.

Gloria Kramer was among the thirteen dead. Little Manuel watched as his mother was cut down before his eyes.

Both father and son became cold to the world from that moment on. At the funeral, after the boy had shoveled the first clump of earth onto his mother's casket, his father took him aside. Kneeling beside his son, Dr. Kramer gripped the boy's shoulders and looked deep into his eyes.

"You are the protector of your mother's memory," the father instilled into his son. "You will learn to avenge this pain through dealing out pain. I shall teach you."

So began the boy's education in inflicting torture and pain. Warped by the events of his mother's death, Manuel Kramer became quite a good student. In fact, he excelled beyond his father's desires. He began working with his father in the dark prisons, in their back rooms where the screams for mercy went unheard by the torturers.

When he had learned everything his father could teach him, he studied further. He was sent to the School of the Americas just outside of Atlanta, Georgia. His craft was perfected. Like his father's name, his own was quite well known among those who wished to remain in power at any costs. He grew in stature and was known for being exceptional at his work.

His father died in 1981, and that sealed away any humanity

the son had left in him. Sealed it deep away, where nothing of the earth could pry open that walled-off area again.

By the time of the second Gulf War and the U.S. occupation of Iraq, Manuel Kramer had well over twenty-five years of experience at extracting information from prisoners by any means necessary. When he heard whispered rumors of what the United States was paying for men who performed services such as his, he didn't believe it. The pay was enormous. He checked with his CIA contacts through the School of the Americas, and the rumors were true. The whispers were real.

Using those contacts, Manuel Kramer signed up. He was soon in Egypt in charge of one of the secret prisons the United States operated outright or paid others to keep open.

So Manuel Kramer, aged forty-nine, stood ramrod straight under the Egyptian sun waiting for the plane to arrive. The plane with the major and his million-dollar contract.

Yes, he was a very patient man that day.

THERE WERE MANY PRISONS SUCH as the Death Factory around the world run by the United States. Abu Ghraib in Iraq had its image cleaned up, and the proper scapegoats were sacrificed before the public's eyes. The most infamous was Guantánamo Bay, Cuba—Gitmo. Since it was well covered by the press and well visited by humanitarian groups, what went on at Gitmo remained timid compared to activities within some of the other secret prisons.

Two other prisons had been documented by the press in Poland and Romania. When they were exposed they were shut down. It was no problem to continue operations elsewhere. There were prisons in Iraq, Afghanistan had at least "the Prison of Darkness" and "the Salt Pit," and Syria was rumored to be another location. Thailand was known. Some were even rumored to be on ships sailing in international waters, well out of the reach of any civilized laws. There was no doubt that the United States had the facilities around the globe for holding prisoners and for extracting information as needed.

The methods, while questioned by many, were never questioned by the administration that set them up. Their publicly stated policies were quite clear. One advocate and author of the administration's policies, a Justice Department lawyer named John Yoo, was asked during a debate in Chicago on December 1, 2005, "If the president deems that he's got to torture somebody, including by crushing the testicles of the person's child, there is no law that can stop him?" Yoo responded with a cold answer that there was "no treaty" preventing that. To a follow-up question, he said, "I think it depends on why the president thinks he needs to do that." Yoo's "Torture Memos" were used to justify and codify the U.S. actions and polices.

There was no doubt that the United States was taking the War on Terror quite seriously. Manuel Kramer saw no problems with the U.S. policy. He had helped keep other regimes' similar mandates enforced for almost thirty years. That the United States was paying quite well for his services didn't hurt.

Egypt was selected as a location for one of the secret prisons because of several factors. Starting with Anwar Sadat in the sixties, Egypt had a long history of battling the militant Muslim elements. Up to his public assassination in 1981, by Wahhabist Muslims—inspired by the warped writings of Hassan el-Banna, founder of the Muslim Brotherhood—Sadat had more than kept these militants in check. The United States noticed. Over the last thirty years U.S. aid to the country was second only to aid to Israel.

Egypt's main police forces, the Amned Daula and Mukhabarat, did their jobs, making sure that the militant forms of Islam did not take over the land of the Nile, the pyramids, and the pharaohs. For decades they ran secret prisons of their own. They had no problem allowing the United States to add one more to stem the growing tide of militant Wahhabism.

They were not concerned with what went on behind the barbed-wire fences. The place was deep in the desert and away from prying eyes.

MANUEL KRAMER WATCHED THE AIRPLANE approach, land, and taxi. He saw that it was the Gulfstream, tail number N379P, that he was expecting. As always, the CIA airplane had delivered the prisoner on time.

Kramer personally supervised the unloading of Jim Simpson and the major and got them into the van. It would be a long trip across the desert back to the prison.

CHAPTER 19

Make assessment by asking background and nonpertinent questions which will indicate whether or not the approaches chosen will be effective.

—FM 34-52 Intelligence Interrogation, May 1987

CUSTER SENT THE WORD OUT WHERE to meet. Paris. It was a good location to work from. He booked two adjoining suites at the Central Hotel Paris, double- and triple-bed rooms.

He and Hargis flew out of D.C. while Van Zandt, who had been enjoying his paid island vacation, headed for France on his own. Winkler had his wife, Neci, drive him to Hartsfield in Atlanta. His daughter was still young enough to want to be with her parents. It took promises that he would bring her something special from France and that all three of them would journey there soon to pry her from her daddy. Hickey would get there as quickly as he could from Iraq. With a little help from Charles Simpson, Hargis's new rifle was shipped to a bonded warehouse, where it waited for movement out of France.

It took two days for all of them to get together. They met to dine on seafood in a private room at La Mediterranée. By unspoken agreement, the conversation was casual. No shop talk.

After the meal they returned to the hotel, opened the common door between the two suites, and sat down for their first briefing as a group. Custer started by telling the story of what had brought them back together. Hickey filled everyone in on the events in Baghdad. When he was finished, Custer asked if anyone wanted to return home. No one stepped forward to cross the metaphorical line in the sand.

They were all in. Custer smiled.

"The first thing we'll need is new identities," he said. "We need to get these fixed up." Custer held up a handful of the blank passports that Van Zandt had secured in New York City. Custer looked over at the quiet man from Orlando.

"I can handle that," Van Zandt said. "I'll just need a new name for everyone and passport photos."

Custer became Bill Hafner. Hickey decided on Ben Rumson. Hargis transformed to Dan Daly, and Winkler, being the 1972 Miami Dolphins fan he was, chose Paul Warfield. Van Zandt took the name of Michael Daniels.

Once they could get the passports in line, they would move via cash transactions as much as possible. If they had to have a credit card for anything, they would use prepaid cards. Custer would go to a French bank and arrange for $100,000 to be transferred to Paris. When that was in, the group would disappear off the grid.

Custer roughed out the plan. The next day he and Hargis would go get the cash, buy enough prepaid credit cards for everyone, and also find a few gold coins for each man to carry. In a world of floundering paper notes, gold always talked. He assigned Hickey and Hargis the task of the finding five pay-as-you-go cell phones with international abilities. He also wanted three satellite phones. Everyone was to go shopping, too.

"Pants, shirts, underwear, toiletries, watches, and anything else you think you need, buy it here." Custer explained, "The stuff we have here now, everything we packed and are wearing, gets shipped back home. We're all getting reborn as of tomorrow."

Van Zandt got the toughest assignment. As well as having to find an above-average forger to alter the passports, he was to ask around if there were any other men who could be hired for the operation: mercenaries.

Custer didn't want to hire mercs unless he had to. Everyone in the room intimately knew each other. When they found out where Simpson was, they would see if more men would be needed. Van Zandt nodded. He understood.

Weapons would have to be acquired, of course, but that was another thing that would have to wait until they knew Simpson's situation.

With everyone caught up and briefed and given assignments for the next day, the men went down to the bar for a drink before heading to bed. It would be their last night in the fine hotel. Tomorrow they would find new quarters of a more common type. Someplace where cash was accepted, and where for a little extra cash questions would not be asked about the five men.

BACK IN MIAMI, JUDY WAINSCOTT had been busy. Custer had handed her a tough assignment, but to her those were the best ones. *Better to hunt, skin, and eat a bear than a rabbit,* she reminded herself. Her first editor had taught her that phrase long ago, and it had stuck. She was not one to be intimidated by the thought of deeply researching a story.

At first, finding Jim Simpson seemed to be an impossible task. How could a civilian, with an ocean between her and Iraq, discover where secret men sent prisoners they didn't want to be found? She knew that there is almost always a trail on missing people. Someone talks, or there is often a bureaucratic chain of paperwork to be found.

It was all of that governmental paperwork plus the work of driven amateurs that lit a small light in the total darkness of Simpson's disappearance. It was dim, but it was a light. She fanned that spark until she had a small fire going. Through her skills, which became as strong as a forest fire, letting her see into the dark crevices of the black ops world.

Starting where everyone today does, Judy Wainscott began her search on the Internet. She started checking references about military transport of prisoners. A little reading of Web sites took her to Planespotters.net. There she delved into the world of amateur "plane spotters."

Plane spotters are people who have a fascination with military aircraft. They come from all walks of life. Hanging out near known military airports, they try to chart interesting planes, such as the stealth bomber or some ultra-secret new test aircraft. Their main tools are a radio, binoculars, a camera, a pen, and a notebook. They photograph the planes when they can and write down whatever they see or hear, including the planes' tail numbers.

This data and the photographs are uploaded onto Web sites or blogs dedicated to the hobby. There other plane spotters from all over the globe can match, confirm, or comment upon the sightings. What becomes interesting is limited to the work some are willing to do after charting a plane's data. What these amateurs exposed sent a shock wave through the world.

Because of what became known as the Chicago Convention of 1944, civilian aircraft can fly over any signatory nation's airspace. Military aircraft need to get permission. On September 17, 2001, six days after 9/11, President George W. Bush signed a classified finding statement and began his War on Terror. In that still-classified document lay the framework that allowed the CIA carte blanche in dealing with terrorists. One of the new tools used by the CIA and the military in their war was labeled "extraordinary rendition."

"Rendition" legally means "to surrender" or "to return." "Extraordinary rendition" came to mean the CIA kidnapped anyone in the world they wanted and could lay their hands on, then transported them to Gitmo or to one of the many other secret prisons they run around the globe. Places where some prisoners just disappeared.

To help keep these kidnappings off the radar, the CIA uses civilian airplanes to transport their prisoners. This allows them much more freedom in their operations. What the CIA got in freedom, though, they sacrificed in visibility, since those planes could be tracked—"spotted." All civilian flights must be logged by tail number or airframe serial number.

When certain civilian airplanes started landing at military airstrips, they were sometimes logged by plane spotters. Other spotters around the globe added what they knew when they saw the same tail number. By exchanging their data on the Internet, these plane spotters allowed reporters to find the key to tracking the planes the CIA was using to transport their prisoners. International journalists such as Frank Laurin, Trevor Paglen, and A. C. Thompson, among others, were able to connect the dots and see where these "civilian" airplanes had been. They were able to plot the CIA planes from where they grabbed a prisoner to where they dropped them off.

It took Wainscott three days of research, reading, and e-mailing with a "Ray" on Planespotters.net to find out that a Gulfstream, with tail number N379P, was the only civilian plane to fly into Baghdad and leave within hours the same week Jim Simpson disappeared. That Gulfstream is better known as "the Guantánamo Express." It was one of the three main planes used by the CIA to transport prisoners to secret locations.

By charting the plane's mandated civilian airport flight logs, she was able to prove that from Iraq the Gulfstream had flown straight to Cairo and then directly back to Smithfield, North Carolina. Smithfield is a known CIA airport, and it was doubtful that Simpson had been taken there. It was possible, and she would let Custer know that, but if she had to put money on the table, it was Egypt where Jim Simpson was being held.

She wrote all of her work up in a concise report and called Custer on his cell phone. He gave her the address of the Central Hotel Paris and told her to FedEx her material along and to keep digging. If she found anything new, she should immediately call him. He would give her his new phone number within forty-eight hours.

VAN ZANDT WALKED THE STREETS until he found a suitable public phone booth. From it he used a phone card to call Li Ang in New York City. The Asian gentleman was always happy to hear the voice of his old friend.

"I enjoyed that takeout meal you made for me," Van Zandt told him. "I'm in Paris now. Do you know anyone here who makes such a fine meal?"

Li Ang asked the quiet man to wait while he checked his phone book. After a moment he came back on the line. Indeed he did have a good Paris contact, and he gave it to Van Zandt.

Now Van Zandt knew where to get the passports updated as needed. Hopefully the Paris forger could also steer him to someplace where Van Zandt could find the rest of the items on his shopping list.

CHAPTER 20

The battle in the prisoner-of-war camp is for the mind.

—FM 21-78 Prisoner-of-War Resistance, December 1981

AFTER BEING CUFFED, UNDER A HOOD, and controlled for hours, Jim Simpson was finally set free of his restraints. He had no idea where he was. He had slept on the plane, so time was a mystery. He thought that sleep came from the suppository that had been forced into him, some drug. After the flight from Baghdad, he had been moved into a vehicle of some sort. He had to step up from the ground quite a bit, and the ride was rough. Simpson figured it was a deuce and a half or some other large military truck that transported him from the airport.

While he couldn't see or hear, he could smell. Even under his hood he could tell that the air was dry. Another desert?

After a long, bumpy trip the truck came to a stop. Simpson was hustled down from the truck, feeling the heat of the sun even through the jumpsuit, and rudely walked into a building and to his new prison cell. He could tell it was a fairly large building, as he had to be led down halls, turned, and prodded along for quite a distance.

He felt the earphones come off and then the hood and blindfold. Even though it wasn't especially bright, the light of the cell blinded him. It took a few minutes for his eyes to readjust. The earplugs were pulled out, and Simpson could hear again. Finally the ankle shackles and cuffs were removed. This was done by one man with two others standing well back in case Simpson tried anything. One held a Taser in one hand and a hard rubber truncheon in the other. The third stood menacingly, ready if needed. Simpson knew better than to tempt the men.

The three men then exited the cell, shutting the heavy metal door behind them. Simpson heard the heavy clanks of bolts being thrown, locks being turned. Left only in his jumpsuit and what had been forced upon him underneath it, Simpson considered his situation.

He was thirsty. He hadn't drunk anything since . . . since when? He had no idea of the time of day. He smiled. It was daytime, he realized. He had felt the sun's warmth as they had moved him from the truck to the building. It was a small victory, but he grabbed it. He looked around the cell.

A dull light illuminated his cell. Looking up, Simpson saw the lightbulbs were ten feet above him behind a narrow wire grid. He sat on an iron cot with a thin mattress atop it. The cot was bolted to the floor. A light blanket and something resembling a pillow were the only bedding.

No sink. No toilet. There was a five-gallon plastic bucket in the corner. He stood and started to walk over to it, almost stumbling after being trussed up and chained for so long. Sitting back down on the cot, he did some stretching to get his muscles as loose as he could. He heard his neck crack as he snapped his head left and right. When he felt up to it, he stood up again. He could walk. He would make himself walk.

He went over and peered into the bucket. Empty. They had left him no water. Simpson knew that this was part of the warder's tool kit—total control. It was their way of saying that they decided what he got and when.

He took off the shoes—some cheap tennis shoes—and stripped the jumpsuit off. Then he removed the diaper and set it aside. He hadn't had to use it, so if he did have to go to the bathroom in the bucket he could use it to clean himself after. He put the jumpsuit and shoes back on and spread out across the cot.

He knew to rest while he could. He would need it.

SIMPSON DIDN'T KNOW HOW LONG he had been asleep when he heard the locks being turned, the metal bolts clanking, and the door to his cell opening. He had barely begun to wake up when three men, rubber truncheons in hand, rushed him. He tried getting up, but the quick blows across his chest sent him back down onto the cot.

The men didn't stop. They continued raining blows down across his chest and legs. He threw his arms up to take the sting of the attack on his forearms. The solid sounding thumps sent shafts of pain shooting through Simpson's nerves, and his brain took instinctual control.

Simpson rolled onto his side, into the fetal position, with his back to the attackers. Helpless, he heard the men's primal grunts with each strike. His back, calves, buttocks, and even the soles of his feet were assaulted. The men didn't strike to maim or break bones. They knew what they were doing. They had done this many times before. They were very skilled at these tasks.

Simpson was still rolled into a ball when he realized the blows had stopped. He heard the door being closed and relocked.

The light had been turned off. Aching all over, but unable to do anything, Jim Simpson slipped into a fruitless sleep.

HE WOKE UP, STILL FEELING where the blows had landed. How long had he slept? What time was it? He had no idea. He felt his way to the corner where the bucket was and urinated. He wondered if there was blood in it now. Without light he had no way to tell. He tried to remember if there was anything he could use as a weapon. He could recall nothing except the bucket.

He explored his metal cot in the darkness. He could find nothing to pull loose. Disheartened, he lay back down and fell asleep. As he drifted off, he tried to think of what he might use to defend himself if attacked again.

HE SLEPT THROUGH THE SOUND of the locks being opened, but the heavy clank of the enormous door bolts being pulled back quickly woke him up. He could smell the odor of his own sweat heavy in the cell.

A shaft of light from the hall shot into the room as the door was opened. Simpson saw the silhouettes of three men standing in the doorway. He didn't see anything in their hands. One of the men barked a long string of commands in a language he didn't understand. *Arabic?* he wondered.

Two men entered the cell, threw back the thin blanket, and grabbed Simpson, each firmly holding an arm. They pulled him up and dragged him toward the hall.

As they reached the door, Simpson sent his right foot in front of the feet of the man on his right. The man tumbled down, taking Simpson with him. The other man holding Simpson lost his grip.

The man Simpson had tripped growled and curled his right hand into a fist. More barked commands from the third man overseeing the movement. Simpson saw the face of the man he had tripped, heard his short words. One didn't need to understand a language to know what was being said.

"Do not fight," the leader told Simpson in heavily accented English. "We are taking you to bath and food."

Simpson allowed himself to be hauled up straight again and to be led down the hall.

He was taken to a communal bathroom and walked to the rear. Five shower stalls were there. The man he had tripped pointed to a chair. A towel and a bar of soap sat atop it. The man grunted and pointed at the shower.

Simpson stripped and took the bar of soap. The water was cold but welcome. He washed himself. He opened his mouth and drank for the first time in too long, his body absorbing the precious liquid.

"Enough!" barked the English speaker in what seemed like far too short a time. Simpson ignored the command. More foreign-language commands, and the man Simpson had tripped walked over and shut the water off. He and Simpson locked eyes. The man grunted again and pointed at the towel.

Simpson dried himself and dressed. The two men grabbed him again and led him through the maze of halls. Simpson saw other cell doors. Each of them had a thin metal strip at eye level in the center. These were all closed, from what he saw. Observation slots to view the inside of the cells. There was also a hinged metal plate along the bottom of every door. Wide enough for a food tray to be slid into the cell, Simpson noted.

His next stop was a small, well-lit room. There was a wooden table and chair near the back wall. Sitting on the table was a plate of food, a bowl of a thick, hearty soup, a pitcher of water, and a pot of coffee. Simpson could smell the rich coffee. His stomach rumbled. The two men released him once they reached the door.

"Eat!" barked the English speaker.

Simpson glanced over his shoulder and stared at the speaker. He was of average build with dark brown skin. Again Simpson thought of the desert. He noted the man's broad fingers and hands.

The man sported a thick mustache. Yes, thought Simpson, the man looked Middle Eastern or Mediterranean.

Omar, Simpson thought to himself, labeling the speaker until he could find out the man's name. Though the man was nowhere near as handsome as Omar Sharif, their mustaches looked the same.

Simpson turned around and studied the other man. He was short, hairy, and wide at the shoulders and hips. The type who would go to fat if not careful. A single brow arched across his dark, beady eyes.

Kong. King Kong, Simpson thought, with all that hair and brute force. Kong closed the door, and Simpson heard a heavy lock being secured. He turned and looked at the food and drink and went and sat and waited.

His body demanded food. Simpson knew it would be wise to eat it. He also knew that in the battle he was engaged in, he must resist where he could. He needed to resist. He crossed his arms and waited.

Half an hour later he heard the door being unlocked. He watched as Kong stepped aside and Omar entered the room carrying a chair. He set it down in front of the table, then left the room.

A tall, thin, pale-skinned man entered. *He doesn't spend much time in the sun,* Simpson thought. The man's pants carried razor-sharp creases. His shirt was wrinkle free and perfectly tucked in. The cuffs were cut just the right length and looked as if they were done in London. Knee-high polished boots. *The man could be on dress parade,* Simpson thought. His eyes were green and cold, like a shark's.

The stranger entered the room and stood staring down at Simpson for a moment. He then moved to the empty chair, sat down, and crossed his leg, letting his long right leg fall down gracefully across his left knee. He smiled at Simpson, exposing perfect white teeth, before breaking the silence. The man's English was quite good but carried an accent Simpson could not place.

"Mr. Simpson, my apologies for your beating earlier," the man opened. "I was not on the premises. I should have left stricter orders."

"And you are?" Simpson questioned.

"My name is Manuel Kramer," came the reply. "I run this facility."

"You mean prison."

Kramer thought before answering. His conversation with Major Hataway and the reason Simpson was here ran through his head. The major had insisted on being at every interrogation. Kramer almost laughed at that idea, he was so caught off guard by the demand. This was *his* prison. He set the rules. "Impossible," he had informed the major. Kramer had placated the major and sent him to a separate building where the troops and the few officers were quartered to sit and wait as the torturer performed his craft. He decided to ignore Simpson's remark.

"You should eat," he replied instead. "The food is safe and not bad. The soup is very good."

Kramer pulled a silver cigarette case and matching lighter out of his pants pocket. He opened the case and took a cigarette before offering the open case to Simpson. Simpson thought a second, then removed one. Kramer smiled and lit his before offering the lighter to his prisoner.

Simpson studied the silver lighter in his hand. It was heavy, sturdy. It looked old. Upon examination he saw the double S lighting bolts etched into the fine silver, the unmistakable symbol of the Nazi SS.

"My father's lighter," Kramer said proudly.

Simpson placed it on the table between them. He rolled the unlit cigarette across the tabletop.

"Not my brand," he simply stated.

"Not bad, Mr. Simpson." Kramer laughed. "Quite good, in fact. I was surprised when you took the cigarette. Your file states you do not smoke. Please, eat your dinner while I talk a bit."

Figuring that he had scored at least one point in the exchange, Simpson decided to eat. The food would give him much-needed energy. He did not know if he would see such a full meal again from his captors. From his Ranger POW training he knew what Kramer was doing. The soft approach. The good cop.

He started with the soup. It was quite good. After a couple of spoonfuls he poured himself some coffee.

"My apologies," Kramer said, "we're out of sugar."

Kramer sat silently smoking until his cigarette was finished. Simpson started on the plate of food now. Some lamb and rice.

"We both know why you are here," Kramer began. "The major is close by. He personally informed me of your theft."

The less Simpson said, the less they had to work with. Without responding, Simpson continued eating.

"That is quite a substantial amount of money you stole."

"How much exactly?" Simpson cut the lamb.

"You tell me." Kramer returned the volley.

"You don't know, then." Simpson smiled.

Kramer pondered the remark.

"I will find out." Kramer indifferently tossed his cigarette onto the cold cement floor and ground it under his boot heel. "You see, Mr. Simpson, I always find out. I am quite good at what I do. I have been doing it for thirty years."

Kramer had calculated that if the major was paying one million dollars for the information, then there must be a lot more money at stake than that. He would find out how much, the password, and where the bank was. He would then dispose of Jim Simpson and decide how much more money to demand from the major, or maybe he would take it all for himself.

"Yes," he continued, "you will tell me everything I wish to know."

"We'll see," Simpson calmly said as he finished his meal and pushed the plate away.

"Mr. Simpson," Kramer warned, "I am an expert at extracting

information by any means. Save yourself much pain and many sorrows. Tell me what I wish to know."

"Simpson, James. Sergeant, United States Rangers, 18120590," came the reply.

"I see," Kramer said. He stood and went and rapped loudly on the steel door.

Simpson quickly slid the knife into his pants pocket. Kramer turned back to face him again.

"I'll let you reconsider your response. We'll talk again in the morning."

Omar opened the door. Kramer exited, letting his final words for the night trail behind him.

"Take him back to his cell. And see that that knife he hid in his jumpsuit is returned to the kitchen."

Jim Simpson was strip-searched before his cell door was closed, bolted, and locked.

CHAPTER 21

Screeners should personally observe the source . . . Screeners should examine the documents captured with the source and any documents pertaining to the source.

—FM 34-52 Intelligence Interrogation, May 1987

IN THE EARLY MORNING GLOW, VAN Zandt stood in front of an innocuous-enough-looking bakery. It was in the Montreuil district near the Parc des Guilands. This was the address Li Ang had given him. It was a fashionable bakery with a brisk business, Parisians flowing in and out of the front door. The sweet aroma of the fresh-baked breads, bagels, and croissants filled the air.

He walked in and, in perfect French, asked for Naomi Levenson, the owner. He had to wait a moment while she finished conversing with one of her regular customers. When her employee informed her that there was a man waiting to speak to her, she walked over.

"Yes?" she asked in French. "You asked for me."

"A friend sent me," Van Zandt replied, still using the native tongue. "He suggested I try your fig bread. He said it is quite good."

Naomi Levenson didn't show any reaction to the question. Her bakery sold no such bread, but it was a code phrase for other items she sold.

Like Li Ang's, her motive for dealing in forged documents was ideological. Her grandparents had survived the Nazi concentration camps and settled in Paris after the war. Her grandfather had been a printer. He used his skills to create documents good-looking enough to help hundreds of Jewish refugees from World War II to escape Europe to the newly formed Palestine. He passed the trade to her father, who continued the family tradition. He in turn trained Naomi when he saw that she understood that sometimes the right people need help from unofficial channels.

Their family was well known in Israel, most especially by the Mossad. They were Syanim, Jewish foreign nationals who are more then willing to provide unquestioning assistance to Israeli operations. Their contributions can be in the form of cover for operators, money, a safe place to stay, or other kinds of assistance. There are Syanim in most countries in the world. Naomi Levenson provided false papers to the Mossad, among others.

"And your friend's name?" she cautiously asked. He told her. She smiled. "Please come back at two this afternoon." She didn't forge for just anyone.

Van Zandt went and did the other tasks assigned him to kill the time. When he returned, Naomi waved him past the long glass counters. He followed her through the kitchen and into her private office. She sat behind a small desk in the cramped office. Van Zandt took the metal folding chair opposite her. He was sure that she had called New York City and spoken to Li Ang. All was in order.

"My apologies for the limited office space, Mr. . . . ?" She let the question hang in the air.

"Van Zandt," he replied.

"Mr. Van Zandt," she continued. "I spend so little time in here. I much prefer my kitchen and my customers."

He silently nodded.

"So what can I do for you?" she asked.

Van Zandt pulled five of the blank passports out from the inner pocket of his overcoat and handed them over. "These need names." He then handed her the list of new names for the passports.

"I'll need photographs."

Custer and he had decided not to hand those over until they knew that she could do the work. They didn't want her to know the faces of the group unless absolutely necessary.

"I can bring those tomorrow morning," Van Zandt informed her. "Can you do the work?"

Naomi had heard this question before. It was a silly question to her, like asking her if she could bake a simple loaf of French bread.

"Of course," she said. "Fifteen hundred euros each." It was her usual price for new customers.

"And when would they be ready?"

"Seven days," she said. "I do the work myself, but my bakery keeps me quite busy."

"Can they be ready sooner?"

"How much sooner?"

"Three days?" Van Zandt asked.

Naomi Levenson thought for a moment. What she had said was true. Her bakery did keep her busy. Her forgery work was meticulous, and none of her creations had ever failed. That took time. Yes, she could finish the job in three days. It would mean late nights and less time with her two sons, but it could be done.

"That would incur extra expenses," she informed the quiet man. "Seventeen hundred and fifty euros each. And that will be three days after I receive the photographs."

Beggars can't be choosy, Van Zandt thought as he pulled off a thick roll of euro notes. He counted off six thousand in bills and handed them over. "The other five thousand when I pick them up."

"But of course." Naomi Levenson smiled as she unlocked the drawer in her desk and dropped the notes into it.

Business concluded, Van Zandt asked her a question. He needed to contact a certain type of man. Men who were looking for security work. Men who wore no official uniforms and did not work for any established security companies. Men who asked no questions for the high wages they got for going into possibly dangerous situations.

Naomi knew of such men. She told Van Zandt where he might meet some of them. Some liked an occasional drink at a small bar she knew of. She had done work for the owner and his customers before. He thanked her.

"Until tomorrow, sir." She stood, extending her hand.

Van Zandt stood also, returning the smile, and they traded handshakes. "Until tomorrow."

She led him out of the office and back to the front area. He was about to walk out the door when he heard her call him.

"Oh, Mr. Van Zandt."

He turned. She held a long white bag up.

"Your bread."

Van Zandt returned to the counter and accepted the bag from her. It was warm in his hands and smelled of figs. As he walked down the street he opened the bag, tore off a piece of the bread, and tasted it.

It was delicious.

VAN ZANDT WAITED UNTIL EVENING to head to rue Miollin and the address Naomi had given him. The modest bar didn't stand out. It was like many others around it. What made it different was that this was where black market small-arms dealers and mercenaries might be found. He had been told to ask for the owner, an old German named Josef Wagemuller.

Wagemuller was eighty-four years old. He had grown up during the height of the Nazi regime. Like most boys his age, he had been in the Hitler Youth and worried that the war would be over before he got his opportunity to do his duty for his country and the Fuhrer. He was barely eighteen as the dream of the Third Reich began crumbling around him and all of Germany.

Trained into one of the last SS cadres, he found himself in his first posting, early in 1945, watching the Russians ever advancing toward the heart of Berlin itself. Too young to be anything but idealistic—he truly believed the mad paperhanger's words of hope and change as the end neared—Wagemuller found himself in command of a small group of old men and boys attempting to hold off the unstoppable tide of Red soldiers crushing their perimeters in more each day.

Panzerfäuste were not much use against a seemingly endless flow of T-34 tanks. The few Mauser 98 bolt-action rifles were far outmatched by the Russian PPD-40 machine guns and the ruthless will of the men who used them. Men who had fought at Stalingrad and Kursk. Men who were merciless in their destruction of Nazi Germany.

As the end approached, his "soldiers" were killed or captured until only he and one World War I veteran were left in the rubble and ruins that the heart of Nazi Germany had become. It was the dead of night and a rare repose from the constant bombardments and attacks.

"You are young," the old man told him. "Run. Escape. Run to the west. If you must surrender, better it be to the Americans or British. The Reich is dead. Maybe you can live. Others will survive. Return one day to rebuild Germany."

Young, afraid, and his ideology shattered, Wagemuller ran west.

He dumped his SS uniform in favor of civilian clothes, and he kept moving. He traveled mainly by night and slept far off the roads during the day. He thought he would die many times as he evaded capture. He had nightmares of that nightly. Somehow he made it to France, and there he found other escaping Wehrmacht and SS soldiers. With nowhere to else to go, some of them joined the French Foreign Legion.

Long ago forged in an attitude of not looking into one's past, the Legion accepted all these soldiers. They were trained and used. Eventually they were sent to Indochina to try to keep that colony under French control. That war raged from 1946 to 1954 when, on a hill named Dien Bien Phu, the French dream of holding their colony died. On May 7, 1954, after fifty-six days of battle, the Viet Minh army, led by General Giap, destroyed the enemy of the Vietnamese people.

After months of being held prisoner, Wagemuller was returned to France. He finished his enlistment and left the Legion. At first he planned to return to Berlin, but he decided to remain in Paris to rest. Slowly the spell of the city took him over. By the late seventies, he found himself the owner of the little bar on the rue Miollin. He had bought it from an Englishman named Freddie who suddenly had to sell it when a mercenary operation in Africa had been betrayed by British intelligence. Freddie had been warned to leave that kind of work forever.

The clientele, men of combat and arms, tested the new owner. When they saw that he could be trusted, they stayed. Wagemuller did nothing to alter the clients he attracted. He sometimes scored a decent bonus for putting people together.

The bar was almost empty when Van Zandt walked in. The only others there were a couple of men, quietly talking, and a lone ex–French para nursing a whiskey at the end of the bar. Wagemuller looked up from drying some wineglasses as Van Zandt entered. He studied the man a moment, then went back to his labors. Van Zandt walked up to the bar in front of the old German and ordered a glass of wine in English.

An American, Wagemuller thought as he found a clean glass

and poured a glass of serviceable wine for the customer. He didn't hate Americans, but he wasn't fond of them either. Without their meddling, the Third Reich would have won.

Wagemuller had done deals with Americans before, but he didn't trust them right off the bat. Too often they were with the CIA or some other spy agency, he thought. More than one middleman in an arms deal had gone to Moulins prison for making the mistake of getting involved with the Americans.

Van Zandt was quiet as he drank his wine. When he had finished the glass, he broke the silence.

"I was sent here by a friend," he said in perfect French. "I was told you might be a man with interesting connections."

Wagemuller looked up, still polishing a glass. "What kind of connections?"

"Certain men and possibly weapons."

"Who sent you here?" Wagemuller questioned.

Van Zandt gave him the French forger's name.

That Jew. A Jew and a woman, the old Nazi thought. Yes, he had used her services once, but only out of desperation when the man he used was sent to prison. Wagemuller didn't want anything to do with the Jews, and this man being an American lowered his interest even more.

"Sorry," he calmly said. "I'm just an old man running a bar."

Van Zandt paused a moment. Then he quickly reached out and grabbed Wagemuller's right wrist. The German looked up, and when their eyes met they locked. Wagemuller was unable to look away. Some preternatural force had taken hold of him. The stranger's gaze seemed to bore deep inside of him. They stood like that for ten seconds, but to Wagemuller it seemed much longer. When the man spoke again, it was with a quiet but very forceful voice.

"Stehen Sie stramm, Scharführer! Vor Ihnen steht ein Vorgesetzter! Ich kämpfte an der Ostfront während Sie in ihrer Hitlerjugend Uniform in den Bergen gezeltet haben. Wir haben gefroren und wir haben geblutet während Sieden selbstgebackenen Strudel ihrer Mama gegessen haben und lernten, wie man Knoten bindet. Ich weilte im Bunker in Berlin während Sie vor den Russen weggelaufen sind. Letztendlich habe ich seine Leiche gesehen."

Wagemuller knew this couldn't be true; the man was too young. Yet he sensed the eternal reality in the man and his words. He couldn't move or speak. When Van Zandt released his grip the old German dropped the wineglass in his left hand, reached over and started rubbing the spot where the quiet man had held him. This was not a man to toy with.

"My apologies, sir." He finally found his words again. "What do you seek?"

Van Zandt told him.

BACK IN MIAMI, JUDY WAINSCOTT had been busy. She did as solid a research and fact-finding job as she had ever done. Now that she better understood the nature of the black operation to move prisoners around, she began looking for where they put them.

She found clues in foreign newspapers, magazines, and a handful of small-press books dealing with the subject. She read interviews with men who had been captured and held without any trials or even charges—held sometimes for years—before it was discovered that they had nothing to do with al Qaeda or any other militant Muslim group.

An interview in *Der Spiegel* with a thirty-one-year-old intern of Iranian heritage who had been held prisoner was her next break. He had lived in London since 1992 and was about to become a doctor. His father had been killed in the first Gulf War, and his mother had managed to get him and his sister out to England.

When the Battle of Fallujah began, his mother had begged him to go get his aunt and his nieces and nephews out of the country. His uncle had been killed by Muslim extremists when he was thought to be too friendly with the Americans. What could he do but go? This was a family matter, and he was now the oldest male in the family.

Mistaken for the enemy, he had been taken prisoner and turned over to the intelligence services. No amount of logic or evidence he presented mattered to those people. He was shipped off as a suspected member of the insurgency. Transported just as Jim Simpson had been, he had no idea where he ended up.

The torture came again and again over months until he confessed to whatever the questioners asked of him. He signed whatever they put in front of him after a while. Almost any man will eventually break. The ones who don't break usually die.

After he had confessed, the torture stopped. It still took his mother and the efforts of a human rights organization three years to secure his release. When he was released all he knew was that he had been somewhere in Egypt and that the prisoners' nickname for the prison was "the Death Factory."

With that nugget Wainscott had more to search for. She found other references to the Death Factory. The more she found, the worse it looked. Many men just disappeared off the face of the earth once they were taken there. Few walked back out from the dark cells and dungeons.

She found three men who had, the Londoner and two others.

One of them, in an interview with an obscure Swedish newspaper, said that he thought the prison was deep in the desert southeast of Aswan, somewhere between that city and the Red Sea. He had heard one of the guards talking about going to Aswan for some R&R to see a "sweet little woman" he had met the last time he was on leave.

After that it was a dead end. Wainscott could find nothing more of the black world's abyss known as the Death Factory.

She typed up what she knew and could prove and then added in everything that had led her to her report. She knew that any clue she could give Custer might be something he could use to find the black hole.

While she was preparing her FedEx package for Custer, he was on the phone to Charles Simpson. He was getting the elder Simpson to write him a letter. A letter that might prove quite useful very soon. It also would be sent via FedEx to Custer's Paris address.

CHAPTER 22

PWs can prevent mental deterioration by playing mental games, working problems in the mind, writing a book—generally keeping their minds active. By so doing, they tend to defeat the captor's system. ***The individual who allows his mind to stagnate is the one who has problems.***

—FM 21-78 Prisoner-of-War Resistance, December 1981

THEY CAME AGAIN FOR SIMPSON at 2:00 A.M.

He woke up as the heavy metal locks on the door were thrown back. Light from the hall flooded his vision. Shapes moved at him with speed and menace. Strong arms grabbed him and yanked him from the cot. Loud yells in a language he couldn't understand. Hard kicks to his ribs and stomach. The food he had just eaten came up all over his cell floor.

Uncaring force took him away, dragging him down the hall. Any attempt to move against that force brought a new series of yells, kicks, and punches raining down upon him. Resistance was rewarded with force. Simpson still fought.

The final destination was a room down a short flight of stairs leading underground. Simpson smelled the others who had been taken here before him. The dried stench of sweat, blood, bile, urine, and feces filled the underground chambers. He heard a haunting, begging moan come from behind one door he was dragged by. A demon-inspired scream vibrated through another. One didn't have to know the victim's language to know a plea for mercy when one heard it.

Simpson's destination was a dark, cold cell with a dirt-covered floor. As he was dragged into the room he could see the stains of whatever had soaked into the earth. A guard on each arm holding him tight, his hair was grabbed from behind by another, his head forced upward to see the pair of heavy chains and manacles hanging from the far wall.

A guttural laugh came from behind him before a savage rubber truncheon blow hit his left kidney. Somehow Simpson remained silent, gritted his teeth through the shot of pain. Another laugh. Orders barked in that strange tongue. Those holding him dragged him to the far wall. He tried to stand to resist, but his bad knee collapsed, making that attempt a failure.

When they got to the wall, he was turned around to face the door. One guard firmly held his arm while the other, with unnecessary force, yanked his other arm straight back and upward. Simpson felt a cold manacle being locked around his right wrist. Now the man holding the other arm pulled him upward, Simpson's feet leaving the ground, until his left arm was poised under another steel loop. Simpson tried fighting back, but the grip was too tight. The other man joined and locked the loop. Now both wrists were all that held Simpson up, his feet dangling a clear foot above the earth.

Not satisfied, both men moved to Simpson's left side, grabbed the chain, and grunted as they pulled the chain behind his body, his arm forced unnaturally straight back behind him. A chain link slid over a thin steel rod that had been cemented deeply into the wall. The two captors went to his right arm now, yanked it back with harsh force, and, grunting, cussing, and sweating from their efforts, forced that arm back also.

The pain started immediately. Simpson's arms were twisted so far back and upward that his body could do nothing but shoot pain signals in his brain. The longer he hung there, the more his weight dragged his body down away from his arms, which were held fast in place.

The two men who had hung him up stared and studied their handiwork. It was good work. Kong stepped forward, said something to Simpson, sent another truncheon low to his right rib area, and laughed.

Simpson looked up and spat in his face.

Fire came into the man's eyes. He almost lost control. He almost forgot Kramer's orders for the prisoner. Not quite, but he still brought the three-foot-long, hard rubber club down across Simpson's left collarbone. The force sent a white-hot shaft of pain shooting through Simpson's torso.

The leader barked orders, and the three men left the cell, the door clanging shut behind them. The lights went out soon after.

HOW LONG DID SIMPSON HANG there? Hours? It felt like days as gravity forced his body constantly downward but the steel loops holding his wrists refused to allow that. Millimeter by millimeter, his body sagged.

Simpson absorbed the pain. He gasped and gritted his teeth and let the pain out in low moans, tried to let it leave him in waves. More intense pain just replaced that which left.

Simpson dug deeper. He stared down below him where his sweat had dripped and stained the ground. It was a dark spot. Details like that forever haunt those who are seriously tortured.

Other thoughts can fill a tortured man's mind, freedom among them. Simpson brought back the memory of the country singer's voice. His father was doing something. Someone would come. Jim Simpson started forcing the pain away as far as he could.

Though that pain was an ever-rising river, he tried to dam the deluge behind a wall of hope and some thoughts of his eventual freedom.

He began to wonder what he would do with his freedom. One thing he realized was how deeply he missed his wife and son. If—no, *when* . . . when he got out of here, he would never venture so far from them again that he was away for more then one night's business.

The flood began to abate.

He realized how deeply he loved his wife. When was the last time he told her that? he wondered. On his last trip to the States? Yes, he had told her, and numerous times on the phone or through e-mails since then, but had he been sincere enough? Had he really let Jan know what she meant to him?

No, he decided, nor Alex, his son. He would let them know when they met again. He would never again place himself so far from them for so long.

What would they do? They had talked about opening their own business, but what kind? Jan wanted a coffee shop. He liked books. Maybe they could combine the two. Simpson started thinking about where in the city of coffee he and Jan would put their new shop. Simpson began to plan the coffee shop/bookstore.

The flood receded.

The lights snapped back on. Simpson looked up as the cell door opened. Kramer walked in, impeccably dressed as he had been before, every crease sharp as a razor. He walked four feet into the room and stood ramrod straight.

"I wished to avoid this, Mr. Simpson." His politeness was almost convincing under the circumstances. "It is bad, no?"

"I've had worse," Simpson bit back. "You ought to try Ranger training sometime. Something like this is like a vacation at Fort Benning."

"I see," Kramer said. "You know it can all end if you just tell us the password for the bank account. It is our money, after all. I am an honest man, Mr. Simpson," the torturer calmly said. "I see no reason to kill you unless I have to. Unless you force me to. All we want is the money and we'll send you home again."

Simpson laughed. "Bullshit."

"No, it is true," Kramer insisted. "There would be nothing you could do once you give us the account password. There would be no reason to kill you."

"What account?" Simpson asked.

Kramer waited a moment before replying, "I see."

He barked some orders, and two men came into the cell from the hall. Each held one of the rubber truncheons. Kramer pointed and commanded in Arabic. The men came to opposite sides of Simpson within two feet of him, the black rubber clubs poised above their heads.

"The password, please," Kramer demanded.

"I don't know what you're talking about," Simpson said.

A barked word and the beating started. Simpson's body became just a target for the hard strikes. The men delivered a savage attack. Each blow sent vibrations through his body. Each one made his body move downward. His wrists held his arms impossibly in place.

The flood rose again, higher than before.

Simpson held it in as long as he could. When the pain demanded release, he looked up and screamed at the top of his lungs. He then locked his gaze straight at Kramer and started praying.

"Our Father, who art in heaven, hallowed be thy name. Thy kingdom come, thy will be done . . ."

Kramer barked louder. The blows became harsher, faster, and harder. Simpson got louder.

". . . on earth as it is in heaven. Give us this day our daily bread. And forgive us our trespasses, as we forgive those who trespass against us. And lead us not into temptation, but deliver us from evil . . ."

Kramer yelled for his men to stop. He approached Simpson and grabbed his chin and forced the beaten man's eyes to look at his.

"You will tell me what I need to know."

Simpson smiled.

"For thine is the kingdom, the power, and the glory, for ever and ever. Amen."

Kramer punched Simpson hard in the face. He struck again. He rained down blows until Simpson passed out.

CHAPTER 23

An interrogator must adapt himself to the many and varied personalities which he will encounter.

—FM 34-52 Intelligence Interrogation, May 1987

VAN ZANDT AND CUSTER RETURNED TO Wagemuller's bar at 2:00 P.M. the next day. That was slow time for the bar. The early risers had come and had their lunchtime drinks and left. The night crowd wouldn't be in for hours.

As they entered, Van Zandt wheeling Custer in, the old German nodded his head to the corner table farthest away from the door. A lone man sat there nursing a glass of red wine. Van Zandt pushed the wheelchair to the edge of the table before sliding into the booth opposite the stranger. Wagemuller came around from behind the bar to the table.

“Gentlemen, I present Herr Henry Schaffer,” the barman said in his accented English. “Drinks?”

Custer and Van Zandt both asked for wine. The bartender brought the bottle of what Schaffer was drinking and two more glasses, then left the men alone.

Henry Schaffer sat quietly before the two warriors. Just over fifty, his head shaved bald for his convenience and not for the fashion of the day, he stared at the men before him through expensive horn-rimmed glasses as he tugged at the tasteful gold and diamond stud earring in his left earlobe.

Just over six feet one inch tall, in shape, Schaffer was the opposite of his appearance to most. Most saw the physical presence, when it was his mind that was sharper than his body. He was a cold calculator when it came to business and an expert negotiator. After doing his time in the German army in his youth he had found that he liked weapons and those who bought them. He moved easily into the international business of arms sales. He apprenticed with Heckler & Koch and Diehl BGT Defence before breaking out on his own.

Germany is number three in world arms sales, behind only the United States and Russia. There was more than enough business for the young entrepreneur as he established himself as a small-arms dealer. Then the Berlin Wall came down. That caused a flood of high-quality arms and munitions to flow into the West from the former Eastern Bloc nations. As these were often illegal arms, it was risky territory for most. In return for keeping the German foreign intelligence agency (the Bundesnachrichtendienst, better known as the BND to most outside of Germany) aware of some questionable customers, Schaffer was left pretty much alone. The BND was very good at what it did.

Henry Schaffer was no fool. He was careful about who he sold what. He well understood the unwritten rules of the bizarre international arms trade.

With the flow of new merchandise, Schaffer's business prospered and his status grew within the world of suppliers of small arms and munitions. As long as he left the big contracts to the big operators, he was left alone.

When Wagemuller had called him with the prospect of new clients, Schaffer had come to the old man's bar to see who these men were. He smiled as he introduced himself again and shook their hands.

"Josef tells me I might be of some service to you gentlemen," Schaffer opened.

"Possibly," Custer replied. He reached into his pocket and pulled out a folded piece of paper and handed it over to the German arms dealer. "We're looking to fill an order."

Schaffer took another sip of his wine before unfolding the piece of paper. He read the list and pondered it. "Quite a small list," he commented.

"We're a small operation," Custer countered.

"Most of these items, I have in stock in my warehouses," Schaffer said. "I see you are seeking two South African Rhino trucks and an M-35 transport truck."

"We heard the Rhino was good," Custer replied. "The deuce and a half we know is good."

Schaffer hesitated before speaking. "The Rhino is adequate. Just don't blow the hose because then you are stuck," he said. "I generally recommend the Oryx MPV or APC. Depends on the need. They are made in South Africa to the U.S. military standards for Iraq. I would have to know more about your operation before making a professional recommendation."

Now it was Custer's turn to go quiet for a moment. "The Oryx APCs will do fine," he finally said. "We can't afford breakdowns in the middle of nowhere."

Schaffer knew better than to try to pry more operational location information out of these men just yet.

"I see." He smiled. "There is the question of your—" The

German paused. "Credentials. They make a difference in these matters."

Custer pulled out the letter Charles Simpson had written for him on Pentagon stationery and handed it over to the German. Something of a white lie, the letter stated that the men bearing it were working with the cooperation of the United States military and that any necessary paperwork for moving arms across national borders would be provided upon request by the proper authorities.

Schaffer studied the document with interest. It smelled of black ops. He had dealt in that realm before. It usually meant no questions asked by the proper authorities and quick, full payment, usually in cash. Looking up again, he smiled at Custer.

"I will need a copy of this, of course," he stated before handing the letter back.

Custer hated paper trails. Especially since he had found out that the Belle Glade operation was known.

"Just let me know when and who to send it to." Custer smiled back. He would spread that letter around only if absolutely necessary.

Again, Schaffer decided not to push. "And payment?" he asked.

"Not a problem," Custer replied. "Just let me know how you want it paid and where, and it will be there."

Schaffer had another sip of his wine and then pulled out an expensive Pelikan fountain pen. He began going down the list and marking the price by each item. When he had finished, he looked up at Custer.

"What is your timeline?" the German asked.

"Yesterday," Custer replied.

"I see," Schaffer said, inwardly smiling. The necessity of speed brought a slightly better profit to any deal. He made more marks on the paper and handed it back to Custer. "Those are my prices," he commented. "As I said, I have almost everything you request in my warehouses. It is just a matter of gathering them in one spot and shipping them to your final destination. The shotguns and the trucks I do not have in inventory. But I see no problem delivering them per your immediate demands. You will note, I have added twenty percent onto the cost of those for the necessity of speed."

In fact, Schaffer hoped that he might only have to spend a ten percent premium at most to get the trucks delivered on time. If this deal came off as he hoped, it would be a profitable one. If it was he would take Debbie, a beautiful young American on vacation whom Schaffer had met at a wine shop, out and they could sample a good Château Latour 1982. She was worth the expense.

Custer reviewed the list. He hardly knew the prices of international arms, and he was sure that the man in front of him was padding them. Fred Custer knew when to give in, though. He didn't have an option here. He added up the total.

"How do you want payment?" he asked.

"My Swiss bank account would be best," Schaffer stated.

"Twenty-five percent up front. Half when we see the goods boxed, addressed, and in a bonded warehouse, and the final payment when we pick up the trucks," Custer demanded. He wasn't trusting anyone he had no history with.

Schaffer thought, took another sip, then thrust his hand out.

"Agreed," the German said with a smile.

The men shook hands. Schaffer then took out a business card and wrote on the back of it.

"My bank account number," he said as he handed the card over.

"The first payment will be in it before the day is out."

"Good," Schaffer commented. "I shall begin gathering the items and get the special weapons and trucks ordered. Where will I be delivering them to?"

"Cairo," Custer said. "I also need some modifications on one of the Oryx APC trucks."

"What kind of changes?" Schaffer asked.

Custer told the German what he wanted. Together they made a rough sketch on a piece of paper. Schaffer looked over the drawing.

"It can be done. A little cutting, some custom-made bulletproof glass, a higher passenger seat. This is possible. It will cost, of course."

"Of course." Fred Custer smiled.

There was silence as Schaffer thought.

"Everything will be there within five days," Schaffer noted. "My own goods I can have there tomorrow if need be, but the trucks will take a bit longer."

"Five days is acceptable," Custer agreed.

"Good. Good," Schaffer commented. "Now that business is over, will you come and have lunch with me? My treat, of course."

"As much of a pleasure as that would be, Herr Schaffer," Custer stated, "I am afraid that we have another engagement already."

"Ah, that is too bad," Schaffer said. "I am sure that you would be interesting lunch companions."

"Perhaps another time," Custer added.

"Well, then, I shall excuse myself and get to work on your order." Schaffer slid out of the booth and stood. He firmly shook each man's hand.

"We'll have the destination address to you this afternoon. It has been a pleasure," Custer commented.

Schaffer bowed slightly. "The pleasure has been all mine, gentlemen."

As he started to leave, Van Zandt spoke his only words to the German arms dealer.

"Auf Wiedersehen," the quiet man from Orlando said.

Henry Schaffer was not sure he liked the tone in the phrase. There was a lurking menace behind the delivery. *Do not cross us,* it seemed to say.

Being an honest man—one didn't last long in his business

without being that—he had no intention of cheating these men. Making a little more profit, yes, but cheating them, never. Still, after hearing the tone in the quiet man's voice, Henry Schaffer decided to finish this transaction as quickly as possible.

Custer and Van Zandt watched the German arms dealer walk to the bar, hand Wagemuller a hundred-euro note, and leave.

They sat and waited for their next appointment.

CHAPTER 24

The interrogator must have an exceptional degree of self-control to avoid displays of genuine anger, irritation, sympathy, or weariness which may cause him to lose the initiative during the interrogation.

—FM 34-52 Intelligence Interrogation, May 1987

MANUEL KRAMER KNEW WHAT HE WANTED to do with Jim Simpson next. It was an old technique he had learned from his father. In many ways it was the cruelest torture he could inflict upon a man. The torture of the mind.

He called his men in and gave his orders.

JIM SIMPSON WAS LYING ON his rough cot when they came in for him, too spent, too terribly abused, to sleep. His shoulder sockets sent throbbing memories of his last torture session to his brain with every pulse of his heart.

He barely had the strength to lift his head when his cell door opened and two men came at him, with one more standing in the cell doorway. The man Simpson had labeled Omar was in charge of two other unknown guards.

After Omar barked his orders, the two men grabbed Simpson's arms, oblivious to the new pain they inflicted upon him just by moving him, and pulled him to his feet.

His feet. He was too beat up to use them properly, so the two men just dragged him along. Through the cell, out its door, and down the halls of the Death Factory.

"Where are you taking me?" Simpson managed to choke out of his dry throat. The sound of his own voice was strange to him. It sounded odd, like some alien living in his body was using it as its home. When had he last had anything to drink? he wondered to himself.

There was no response from the guards or Omar. Only Simpson's forced movement through the dark halls and down the stairs. Down the last corridor of Kramer's palace of torture.

The lights above were spaced for a purpose in this long hall. Bright light and cold dark alternated like squares on a chessboard leading to a finale at a thick iron door. A door buried in the darkness of one of the squares.

An unmercifully thick iron door crisscrossed with heavy bands of iron, its only relief, if it was that, was a one-foot-by-one-foot square cut into the center at eye level. In that square, every four inches, vertical half-inch bars were deeply welded under the iron covering of the door. An unnaturally bright white light seeped from inside the room behind the iron door, invading the blackness just outside.

"Where am I?" Simpson demanded.

There was no response as Omar carefully swung open the door. The hot light streamed out from inside the room, filling the hallway. Simpson stiffened in resistance as the two guards tried taking him into the room. One grunted something, and the other used his free hand to punch Simpson in the gut. He folded and softened. They pulled him into the room. Omar had already walked into the center. Omar turned and faced his prisoner.

"The end," he said in heavily accented English. "You are in the final room."

Simpson was forced farther into the room, stunned by its whiteness. It was as sterile as a Mayo Clinic operating room. Flawless white-painted walls and white tile, both lit by far too much artificial light from above. Some industrial-strength xenon or tungsten lamplight filled the room with an extra-white luminosity, lamps designed for a far larger space. Simpson's pupils dilated as he was brought into the center of the room.

"Not final for you. Not tonight," Omar continued. "The commander has plans." That was as far as Omar's limited English could take him.

As his eyes adjusted, Jim Simpson saw "the machine" for the first time. That was the gruesome torture device's nickname among the guards.

Hand built, at great expense, to Kramer's exacting specifications, the machine was his dream of the ultimate torture device. It was the result of twenty years of Manuel Kramer's slow descent away from humanity, the ultimate symbol of his contempt for his fellow man and his ever-growing love of the darkness he swam in.

The main area was built of three-inch-thick aluminum sheets. There were four of them, each with a heavy clamp near the corner. That way the victim could be strapped in quite securely. Once clamped in place the victim could be manipulated into almost any position the human body can be forced into.

There were hinges between the four large metal sections. Depending upon which hinges and pieces of metal it was on, the victim's body could be twisted, spread out like an X or folded like a U. By keeping the two pieces on either the left or right side together and lowering the edges down or up, the machine could spread a man into an inhuman V shape. Pneumatic cylinders controlled all of this beneath the main table area, and those provided the finest control available, down to millimeters as needed. An adjustable leather strap allowed the torturer to completely immobilize the victim's head.

Long electric wires and thin water hoses grew out from beneath its massive frame to hang above the victim's head. The ends of those had special connections to which wires and tubes could be attached per the torturer's decisions. An IV pole top was welded onto each side to allow the complete use of the many drugs the modern age has introduced to torture.

All of this was controlled by a state-of-the-art computer console. A torturer with training could make the machine move and float at his will. It was an orchestra waiting to play, and Kramer was its maestro. He had conducted many symphonies of pain on the machine.

Jim Simpson stared at the machine in growing terror. He could sense its evil purposes. Silently he began to pray for strength.

But the machine was not his fate that night. Kramer had a much more devious use for it.

Jim Simpson was dragged backward and forced into a heavy metal chair that had been bolted into the floor near the wall opposite the machine. His wrists and ankles were securely held under thick leather straps. His head was frozen in place by another strap so that his eyes were aimed straight at the machine. Finally an ugly rubber ball gag was forced into his mouth and tightly secured. Simpson could taste the hot fear of those who had worn that gag before in the sweaty taste of the rubber.

The three men left the room then. Jim Simpson could only stare ahead and wonder what tonight's session was going to be. He looked around at the only other objects in the room. A freestanding coatrack with clean white medical coats hanging on it stood in one corner. A waist-high, three-shelved rolling metal cart rested beside it. Only the top shelf of the three had anything on it. A spotless white cloth lay across the top shelf, on which Simpson saw medical instruments, a couple of syringes, and vials of drugs.

He sat like that for fifteen minutes.

When he heard noises again, it was the sounds of shuffling feet and hard boots on the outer hallway. Omar entered, followed by two guards who were trying to get a man into the room. He was a gaunt man, barely five foot four and weighing 110 pounds if he was soaking wet. He had been resisting the trip down the long hall, but as soon as he saw the machine he redoubled his efforts. He had tasted the hellish device before.

Fight as he would, he was no match for the brutish guards. A couple of fists and a truncheon blow and he was soon past the doorway and deep into the room. He was cuffed in and tightly secured to the metal framework. His physical protests were no good.

Though he spoke a language Simpson did not understand, Simpson understood every plea for mercy and begging word the man spoke. Immune to such pleas, the guards used another ball gag to mute the man to a series of grunts and groans.

The two guards left then, and only Omar remained. He walked over to the man strapped on the machine and then reached up and grabbed his nose and clamped it tight with his thumb and forefinger. He turned to Simpson, smiling.

"See?" He laughed.

The man couldn't breathe now. He couldn't move his head enough to struggle to any useful effect. Omar just laughed louder and watched. Right when the man was at the point of passing out, Omar released his grip and laughed still louder. He walked halfway toward Simpson and bent over so he was staring straight into his eyes.

"See?" Omar laughed again. "You see more soon." He laughed even louder at the thought.

A rage he had never known began to build up inside Jim Simpson. He had heard of men like this—pure sadists—but he had never encountered one. All he could see was innocence being tortured and a former human being who had sunk too far back into the swamp of inhumanity.

Jim Simpson knew that if he ever got the slightest opportunity he would make Kramer, Omar, and anyone else at the Death Factory pay for their falls from grace. He used that hate to build upon. He used it to help him survive that night. He tried burning holes through Omar with his eyes, wishing they shot laser beams of pure white energy.

The sound of precise steps coming down the hall got Omar to stand up straight and face the door. Simpson turned his eyes toward the door and watched as Kramer entered the room, turned, and closed the heavy metal door behind him.

Kramer silently walked over to the coatrack, removed one of the medical coats, and slipped it on over his custom-tailored clothes. He then turned and examined the instruments atop the rolling cart. He picked up and examined two items before setting them down and deciding on a third. Then Kramer walked to the middle of the room before addressing Simpson.

"Mr. Simpson," he began, "I am so sorry to disturb your rest tonight. But I felt it was necessary." Kramer held up the medical tool and carefully examined it. It looked to be a curve-tipped hemostat, as far as Simpson could tell. "I thought I would give you a demonstration in hopes of changing your"—Kramer paused—"attitude."

Kramer nodded to Omar. The sadistic guard reached into his pocket, pulled out a handheld Taser, and stood next to Simpson. Kramer stepped toward the machine with the terror-stricken man strapped to it.

"This man also has been most uncooperative," Kramer stated. "We have tried being gentle with him, but, as with most of our guests, he has failed to take advantage of our hospitality."

Kramer turned back and faced Simpson.

"You shall completely watch my discussion with him." Kramer threw his thumb back over his shoulder, pointing at the victim. "If you attempt to keep your eyes closed, my associate will shock you."

His attention on Kramer, Simpson wasn't watching Omar. Suddenly he felt a jolt of hot electricity shoot through his lower body as Omar applied the open electrodes of the Taser to Simpson's thigh. Simpson's body rebelled, his muscles unable to control themselves. His vision blurred. Simpson's flesh tried to jump from the chair, but he was too well secured. After a moment he could see clearly again, and he was staring at Kramer.

"That is an early model of the Taser. A mere twenty-five thousand volts," Kramer noted. "Quite painful but hardly dangerous except to the elderly or unless one has a heart condition. So I urge you, Mr. Simpson, for your own well-being, do not attempt to close your eyes." Kramer indicated Omar with a nod of his head. "His sole purpose here tonight is to make sure you do not close your eyes. Our friend here"—Kramer turned and walked over to the side of the machine—"has resisted telling us what we need to know. Tonight I shall convince him of why he should change his mind."

Kramer bent toward the man, made sure his head was tightly held down, and attacked the man's ear canal with the long hemostat. Simpson heard the muffled scream seep through the gag.

For the next hour Jim Simpson watched as the other prisoner was tortured. The man was never asked any questions. Only statements were made to him in a language Simpson didn't understand.

Jim Simpson needed no translation of what he saw, heard, and felt for that hour. He shivered in his bonds at the assaults. He silently prayed, and when that wasn't enough Jim Simpson let the rage he felt inside slowly build within him. He made a vow to correct this injustice before him no matter what it took. Twice he closed his eyes on purpose to feel the pain and to channel it into his rage.

He understood why Kramer was trying what he was. It was psychological warfare. Apparently Manuel Kramer did not understand the man he was attacking. It would take a lot more than that to break Jim Simpson. Much more.

CHAPTER 25

The direct approach is the questioning of a source without having to use any type of approach.

—FM 34-52 Intelligence Interrogation, May 1987

CUSTER WAS GATHERING HIS OWN INTELLIGENCE. Having some time before their next meeting at Wagemuller's bar, Custer and Van Zandt found a public pay phone, and, using an international calling card, Custer called Charles Simpson at the Pentagon. He was brief but concise in what he asked for. Was there any way that the senior Simpson could get them satellite images and anything else on the Death Factory?

"I'll see what I can do," Simpson responded. "It's out of the general's usual AO, but it shouldn't be too tough to twist a few arms and call in a couple of old favors. How should I contact you when I have anything?"

"Call my cell phone," Custer replied and gave Simpson the number to his new phone. "Are we good?"

"Five by five," the elder Simpson responded, using the common radioman's response for "the message was received and understood as strongly as it could be."

"Roger that," Custer sent back before hanging up.

Checking his watch, he saw that they still had two hours before they were to meet other men at the old Nazi's bar.

"Lunch?" he asked Van Zandt.

"I used to know a good place near here," the quiet man responded. "Let's go see if they are still open."

The two old warriors traveled through the busy Paris streets, invisible to those passing them. If any Parisians even glanced at them, their thoughts were *Just American tourists.* After lunch they headed back to the bar. There was still business to be done here in Paris.

Custer was confident in his team, and he could buy all the equipment they would need, but he felt a couple of men short. With Hadad unable to be there, he wanted enough hands to get the job done properly. He knew what he had to do—break into a highly guarded CIA-funded, Egyptian-run prison, free Jim Simpson, and get out. They would get no second chance.

Van Zandt had told Wagemuller that they were looking for a couple of good mercenaries. Men with solid military combat experience who could be trusted to stay loyal to the team because of the good pay. Wagemuller told Van Zandt that he would pass the word and see who was available.

The German was good as his word, and he had found a few men who were more than willing to take the work. The question was, did Custer want them? The day before, Wagemuller had given Van Zandt the short list of those in Paris currently and willing to take the money. They were given times spaced thirty minutes apart to come to the German's bar and meet Custer and Van

Zandt. Using the Internet, Van Zandt had done what research he could on those men.

While Custer and he were at lunch, they had discussed the men and Van Zandt's notes. After settling back in at Wagemuller's bar, they began the interviews.

The first two men came in together. Clearly, they were a team, both former British para soldiers from the same unit. There was no doubt about their credentials. One of them had even written a fiction book based on his time in Iraq. On the Internet Van Zandt had found some interesting corrections by others in the unit to the author's recall of events. There was enough discrepancy to bother Custer, and the two men were thanked and told that they might be contacted again.

The next man came in alone. He claimed status as a former New Zealand SAS trooper, so there should have been no doubt to his military training. Custer and Van Zandt sat and listened to him as he told them of his exploits.

Those who didn't know Fred Custer would never think that the man in a wheelchair had ever been in the military, much less in the elite U.S. Special Forces. That worked to his advantage. He sat and listened to the man, knowing a lie when he heard one. Custer doubted that the man had ever served with any decent outfit, much less the New Zealand SAS. He dismissed the man with a wave of his hand, and after they were alone he had a quick word with Van Zandt.

The stoic man went to the bar and spoke quietly to Wagemuller. The old German shrugged his shoulders and said something in return. Van Zandt didn't pursue it. He just came back to the table.

The next man didn't show up. Custer was beginning to wonder if they would have to go with just his men when two imposing figures entered the Paris bar.

The first to walk in filled the doorway. He had short-cropped blond hair and removed his Oakley sunglasses to expose deep blue eyes, which looked around the bar before the man strode over to Wagemuller. Standing an imposing six feet three inches and weighing in at 240 pounds of thick, well-toned muscle, the man looked more like he was chiseled out of white granite than born of flesh and blood. The Russian known as Kamenev had started fighting in Afghanistan in the late eighties and had never looked back at the poor village he had sprung from. He confirmed that the men he wanted to see were at the bar before motioning the second man in.

If Kamenev was white granite, then Domaac Gat Tut was black obsidian—razor sharp when an edge is put on. Six feet six inches tall, the Nuer tribe warrior from Southern Sudan almost had to stoop to enter the bar. Not as thick in the chest and legs as Kamenev, Domaac (a name meaning "bullet" in his native tongue) looked no less imposing than the Russian.

With six parallel razor-cut scars across his forehead (his coming-of-age tribal *gaar* markings) and not an ounce of fat, Gat looked at the world with an intense gaze from his dark eyes. The African warrior didn't back down to anyone. He had been fighting against the Northern Sudanese Muslims since he was a young teen. For more than twenty years he had fought and killed, most recently for the United States as a contract soldier in Afghanistan.

How the two men came to be a team and liked each other seemed to be an impossible tale. Yet there they were, Mutt and Jeff.

After joining up in the same unit in Afghanistan and being randomly assigned to the same machine-gun nest behind a wall of sandbags, the two men had survived a savage week of combat together in the cold mountains of northern Afghanistan fighting off invading Taliban. Like a well-oiled piston and rod, the two men were just right together in combat.

They came to the table and shook hands as they introduced themselves. They filled the booth bench opposite Van Zandt to the point of Kamenev spilling out over the edge of the seat. Custer watched from the end of the table in his wheelchair.

Domaac had been educated by Christian missionaries, and his English was far superior to the Russian's. He did the talking for the team. After the usual introductions they got down to business.

"The work is drying up fast in Iraq," said the Sudanese. "And we have been to Afghanistan, him three times now." The black warrior thumbed over at his partner. "I'm tired of it there. Too cold. And once a lifetime is enough there, so we are pushing our luck there. I want to earn enough to go back to my village in the south."

"And him?" Custer asked.

Domaac grinned. "He's not sure what he wants to do." Kamenev started speaking to his comrade in Russian. The Sudanese laughed and shot back a couple of words. "One day Kam will figure himself out. Until then all he knows is fighting."

"Well," Custer said, tempting the pair, "we might have some work for you two."

As they talked more, Custer knew he had found his men. As long as they checked out, they were more than perfect. Both were seasoned warriors with at least twenty years' experience, and they wouldn't freeze under fire. Gat (he preferred just his middle name for most Westerners) not only knew Africa but spoke his tribal Nuer, Somali, English, Arabic, and enough Italian and Russian to be understood.

Kam had begun his military service as a nineteen-year-old boy serving under the tough General Boris Gromov in his 40th Army. Gromov was the last Russian to leave Afghanistan on February 15, 1989, as he walked across the Friendship Bridge, which spanned the Amu-Daria River. Kam had stood on a ridge looking back as his top commander ended the nine-year effort by the Soviet hammer to break the tough Afghanistan anvil. The anvil always breaks the hammer in the end.

After the Wall came down, Kam had mustered out of the Soviet Army a much harder man than he had entered it at nineteen. Like many other out-of-work veterans, he had worked as an enforcer among the Russian mob in Moscow through the nineties. Because he had been there for the Russians, he was able to get back into combat when the United States invaded Afghanistan as part of Operation Enduring Freedom. He bounced between there and Iraq, depending on the pay, until he had hooked up with the tough African. Despite their differences, they found they had much more in common, and now they were a team.

Gat's military credentials were no less impressive. Learning to fight as soon as he was able, he had his early baptisms under fire against the militant Muslims who held the top two-thirds of his country. He didn't fight for Sudan so much as he fought for his village. A wise man once said, "All African politics are tribal." Gat was proof of that.

Like Kam, he found that working for the Americans paid far better than anything else in the world he could do. The money he sent home supported his wife, children, and close family. The small arms and ammo he could rarely get sent home were very welcomed by those fighting the Muslims in the north. With serious combat time in Iraq and Afghanistan, Gat had proven himself under fire numerous times.

Van Zandt got their names and the information about the units they had served with for the U.S. military. While Custer kept them talking at the table, Van Zandt stepped outside and called Charles Simpson at the Pentagon. Simpson would run their names through the system and see what their records said. It would take him six hours to track down the records and even talk to two commanders who had worked with the two men. His information only confirmed what Fred Custer already knew: These were his men.

Prices were agreed upon, $50,000 a man. Half payable before they left Paris, payable however they wanted, and the other half when they were finished. Both men provided the names of the people the money should be sent to if they were killed in combat.

They left the bar and found a Paris photo booth. For two dollars American each, the new team members got black-and-white photos. While Custer got the pair checked into their hotel, Van Zandt called Naomi Levenson and used the photos to get passports made for the two new members of Custer's latest A-Team.

Kam and Gat were settling into their hotel room about the time that Jim Simpson was being strapped down in the room with the machine.

BY THE TIME THAT JIM Simpson was witnessing the other prisoner's torture, Henry Schaffer was having a drink with Adam Jacobi. The two men were having Sancerre wine and goat cheese at the quiet La Tartine on rue de Rivoli.

Based in Paris, with a quite legitimate cover as a fine arts dealer, Adam was with the collections department of the Israeli Mossad. Among his many jobs was the collection of raw intelligence from the field, which he communicated, unedited, back to the Tel Aviv Mossad headquarters. His job was not to analyze it, which he was more than capable of doing, but just to gather it and send it in.

Schaffer had contacted him for a meeting as soon as he had discovered that Custer's operation was going to be somewhere in Africa and was starting in Cairo. Schaffer knew better than to let anything with him connected to it that went on anywhere near Israel happen without notifying Jacobi. Fine wines and beautiful women cannot be enjoyed if one is in prison or dead.

Schaffer slid over an envelope that held a list of what was being procured by Custer and his handwritten notes of everything he knew about Custer and Van Zandt. It wasn't much, but then Schaffer didn't think it was his job to do anything but report what he knew to the Israelis.

With a smile, Adam Jacobi accepted the information and slid the bill for the wine and food over toward the German arms dealer. Schaffer smiled, knowing he was staying well within the unwritten rules of the game of international arms sales.

As the two men were exchanging paper, Naomi Levenson was also busy. She was rolling dough in her kitchen after finally getting her children to bed. She didn't need to report to the Israelis. She had done that two hours ago via an e-mail to her contact, who lived in Jerusalem. She had written her contact right after she had finished creating all of the passports for Van Zandt.

Both pieces of information would be read in offices in Israel within twenty-four hours. The tiny country had to be beyond efficient in such matters. Its existence depended on such solid human intelligence work.

While the Israelis would know the false names of the men in the operation and that there was some Pentagon connection, they would not know where and when the operation was to take place. By the time they could put all the pieces together, Fred Custer and his men would be well past their timetable for having finished the rescue mission.

Custer, the ever thorough planner that he was, had anticipated that some word of his operation would get leaked to an intelligence agency. He was prepared for that. All the men had extra passport photos. Custer handed those over to Van Zandt and asked him to make a call to see if what Custer wanted done with the extra photos could be pulled off in time.

Van Zandt checked his watch and went to make that call.

CHAPTER 26

IF THE ENEMY DOESN'T LIKE YOU, YOU'RE DOING WELL.

—FM 21-78 Prisoner-of-War Resistance, December 1981

MAJOR HATAWAY WAS NOT A HAPPY man.

Ever since he had arrived at the facility he had been basically ignored. He had access to the mess and some of the other buildings, but not all of them. The main building, the one he had watched Jim Simpson being taken into, was off-limits to him. There was only one entrance, and there were two armed guards at it 24/7. No one got into that building without permission. That permission came only from Kramer.

Hataway kept demanding to meet with Kramer, but those pleas almost always went ignored. He did get to meet with the master of the camp twice, but both of those meetings were short and to the point.

"Where is that hundred thousand dollars you promised me?" Kramer had questioned Hataway both times.

The problem was that Simpson had drained almost every dollar from the company bank accounts. There was a little cash flowing in from old contracts, but the sudden destruction of the PIS facility in Baghdad had put a major crimp in the company's operations. The investors in the USA were asking questions. Hataway had managed to stall them off, but their demands for clear answers were moving to the point of insistence. There was word that they were sending auditors to Baghdad and that Hataway had better be there to greet them.

If Kramer could break Simpson quickly, Hataway thought that he could get the money back and soothe things over. But that wasn't going well. Hataway also suspected that there was the possibility that Kramer had broken Simpson and knew what was at stake. That thought worried Hataway. Those worries led him back to the bottle at night.

Kramer was more than happy to approve the fifth of Jim Beam that Major Hataway started requesting after dinner each evening. He made sure the major was well supplied.

If all went as Kramer had planned, then Hataway would disappear in the deep Egyptian deserts at the same time as Jim Simpson.

KRAMER WAS BUSY ALSO. HE wanted every tool available to him to crack Jim Simpson. He would try two drugs, Rohypnol and scopolamine. Fifty milligrams of Rohypnol—better known as the "date rape" drug—lowers a person's inhibitions. It causes intoxication and short-term amnesia.

Scopolamine comes from a Colombian tree called burundanga. The drug makes those who are given it totally compliant.

Possibly too compliant. They will tell you anything, agree to anything. The problem is that it might not be the truth. They might just be trying to tell you what they think you wanted to hear.

Kramer had the Rohypnol in stock. He had rush-ordered the scopolamine and expected it to arrive in two days. He would let Jim Simpson rest a day and then use the Rohypnol the next morning. He would have fifty milligrams slipped into some orange juice to hide the taste.

JIM SIMPSON WAS ALSO THINKING. He was recovering after the previous night, when he had been forced to watch the other man's torture. He knew if he told Kramer what he wanted to know he would be killed. He had to fight back. He had to find a weapon against the torturers. He needed time because he was sure that help was on the way.

As he lay on his cot in his cell looking up at the ceiling, Jim Simpson began to hum a tune. It was the song sung by Chely Wright he had heard back in Baghdad.

As he let the melody soothe him, he came up with how he would fight back against his captors. When he was finished with that he began to plan the coffee shop/bookstore he and Jan would open when he got home.

CHAPTER 27

Once the interrogation element has arrived at the designated holding area, the senior interrogator establishes a site for interrogation operations.

—FM 34-52 Intelligence Interrogation, May 1987

FRED CUSTER WAS IN HIS HOTEL room when the front desk called. An overnight package had just arrived for him. He wheeled himself to the elevator, rode down to the front desk, and retrieved the package.

It was from Charles Simpson. Custer went back to his room before opening the thick envelope. It was full of detailed photo-recon photos and reports of what Simpson could gather on the Death Factory. With the intel the team needed now in hand, it was time to plan the assault and fully brief his men. First, he sent Van Zandt out to find maps of Egypt.

"The more detailed the better," Custer requested. "But find them quickly and get back here."

While Van Zandt was out buying the maps, Custer carefully reviewed the material he had been sent. He had a good idea how he wanted to pull the operation off. He called Schaffer and was assured that all his material needs were on schedule and would be waiting for him in Cairo when they were due to be there.

When Van Zandt came back two hours later with enough maps for the entire team, Custer called the rest of his men to his room. He called room service and ordered two pots of coffee, one of tea, and other drinks and light snacks. They might be going over the plan a long time.

When the men had all settled in, Custer started laying out his plan.

"First, commit everything to memory. No one carries any notes from this room," the old warrior began. "No writing on the maps yet. We'll do that if we have to once in Egypt. Second, from now on, we travel in threes if any of us even leave our hotel room."

Custer was hardly worried about his men. It was the two mercenaries he was thinking of. He was fairly sure of them, but he wanted to be absolutely certain that they didn't go sell them out. He couldn't imagine them being able to secure more than the $100,000 he was paying them from any intelligence agency—not with what they knew—but he wanted to make sure. He wanted that "Fred Custer 100 percent certain" in his mind. The agents of the French National Defense General Secretariat—the SGDN—were very good at what they did. They had broken up more than one private operation being staged from their country.

With those caveats Custer handed out the maps and began telling the men his plan. Seasoned soldiers all, they sat and listened until their commander was done. There were some questions and clarifications, but overall the idea seemed sound to everyone in the room. It was as good a plan as they could come up with to spring Jim Simpson.

Custer's plan was solid up to freeing Simpson and getting away from the Death Factory. After that he needed some assistance. Custer turned to the Nuer warrior. He knew Africa best.

"I want a doctor, a nurse, and a full kit of medicines available when we get Simpson out," Custer told Gat. "We have no idea what condition he'll be in. We'll have field first aid kits and some plasma, but I want a fully qualified doctor. Hopefully one who has seen combat in case we sustain any casualties."

Gat thought a moment. "Budget?" he asked.

"Not a problem," Custer replied.

"I'll call my father," Gat said. "He has contacts."

"Good," Custer said. "We'll have the trucks, but where to go with them afterward? We might only have a few hours lead time. The prison is in the middle of the southern deserts of Egypt. We can head east for the Red Sea or west hoping to sneak quickly in and out of Libya and into Chad. Northern Sudan is out. Too unfriendly to Westerners. If we can get into Southern Sudan we'll be OK."

Gat spoke up. "Eastern Chad isn't very friendly to Americans right now. Plus there is a lot of tension between Chad and Sudan. That can be a hot area."

It was here that Custer sprang one of his surprises.

"How are they to Canadian relief workers?"

"Much safer," Gat stated after a moment of thought.

"We will have a second set of passports soon," Custer announced. "Forgeries, but quite good forgeries. As soon as we leave the prison with Simpson, we destroy the U.S. passports and go with the Canadian ones."

Van Zandt had called his old Chinese friend in New York again. He had been told that of course Li Ang could do a set of Canadian passports. All it took was money and time. Van Zandt had FedExed the extra passport photos to the Chinese restaurant. Charles Simpson had been called, and he located a suitable photo of his son, which was used to create a forged passport for him. The photos were expected back in Paris, attached to flawless forged Canadian passports, the next day.

Custer planned to dump Naomi Levenson's passports as soon as he could. Once they left the prison they would be off the grid again.

"A Canadian relief group in fully armed APCs?" Hickey chimed in.

"Hey," Custer replied, smiling, "we'll be escorting a wounded man through dangerous territory."

"It's crazy enough that it might work," Hickey said.

"I hope we never have to find out," Custer said. "I would rather go east to the ocean and get a pickup by boat and float to Yemen or Saudi Arabia. Much safer places to bug out from."

With the basic plan established, the men went over the drive to the prison and the plans for assaulting it and freeing Jim Simpson. They went over the plan again and again until every one of them knew it like they knew how to fieldstrip and reassemble a rifle.

When the briefing was over, Gat asked to speak to Custer in private. Custer asked if Hickey and Van Zandt could also listen to what he had to say. Gat thought a moment and agreed.

The three older men listened to what the African proposed. They conferred in front of Gat. If he could do what he said he could do, they would more than agree to what Gat had in mind.

Gat left the briefing to go call his father. He would gather the tribal elders and talk out what their young warrior was asking of them. What Gat proposed interested both Custer and his men and the tribal elders.

CHAPTER 28

The approach phase actually begins when the interrogator first comes in contact with the source and continues until the prisoner begins answering questions.

—FM 34-52 Intelligence Interrogation, May 1987

JIM SIMPSON WAS DECIDING BETWEEN USING dark cherrywood or light ash for the bookshelves in the coffee shop when he heard the clang of his cell door being unlocked. It was Kong and Omar beckoning him out of the cell.

Knowing he was still at war, he quickly thought it out. He saw no point to resistance, so he folded his hands behind his back and walked out the cell door as if the two guards weren't even there.

Kong led the way, with Omar well back, Taser in hand, in case Simpson tried anything. They led Simpson back to the room he had first met Manuel Kramer in. The room where he had been fed the only good meal of his internment. Once back in that room

Simpson saw a full breakfast waiting for him—an omelet, sausage, fruit, toast, orange juice, and coffee.

"You eat," Kong informed him. "The commander will be here soon."

Seeing no reason not to eat, Simpson sat down and began his breakfast. He had no idea that his orange juice had been spiked with Rohypnol. Had he been given a full dose of the drug, Simpson would have passed out for somewhere between eight and twelve hours. Kramer, knowing Simpson's weight and the effect he wanted on the prisoner, had reduced the dose.

Once he had drunk the orange juice, the drug would take around thirty minutes to take effect. After two hours under the influence, Simpson would be at the drug's maximum effect level. His inhibitions would be lowered, his judgment would be blurred, and his speech would slur.

Kramer had ordered Kong to wait until Simpson had finished the orange juice and then come notify him. If Simpson hadn't drunk the orange juice, then he would have been force-fed it.

Due to his honest nature, Simpson anticipated no such trickery. He drank the orange juice never suspecting that he had been drugged. When Kong left the room to go get Kramer, Simpson didn't think anything of it. Omar stood and watched Simpson as he ate.

Jim Simpson had long ago planned his strategy of battle for when he next met Manuel Kramer. It was time for him to be on the attack. He knew how he would attack when he and Kramer next clashed.

It was twenty minutes later when Simpson began to suspect something had been done. He was getting woozy. As he approached thirty minutes after the drug's ingestion, his suspicions were on high alert, but it was too late. By the time Kramer arrived, Jim Simpson was under the full effects of the drug. He was quite relaxed.

When Kramer entered the room, Simpson grinned, slid his

chair back, threw his feet onto the tabletop, ankles crossed, and held his coffee cup between his palms.

"Kramer." Simpson grinned and pointed a finger at the torturer. "I don't like you." He sipped some coffee.

Kramer whispered something to Kong, who moved over and removed the coffee cup from Simpson's hands. Kramer didn't want the caffeine working against the Rohypnol. Kramer once again sat down in the chair opposite Simpson.

"Why is that?" he asked. "I thought we were getting along just fine, Mr. Simpson."

"Ha!" Simpson laughed back. "You only want me for my money." The last word was slurred.

"But you stole it," Kramer countered. "I am being paid to get it back to its proper owners."

Jim Simpson had to pause a moment, thinking how to reply.

"They stole it," he finally countered.

Manuel Kramer didn't care who stole the money. All he wanted was the name of the bank where it was and the password for the account. Once he got those it would be his money. He decided to try to sway Simpson through an emotional appeal.

"When you tell me what I need to know, I'll send you back to your wife and son," he tried.

"Bullshit!" Simpson didn't even have to think on that answer. "You'll kill me and bury me in the desert wherever . . ." He paused, eyes closed, thinking for a moment. "Just where the hell are we, anyway?"

"Egypt," Kramer replied, actually being caught off guard by the question. Besides, it didn't matter if Simpson knew. He would never use the information.

"Well." Simpson paused between words. "I'm never coming here again."

Jim Simpson went back to his strategy of attack now. He had been working on it in his cell when Kong and Omar had come to get him, so it was floating through his mind. He swung his feet down, pulled his chair to the table, leaned forward and whispered to Kramer.

"You want to know something?" Simpson asked.

"Of course," Kramer replied.

Simpson brought his words down to a whisper. "Better send them away. I'll only tell you."

Kramer thought a half minute. He could more than handle Simpson under the effects of the drug. He barked some words, and Kong and Omar left the room, closing the door behind them.

Simpson put his hands on the table, fingers intertwined, and rested his chin atop them. He closed his eyes.

"You're not going to sleep, are you?" Kramer asked him.

"Nope," Simpson replied. "Just praying the Lord's Prayer. So you be quiet till I finish, you godless heathen."

Kramer decided to allow this as long as the prisoner didn't fall asleep. After a moment Simpson opened his eyes again and stared at Kramer.

"So you think I am going to tell you where I put the money?" Simpson asked.

"Mr. Simpson . . . Jim. May I call you Jim?" Kramer tried the soft approach.

"Sure," Simpson replied with a smile.

"Jim," Kramer continued, "you are going to tell me in the end. Frankly, I have been gentle with you up to now. My techniques will get progressively more"—Kramer thought again—"persuasive from here on out."

As if on the devil's cue, a scream from one of the torture rooms echoed through the halls and into the room they were in.

Simpson thought back to the beatings, the pain, and other tortures in his cell. Even his drug-addled brain didn't think those had been gentle.

"Still won't tell you," Simpson said.

"In the end you shall," Kramer replied.

They were silent for a moment.

"Here's what I'll tell you," Simpson offered. Kramer sat up a little straighter and leaned in some.

"PIS is a big company. Well connected," Simpson began his attack. "The major knows some people. Some of the wrong people to get mad at you." He closed his eyes again before continuing. "You need to look at what happened to Dan Casolaro."

"Who is he?" Kramer asked.

"Was," Simpson corrected. "Who was he. One of the early investors. He was looking into the major and he got too close and he had an accident. A bad accident. The kind you should have."

In fact, Casolaro was one of the first-level investors of PIS. While he had died in a car accident, he was not looking into anything the major was doing. As long as the profits were flowing, he was happy to drive his silver Acura MDX and go to church socials with his wife and cocaine parties with his other women.

It was while driving home one night from one of those parties with his current alternate companion that he had crashed his pretty SUV, killing them both. Since he was a well-respected citizen in a small enough community, the police did what they could to keep it quiet. The usual lies were printed in the local newspaper and church newsletter.

It was murky enough for Jim Simpson to use as a weapon against his captor. He would let the thought stew in Kramer's mind. Let him wonder what was the truth behind Casolaro's death.

"Accident," Simpson repeated and then laughed. "The major is connected, Kramer"—Simpson opened his eyes and pointed at Kramer—"and once he gets what he wants, don't think you won't have an accident."

"I can more than protect myself, Mr. Simpson." Kramer's voice was stern.

Simpson laughed again.

"From the CIA?" he fired back. "The NSA, military intelligence, and the other agencies of the United States? The USA can take out anyone they want. They knock over countries the way Dick Butkus knocked over linemen. You wouldn't last a month."

Kramer tried to regain control. He didn't like where this conversation was going.

"Mr. Simpson." He paused, remembering his soft approach, and smiled. "Jim. I work with the major. Nothing will happen to me. It is you I am worried about."

Simpson ignored the last words and sent in a flanking maneuver.

"Casolaro was an investor," he emphasized. "You, you're just hired help."

Kramer lashed out at the insult. No one insulted him! His hand struck Simpson's cheek. Simpson laughed.

"Want me to teach you to pray?" Simpson verbally slapped back.

"Mr. Simpson"—no soft approach now—"I will get what I want to know from you. It will be very painful but not fatal. I would consider it a professional failure if you die before I extract the information I require."

Kramer knew that the drug had failed. He would need stronger inducements for Simpson. He began to plan them.

He called Kong back and ordered Jim Simpson back to his cell.

What Simpson had said to him had bitten deep. He would have this strange death of Dan Casolaro investigated. Until he received that information, he would take out his growing frustrations with Jim Simpson on another prisoner.

Yes, there was a young boy, no more than seventeen, who had been brought in yesterday from Afghanistan. The boy had insisted that he was just a goat herder who had made an enemy of a local war chieftain. The boy claimed that the man had sold him for $1,000 American as a drug runner and Taliban affiliate.

Kramer and his machine would find out the truth.

Release

CHAPTER 29

From the moment of capture until escape or release, you must resist the enemy by all means available. It is not a time in which you are permitted, either by the enemy or by your obligations as a soldier, to hibernate in peace. Your responsibilities as a fighting soldier are not over.

—FM 21-78 Prisoner-of-War Resistance, December 1981

CUSTER AND HIS TEAM LANDED IN Cairo at 1347 local time. Everything in Paris had gone as planned. The future plan was to pick up the vehicles, arms, and equipment, then move as quickly as possible south.

After inspecting the German's arms and goods at a bonded Paris warehouse, Custer called the bank and had the final payment sent to Schaffer's account. He was confident that the private arms merchant would have everything in Cairo on time, and he was correct.

The Oryx APCs looked great. They decided to take them out

for a test run while Hickey took the M-35 supply truck—best known to U.S. military men as the "deuce and a half" for its two and a half ton weight—and loaded it up with what food and water supplies they needed. Hickey took Gat with him to translate in the market.

Custer excitedly took his special seat in one of the Oryx APCs. It had been modified especially for the wheelchair warrior. Custer had ordered the 360-degree ring mount atop the tough APC with a special pneumatic seat mounted under it.

Seat-belted into the chair, he could rise up through the hole in the roof and man the weapons he had had installed. On his left was a 40 mm MK-19 belt-fed grenade launcher. To his right was a sturdy old 7.62 mm belt-fed M-60 machine gun.

Custer could have found a more modern machine gun, but he was used to the M-60, liked it, and knew he could deliver solid effect on target with one. Between the two weapons, Fred Custer could lay down a devastating rain of support firepower for the team. Even the usually stoic Van Zandt smiled seeing Custer in his new weapons platform.

Custer, Van Zandt, Winkler, and Kam would take the trucks out for the test run without any weapons mounted on them yet. Get used to the trucks. Custer had thought Hargis would want to tag along but found out otherwise.

"Hell no!" the Texan exclaimed. "I'm going with Hickey to market. Don't get a chance like that often. I can always sit in a damn old truck. Maybe I'll buy a big hookah to puff on while we're on the road."

Custer laughed, and the teams split up.

Hickey had his orders. He was to fill the big transport truck with enough food and water for the team for a week. In addition to that, he was to buy local foods, fresh fruits, and anything else that would look good to a soldier posted in a remote desert camp. And booze. Custer told him to get lots of local beer and whatever good liquor he could lay his hands on. Custer's battle plan was dependent on such things.

No one smart goes into the Egyptian markets without a local guide. Anything can be bought in Egypt, but one has to know where to go. Hickey found their local guide in a smart, young taxicab driver nicknamed "Tee." His English was great and his Arabic better. He had served some time with the U.S. Army in Iraq as a translator.

After they explained what they wanted and Gat was convinced the taxi driver could deliver, Hickey paid the young man enough to park his taxi for the day and go with them.

"Tee. You just call me Tee," he said, looking up from Hickey's shopping list. He was in the passenger seat of the deuce and a half as they rolled through the streets of Cairo.

"Go right here. Then two blocks and a left. We'll have to park this truck as close to market as we can. And as we load in someone will have to stay with the truck."

Gat volunteered to guard their goods as they were loaded in the truck.

"I love Egypt," Tee continued. "I'm from Libya, but I love Egypt. But like anywhere else these days, you can't leave anything unguarded."

Tee guided them to a local garage where he got his taxi worked on. He knew the owner well, and for a few Egyptian pounds that man was more than happy to let them park the truck and tote their purchases to it.

Tee took them to what they wanted, a real middle-class market. There are markets all over Cairo. Some cater to the tourists selling anything from fine handcrafted goods to mass-produced trinkets from China. The poor, the middle class, and the rich have their markets in their neighborhoods. The food is fresh and good and cheap if one speaks the local language.

The Libyan zipped through the market with the shopping

list. He would suddenly stop at a booth and start talking in the local Arabic dialect. If he didn't like the price, he would throw his hands up and start to walk away, only to be called back by the merchant. He usually got what the team needed at decent prices. Hickey just followed his guide and paid. Hargis had disappeared.

Load after load went into the back of the M-35. After a few hours they had almost everything they needed.

"The beer was easy," Tee said. "Everyone sells that. But good hard liquor, that's something else. We'll go to a hotel for that. I know the manager well." Tee stopped and turned, facing Hickey. "You guys want women?"

"No," Hickey replied. "We're here for business."

"So are the women I know. I love Egypt!" Tee smiled. "OK, off to the hotel."

They soon secured the bottles of whiskey, scotch, rum, and vodka they wanted. More pounds went from Hickey's fist into the palm of the hotel manager. Tee and the man talked in Arabic before Tee turned to Hickey again.

"He wants to know if you need hotel rooms for tonight," Tee said.

"No," Hickey replied. "That won't be necessary."

The plan was to load up what they needed and start south immediately. They would find someplace to stay once they got out of Cairo. A small mercenary force with guns and ammo doesn't want to hang around in big cities unless absolutely necessary.

"What we need now is a printer," Hickey told Tee. "You know Kinko's?"

"Sure," Tee replied.

"Like a Kinko's," Hickey requested.

"I know just the place." Tee smiled. "The Novotel El Borg Hotel. Four star. Full business center. I know the concierge there. If he can't do what you need at the hotel, he can get anything done quickly. For a fee, of course."

"Of course," Hickey replied.

"Everything can be found in Cairo." Tee smiled again.

They went off to the hotel, leaving Gat behind to guard everything.

"Tell Hargis to stay put when he shows up," Hickey told the African.

"Yes, sir." Gat saluted back.

Hickey knew the Nuer warrior would guard the goods with his life.

With that, Hickey and Tee went back to Tee's taxi and headed for the Novotel El Borg Hotel. Once again, Tee's connections and Hickey's Egyptian pounds were a winning team. The concierge soon had the pair in the hotel business center. Hickey handed over a 2 GB flash drive to the smiling woman in charge of the business center and waited.

On that flash drive were electronic copies of forms to be printed off. In this e-world, it was no problem for Charles Simpson to dummy up official-looking Pentagon forms for everything Custer and his men carried and e-mail them to the team in Paris.

If stopped and questioned, they could show quite real manifests for the weapons, ammo, and trucks they were using. On paper, they were transporting everything to the Death Factory for delivery. The forms should get them through any inspections in Egypt. All Hickey had to do was get them printed in triplicate on carbonless paper to make them look more authentic.

It took a little over an hour for the hotel business center to print the forms off as Hickey requested them. He and Tee waited in the bar, sipping on a beer each.

"So, what else do you need today?" Tee asked.

"I think that's everything," Hickey replied. "When we get back to the truck I'll pay you off."

Always the entrepreneur, Tee said, "Well, if you think of anything else, let me know."

They talked, and Hickey found out about the young man's time in Iraq with the U.S. Army.

"I love you Americans," Tee said. "I'm saving up to move there. Maybe L.A. Or Texas. There are a lot of us in Texas."

"Well, here's to you getting there." Hickey tipped his glass toward the young man.

They picked up the forms and took Tee's taxi back to the garage where their truck waited. As Hickey got out of the taxi he saw Gat, a perplexed look on his face, point into the truck cargo area with his thumb. Hickey walked over and stared.

Hargis beamed a smile back at him between taking big puffs of smoke on what had to be a six-foot-tall hookah.

"Want some?" Hargis asked. "This Turkish tobacco kicks ass."

Hickey could only laugh. He turned and thanked Tee.

"You did a great job, soldier," Hickey told their guide. "This will help you get to America."

Hickey handed Tee a thick wad of bills. The taxi driver's eyes popped out as he counted it. It was more than he made in six months driving taxis.

"You sure?" he asked Hickey.

"You earned it," Hickey told him. Without Tee's efficiency it would have taken them a couple of days to do all that they had done in a few hours. It would have cost them a lot more, too. Tee jumped with excitement and headed to his taxi.

"Anything you need, you call Tee," he shouted back as he hopped into his taxi and started it. "Ask anyone in Cairo about Tee. They all know me. Maybe soon in L.A.!"

Tee drove away shaking his fistful of Egyptian pounds out of his taxi window.

"I love Egypt!" the men heard the happy Libyan shouting as he drove away.

"Let's get back to the warehouse and see if Custer is back," Hickey commanded.

Gat drove with Hickey in the passenger seat. Dave Hargis sat in the back of the truck blowing rich tobacco smoke into the air.

Custer and the rest were waiting when Hickey and the M-35

got back to the bonded warehouse. The trucks had worked out fine.

"Top-notch equipment," Custer told Hickey.

Custer and his men had already loaded up everything else in the warehouse, and they were ready to roll. As the sun was falling, they drove south away from the city. The sunset was that uniquely golden glow only found in Egypt.

CHAPTER 30

All professional interrogators must be convincing and appear sincere in working their approaches.

—FM 34-52 Intelligence Interrogation, May 1987

THE CONVOY HEADED SOUTH ALMOST NONSTOP. It was a little over four hundred miles from Cairo to where the Death Factory was located deep in the southern Egyptian deserts.

They traded driving chores as needed and only stopped for fuel or to take a brief rest and stretch their legs. The main highway south was good. It paralleled the mighty Nile to just past Aswan, where it terminated at Sadd el-Aali, the Aswan High Dam, which sat atop the large Lake Nasser.

The team's cutoff was Aswan, though. From there they would head southeast on older roads toward their target. Averaging fifty miles per hour was no problem for the little three-vehicle convoy. Most of the trip was done the night they left Cairo. There was far less chance of anyone stopping them that way.

Once they got past Aswan and cut off the main road, they parked the trucks well off the road and sat out the heat of the day on a remote piece of desert with no one around for miles.

They wanted to arrive at the torture prison at 0330 and start the attack at 0400, that being the time when most people are in their deepest sleep. Custer and his men would have surprise. They needed every trick the old soldiers knew.

As they hid from the sun inside the APCs or under the canopy of the deuce and a half, they loaded magazines, mounted the grenade launcher and M-60 for Custer, and prepared to do battle.

They hadn't seen a soul, much less another vehicle, since they had parked, so they tested the new weapons the German had sold them. They rang off a clip each through the various rifles and pistols each man preferred. Custer tried out his machine gun and 40 mm grenades. Everything worked great.

Gat sat and watched and then pulled out the weapon he'd had Custer order through the German, an Atchisson AA-12 shotgun. Basically just a 12-gauge steel tube mounted onto an M-16-type buttstock and forearm, with its 20-round drum attached the weapon delivered devastating close-combat results.

With a wide selection of different types of ammo—slugs, 00 buckshot, or the explosive Frag-12 ammo, which they had secured a few rounds of—there was little the Nuer warrior couldn't face with his weapon of choice.

"He's a wizard with that," Kamenev told the rest. "Once, Gat took on twenty charging Taliban from his hole. None got close. He reloads drums of ammo faster than they run at him."

"Where were you?" Custer asked.

"In another foxhole handling the twenty charging me," Kam explained as he rested his AK-47 on his hip.

Hargis calmly sat watching everyone, sitting atop a crate of oranges, puffing his hookah at the back edge of the truck. When everyone else had tested their weapons, he carefully laid the hookah tip down and pulled out a long wooden box.

Inside was his CheyTac Associates .408 sniper rifle system. He spent a good thirty minutes putting it all together while Hickey and Kam walked out into the desert and set up empty bottles at various distances up to a thousand yards.

After a final puff on his hookah, Hargis got down from the truck and set up a sniper's position atop a small sand dune. As the rest watched, he let the amazing CheyTac computer systems gather the data they needed. Once everything was green-lighted, Hargis calmly breathed in, let out a half breath, and zeroed in on the first target.

He fired three shots and did some adjustments zeroing the weapon to his needs. The .408 rounds boomed through the dry desert as Custer and Hickey spotted the targets through binoculars. Bottle after bottle shattered as the old Texas sniper did what he did best. After the zeroing, ten rounds took out ten bottles with perfect precision.

"Damn good rifle," Hargis flatly stated. "This one ain't going over the side of a boat," he said, referring to the post–Belle Glade operation.

As the sun dropped in the sky, the men made a fire to cook some hot chow, cleaned weapons, loaded more clips than any of them could possibly use, slid those clips into their webbing, and adjusted that for each of them. They all switched into desert camo uniforms, desert boots, and helmets. Everything was adjusted until it fit as each soldier liked it.

When it was country dark, the night-vision goggles were taken out, added to the helmets, and tested. Like everything else, they worked fine. With the equipment and weapons checked, double-checked, loaded, and ready they cooked dinner.

It was a large meal to fuel them up for the pending battle. They burned the U.S. passports the Frenchwoman had made for them. They were Canadians now. Then they ate and traded war stories. Kam and Gat were able to add new ones to what Custer's former Green Berets knew from each other by heart. The Russian and African warriors were truly interested in their A-Team's Vietnam war days.

As the food settled into their stomachs, each man drifted just a little bit apart from the others and went quiet. They all were doing what soldiers usually do before a battle. Thinking about loved ones back home, praying their soldier's prayers for forgiveness and that, somehow, they be spared from a final bullet. But if they were taken, they prayed, then let it be clean and quick.

No soldier wanted to feel that gut shot or see the foaming pink blood that meant one to the lung.

Custer ordered that everyone try to sleep. He would take the first watch and wake someone up. They would depart at 0100 for the Death Factory and their mission of mercy for Jim Simpson.

Before he went to sleep, Gat took white ashes from the fire and dumped them into his helmet. He gradually added water from a one-liter bottle, mixing it in with the ashes.

"His tribal war face," Kam told the rest before he rolled onto his side to get some shut-eye.

When Gat had the ashes and water to his liking, he got in front of one of the mirrors of the deuce and a half and started applying them to his face. He started with a large plus-sign shape in the center of his forehead. After that he added circles, spots, and lines across his cheeks, chin, nose, and both eyebrows. When he was finished, he turned and faced the others.

There was nothing but grim steel in his eyes and physical bearing. A true warrior from an old tribe of warriors ready for battle. He looked like a soldier of Death himself come to assist in the harvest. The others fed off of that warrior spirit and prepared for the coming strike.

There was little sleep in the camp before they set off at 0100.

CHAPTER 31

Every source has a breaking point, but an interrogator never knows what it is until it has been reached.

—FM 34-52 Intelligence Interrogation, May 1987

THEY EASED TO A STOP FIVE klicks from the Death Factory at 0300.

Custer was mounted up in his special chair, torso and head sticking out of the top of the APC, in front. Gat was his driver. Hickey followed, driving the sturdy M-35. Van Zandt drove the other APC last in line with Hargis in the passenger seat.

The plan was simple. Sometimes quick, simple plans work best.

Charles Simpson had gotten them the satellite overflight images. From those they had studied the Death Factory. It wasn't a very large facility. Basically, it was three buildings surrounded by a chain-link fence two hundred meters on each side. Razor wire in tight, close-cutting lines of steel had been spun out across the entire length of the chain-link fence. Guard towers at the southeast and northwest corners looked over the compound.

To someone facing the front of the complex, to the right, there was a small barracks, which the guards and staff all shared. The team's estimate was that there would be twenty to twenty-five personnel max at the prison.

In the center of the complex was the main prison facility. According to the CIA specs for the construction contract the elder Simpson had acquired, it was a simple layout. That person staring through the front gate would see the front of a sixty-meter-wide structure. Behind it, going back two hundred meters was the main building.

A small guard room was up front. Behind an inner door in the back of that room, the bulk of the first story was made up of cells for the prisoners, divided equally down each side. There were kitchen, generator, and storage rooms in the very back.

There was a second floor underground. One-third the size of the main building, it held the interrogation rooms. That was where the prisoners were led down to for the serious work at hand. At the end of a hall below, opposite the front of the structure, was Kramer's machine room. Behind that was the big generator that kept electricity going to the prison.

Finally, to the observer's far left was the smallest building onsite: Kramer's private quarters with two extra rooms for visitors and a small private kitchen. He did not eat the main kitchen food. It was in one of those spare rooms where Major Hataway was kept. He was in a booze-induced sleep as Custer and his convoy rolled to a stop.

The plan was simple. Most of the guards would be asleep. There was a guard apiece in each tower and two at the front gate as well as the two men always posted at the main building entrance. There would probably be a skeleton staff within the prison itself. All of them were military trained but not top-quality soldiers. They had been picked for their ability to run and brutalize prisoners, not to face live fire from real soldiers. Like schoolyard bullies, their stronger attributes were terrorizing those who couldn't fight back, or at minimum being able to watch as the prisoners were tortured.

Hargis and Van Zandt would peel off from the convoy, lights out, and roll quietly to a spot about a thousand yards southwest of the Death Factory. In the intel photos, they had spotted a small berm that was a good elevation for the sniper. He would set up on top of the APC and wait for the 0400 attack time, or start shooting earlier if things started up before then.

His first job was to take out the man in the guard tower closest to him and then take on targets of opportunity. All the other team members had special markers on the front and back of their helmets and uniforms so that the deadly sniper could easily tell the good guys from the bad ones.

Van Zandt would skirt the perimeter to the west side. He was to cut the wire and get next to Kramer's quarters. If the fence was wired, he would have to wait until 0400 and blow a hole through it with some Semtex plastic explosive and then get inside the perimeter. Once inside he was on his own.

Winkler, their best tracker/scout and outdoorsman, and Kam were on their own also. As Hargis and Van Zandt went away from the convoy, they would take off on foot to the east side of the prison.

They had the biggest initial jobs. Their first task was to take out the other guard tower. Next they had to get through the chain-link fence before the attack time. Winkler said there was no electric fence he had ever met he couldn't slip around.

They then had to take out the guard barracks. Their plan was to place claymore mines at the windows on both ends and a couple in the middle and blow them all when the shooting started or at 0400. Each claymore mine sends approximately seven hundred steel balls flying through the air up to one hundred meters in a sixty-degree arc in front of it. No one wants to be inside that rain of steel and fury.

After firing the mines the two men would toss frag and stun grenades through the windows, then go into the building to make sure no one inside was still a threat. It was unlikely. Those not wiped out by the claymores would be cut apart or stunned by the grenades.

There was also a radio tower in the back of the largest building. They were to blow it down at the same time the attack began. They had more than enough Semtex for the job. Semtex was what the German arms dealer had on hand. They all knew how to use it. Those tasks done, they were to proceed toward the main building to assist as needed.

Custer and Gat would lead Hickey's truck to the front gate. Hopefully they had the paperwork and goods to get past the front gate and to the back of the main prison building, where the kitchen area was. Hickey was to drive the M-35 back there while Custer and Gat parked their APC directly in front of the building, where the front guard area was. Gat was to take out the two front gate guards before the breach of the actual prison began. Custer would handle the two guards posted at the main entrance door.

If all went well, every team member would be in place at 0400, when the shooting would begin. They planned that such a devastating initial attack would kill or wound out of action most of the staff of the Death Factory. The team would kill or capture everyone in their assigned buildings before they all took on the big building. Hargis would roll over at 0415 to 0430, depending on how things went.

They gave themselves one hour to clear the prison and locate Simpson. Depending on his condition, they planned to be on the road again by 0600 at the latest and on their way to their rendezvous. If all went well, they would be finished and well away long before any reaction force could be sent in.

All the men were to be in their initial positions by 0330. If Custer and Hickey couldn't talk their way through the gate, they would just blow the guards away and ram through the fence in the trucks. If that happened, everyone else was to just *go*!

As their watches ticked to a simultaneous 0310, Hargis and Van Zandt took off for their berm. Winkler and Kam started humping east; they would cut back north to stay out of sight.

Custer, behind his 40mm and M-60, gave those groups ten minutes before he slammed his palm down hard twice atop the APC.

"Let's roll!" he yelled.

Gat started the engine on the APC, and Hickey cranked the deuce and a half to life and followed. Their vehicles kicked up the desert dust, and their headlights cut through it. From afar, the two trucks looked like spectral beasts floating through clouds before their attack.

CUSTER AND HIS MEN WEREN'T the only ones who knew the benefits of 0400.

The human body, physically and mentally, is at its weakest then. Deepest in sleep if one is asleep. Most suicides occur between 0300 and 0400. Manuel Kramer well knew all of this, and he was using it on Jim Simpson that night. He had, in fact, begun the cruelest torture session on Jim Simpson at noon that day.

Still recovering from the Rohypnol, Simpson couldn't resist much when Kong and Omar came into his cell and tied him firmly to his cot. They next hosed him down with cold water, leaving him quite awake and shivering.

Then the music began. Large speakers were wheeled in, and suddenly rap song after rap song was blasted through Jim Simpson's cell so loudly that at times the bass made his metal cot vibrate. It was impossible to sleep with that noise, which went on nonstop from noon until 6:00 P.M. But the sounds were not done.

Kramer had located a U.S.-produced CD of Halloween sounds. There were sections with booming shrieks and yells, bone-crunching snaps, and witchlike cackling. Kramer had edited the best sounds into a fifteen-minute orgy, dumped it onto an MP-3 program, and had it looped over and over on his victims.

For Jim Simpson, those sounds played from 6:00 P.M. until midnight.

Then the sounds just stopped. His lights were darkened, and all his mind could do was wonder where the next audio attack would come from as the howling shrieks echoed in his head.

Kramer left him like that for two hours.

Then, without a word, Kong and Omar got Simpson out of bed and dragged him to the floor. They bound his wrists and ankles. Their hard rubber truncheons came out then. They beat Simpson on every part of his body. They raised welts, made bruises, and broke skin. He could do nothing but take it.

When that stopped, the guards washed him completely in another stream of cold water. They next dragged him down the hall, downstairs, and to the room with the machine in it.

They strapped Simpson down tight onto the strange table under the hospital-white bright lights. Then the guards cut away his clothes, connected the electric leads, and forced a thick rubber mouthpiece in between his teeth. The kind used for electroshock patients.

Then they rolled the little cart over to where Simpson could just see it if he looked down. The two guards left the room and slammed the door shut, leaving Simpson alone to think of what was coming.

He was left alone like that for an hour, imagining and trying to shut it all out.

Simpson knew this was going to be bad. He had trained for this as a Ranger and prepared his mind as best as he could while at the Death Factory, but no training can ever truly prepare a person for the real thing under the hands of a master torturer like Kramer.

It was 0300 when Manuel Kramer, fresh from sleep and as immaculately dressed as ever, entered the room.

He removed his military dress coat and slid a white medical coat on. He checked the items atop the little rolling cart. He slipped a stethoscope around his neck before taking an electronic blood pressure monitor and strapping it around Simpson's upper arm.

He coldly read the numbers before using the stethoscope to listen to Simpson's heart and breathing. The blood pressure, breathing, and pulse were all a bit high, but Kramer had expected that. Fear and tension caused it. He removed the blood pressure monitor and set it aside. He snapped on latex gloves. Then he slid Simpson's eyelids back and examined his victim's pupil dilation. He went on to survey the bruises and open wounds on his victim's body.

It was all good. Very good. Exactly as he had instructed, and perfect for this night's work. Kramer stepped back from the machine, then turned and faced Simpson.

"Mr. Simpson," he began, "I have been far too kind to you. Tonight is about pain."

Kramer went toward the little cart and picked up a glass vial with a liquid in it. He held it close so that Simpson could see the label.

"This is Sulfazin," he continued his lecture. "The Russians discovered the uses I prefer it for. Local pain wherever it is injected. Quite an excruciating pain at the site of injection, Mr. Simpson. One"—Kramer paused, thinking—"guest of mine informed me afterward that it was as if hell itself was being inflicted upon her body one small injection at a time."

Kramer stepped back again. "Tonight, you visit hell. But first . . ."

Kramer stepped over to the control panel for his machine and twisted a large black knob. A shaft of electricity flowed through Simpson, making him twitch under the restraints. He bit hard into the rubber mouthpiece.

Kramer doubled the amount.

Simpson could only force muffled screams through the mouthpiece. His flesh strained to break free of the terrible pain, but to no effect. He was strapped in too well. Kramer paused the torture and waited a few seconds.

"Feel free to bite through the mouthpiece," he said. "Others have. We have more of them."

Kramer increased the intensity of the electricity yet again. Even after he shut that off—a long twenty seconds that Simpson felt must have been five minutes—Jim still felt the effects.

Calmly Kramer rechecked Simpson's vital statistics.

"Soon you will think what you just felt a pleasure," Kramer informed him.

Simpson could only watch in horror as the demented torturer filled a syringe, turned, and pressed the needle right next to an area on his shin where his flesh had been broken open by the beating earlier. Kramer injected half the contents of the syringe before moving to a forearm with another open wound. He injected the second half there.

"Soon, Mr. Simpson, soon," Kramer warned him with a wicked smile. He held the still mostly full bottle of Sulfazin up so Simpson could see it. "Soon you will tell me everything that I wish to know. I have six bottles of this. No one has ever made me go past three of them."

Then the new pain started. Pain, Simpson thought, was too mild a word. Pain he had felt. Everyone feels pain in their lives. This was a smoldering heat that quickly built to a Dante's Inferno wherever the drug was injected.

Again Simpson tried screaming, but the mouthpiece prevented that release. Kramer just laughed and turned the electricity on again. Kramer was a master. Simpson didn't pass out. Kramer made sure of that. He knew what dosages and amounts of electricity he could inflict.

This would be the finest symphony he had ever conducted.

Back and forth it went like that. Jim Simpson had no sense of time. He was lost in a deep, dark jungle of pain and more pain. Electricity shocked his system while the injections punched holes into his soul.

He prayed. He tried thinking of the bookstore. He tried telling Kramer everything that the evil doctor wanted to know. The mouthpiece made all his words grunts and moans.

Kramer didn't care what Simpson was trying to say. He knew he would hear what he wanted to by dawn. Every man has a breaking point, and he knew he would pass Simpson's tonight. He would get what he wanted and then go claim the money.

But that wasn't enough. Not now. Not for this man who had caused him so much trouble. So Kramer injected and spun dials and knobs. He would toy with his prey before allowing him to confess all he knew.

Simpson's ears were ringing. His vision blurred. Every sense he possessed focused on the machine and Kramer's tools and trade and the pain. The intense pain.

Jim Simpson did not hear the explosions going off on the floor above him. He didn't hear the gunfire and grenades. He had no idea that Kramer had stopped torturing him, ordering Kong and Omar to go see what was going on as he waited to find out what had interrupted his night of pleasures.

Jim Simpson just swam in a dark ocean of hellfire pain and prayed he wouldn't drown in it.

CHAPTER 32

A number of circumstances can cause
an interrogation to be terminated.

—FM 34-52 Intelligence Interrogation, May 1987

AT 0325 DAVE HARGIS WAS LYING across the top of the Oryx APC. He had a perfect sniper's position, clear view from above of the entire prison grounds. He was calm and patient. Those are among a sniper's main tools. His night-vision scope lit up the dark in an eerie green glow.

He had found and ranged the guard tower he was assigned to take out. He saw one man standing but leaning lazily against one of the 4 x 4 posts that held a small roof over the guard tower. Hargis had a great chest shot. At this range, with the armor-piercing .408 round he had loaded, even if the man was wearing body armor he was dead.

Hargis panned right, viewing through the scope. He saw little white stripes bobbing in the night just past the far perimeter wire. Winkler and Kam were in place. They were through the wire and setting claymores in front of the barracks windows. *Good,* the Texan thought. He panned to the far left now until he located Van Zandt.

Hargis saw his white marker stripes behind the little building Kramer lived in. Van Zandt was in place also. Hargis caught something in his peripheral vision. The shafts from the headlights of Custer's APC and Hickey's M-35 bobbed up and down as they took their vehicles down the rough road toward the main gate.

Hargis moved his scope over to the front gate where the two sleepy guards were posted. He let the distance and other needed data load into the CheyTac system and locked it in. If Custer and Hickey couldn't get past the guards, those would be Hargis's first shots. Take those peckerwoods out, then pop the guard in the tower.

Through his scope Hargis watched as the two lazy guards became alert. They both raised their rifles, wondering what the two trucks coming their way were doing here. Nothing had ever come to the prison at this time of night. The place was too far off in the desert to get lost traffic from the highway. The two guards were somewhat suspicious and started asking each other what was going on.

Like silent death, Hargis quietly waited, eye locked on the back of his scope and finger poised on the trigger.

WINKLER, KAM, AND VAN ZANDT had no problems with the outer fence. It wasn't electrified. It didn't have to be. No prisoner had ever escaped from his cell, much less out of the main building. Even if they did, most of them were too physically ruined to get far. Then, if somehow that happened, they would be alone with no supplies with miles of desert around them. No, there were not any escapes from the Death Factory.

Simple wire cutters allowed the intruders to get onto the prison grounds. Once in, Winkler went to work setting the deadly claymores as Kam wired some Semtex under the radio antenna.

With a watchful eye on the guard tower he was assigned to take out, Kam carefully pushed the fuse into the Semtex and rolled the wires back to the detonator, far enough away. Once he had it connected, he looked back at the guard tower.

The man was more than asleep. He must have been sitting on something and gotten relaxed. His head was hanging back over the edge of the tower's short ledge. He wasn't even wearing a helmet. When the time came, Kam would shoot him in the head, toss a grenade up to make sure, and then blow the radio tower.

The Russian waited as Winkler joined him. The Apache-trained warrior connected his wires to detonators for the claymores. Ready, he looked over at the Russian and nodded, giving a thumbs-up. Kam returned the gestures. They were ready.

On the opposite side of the prison, Van Zandt waited behind Kramer's small home. He didn't know how many were inside there and he didn't care. When the fight started, he would throw frag and stun grenades through the windows, rush around front, throw more grenades in through the front windows, then bust the door down.

If anyone was still breathing after that, he could more than handle them. Van Zandt was not worried.

CUSTER TRIED NOT TO LOOK like he was ready to cut the two guards apart at close range with the M-60 as the APC rolled to a stop, but he was. They had put the Arabic-speaking Gat in the driver's seat of the first vehicle for a reason. Chances were that he could best communicate with the guards.

Hickey stopped the A-35 and put it in park. He barely opened the driver's side door and had his AR-15A3 tactical rifle ready in case he needed to jump out and take out the guards.

Gat got out and stretched, looking bored, as the two guards walked toward him, demanding to know what they wanted. Gat had a big knife on his hip, which he could have out in the time it takes a cobra to strike. If he needed to, he could take both guards out without a shot being fired.

The guards yelped in Arabic, demanding to know who they were.

"Supply trucks," the big African returned as an answer.

"Supply trucks never come at night," one guard protested.

"I do not know," Gat said, trying to look like the stupid hired truck driver he hoped they thought he was. "Ask him." Gat thumbed back over his shoulder toward Hickey.

Hickey laid the rifle aside and grabbed the weapon he needed now, a clipboard with the faked forms they had printed up in Cairo. He opened the truck door and stepped down onto the desert. He turned his left hip toward the approaching guards and thrust out the clipboard. With his right hand, he unsnapped his hip holster and got a grip on a .45 Colt automatic pistol. They had the guards right where they wanted them, between Hickey and Gat.

Back on the berm, Hargis saw that the two front-gate guards were more than covered. He moved his aim back to the guard standing in the tower. He still had his chest shot. He moved the rifle around, checking out the rest of the prison grounds. He saw a bright hot spot near the back end of the main building. That spot grew in intensity, then dropped back down. A man, leaning against the building, smoking a cigarette. Hargis locked the distance data into the rifle system.

One of the guards took the clipboard and looked at it. He couldn't read a word of English. He started talking to Hickey. Hickey let the guard ask his questions—at least he guessed they were questions—before looking over at Gat.

"What is he saying?" he asked the African.

"He asks who we are," Gat replied. "Why are we here."

"Tell them we're delivering supplies." Hickey started jamming his index finger against the list on the clipboard in the guard's hand. "Supplies!" he emphasized.

The guard barked something.

"He says you come back tomorrow," Gat told Hickey.

"No," Hickey said with a tired look on his face. He looked directly at the guard and started pointing. "You tell him"—Hickey's finger was almost in the guard's face—"you tell him that we've been driving all day. This food will rot soon, and I'm not having that happen."

Gat started translating, but Hickey cut him off.

"Come here." He grabbed the guard with the clipboard by his forearm. "This way." Hickey dragged the man behind the deuce and a half.

The other guard raised his rifle, followed, and started talking with animation. Gat was right behind him, hand on his knife handle. Hickey led the guard around behind the truck where he could not be seen from the compound. He released his grip on the man, grabbed a flashlight, and lit up the truck interior.

"Supplies," he emphasized again. Then he started moving the flashlight beam around, pointing at various boxes as he lifted some of their contents out. "Oranges . . . dates . . . lobsters . . . fish . . ." He held up a piece of Egyptian sun-dried fish.

"Fish?" The other guard moved over to look. He was almost behind the truck now.

"Yeah," Hickey continued, "whatever." He pointed at the list again. "We bring to the camp. You sign."

The guard with the clipboard was thinking about what to do. Deliveries never came at night. He had never dealt with them. He was sure that his direct superior and his next in command were asleep in the little office in front of the main one. He hated waking them up, but he was thinking he would have no choice now.

It was then that the second guard came fully around the back of the truck and grinned. He excitedly pointed to the back of the cargo truck and started yelling with happiness. Hickey moved the flashlight beam over until it shined on the hookah Hargis had bought.

"Hookah!" the second guard yelled excitedly before breaking into a fast string of words.

"Sure, kid, sure." Hickey smiled. "And these." He reached into a box and pulled out a bottle of Stiela beer. He let the men see it before he put it back into the box and pulled out a bottle of Wild Turkey 101. "Whiskey." Hickey grinned broadly.

He handed the first guard a bottle of whiskey. Quickly he grabbed another and forced it into the other guard's hand.

"For them." He looked at Gat. "Tell them those are for them."

Gat translated.

"For me?" the first guard asked Gat in Arabic.

"For you, my friend," the African said with a smile. "But we need to unload the rest or else some of the food will go bad."

Suddenly the two guards were in agreement. Yes, these supplies must be unloaded now.

"You follow us," the main guard told Gat. "We'll open the gate."

Gat gave Hickey the good news in English. And like that, Custer's two trucks were inside the perimeter. The second guard ran back and closed the front gate and took his post again.

As Gat parked the APC with Custer atop it thirty meters from the front of the main building, the first guard hopped onto the M-35 and directed Hickey by pointing to the back area where the kitchen and storage were. Hickey just smiled and let the man lead him.

Once in the kitchen door area, Hickey backed the truck up and got out. As he met the guard at the back of the truck, Hickey folded his fingers at the joints and hit the man in the throat. Choking, the man never knew why this stranger grabbed him and slammed his head against the back of the truck again and again until he was knocked out.

Hickey got the man out cold before clicking the disposable plastic handcuffs on the guard's wrists and ankles and tightening them down. Then he duct-taped around those and over the guard's mouth. Hickey dragged the man to the passenger side of the truck and tossed him up into it.

With the man out of commission, Hickey grabbed his webbing and strapped it on before taking his AR-15A3 and getting ready to go into the building. He slid the bolt back, making sure a shiny, new brass round was waiting in the chamber. Checking his watch he saw it was 0352.

Everyone was in place with eight minutes to spare. The clock was ticking.

AT ONE MINUTE TO 0400 Hargis stopped looking at his watch. He started taking deep, controlled breaths and focused through his scope aimed square on the tower guard's chest. The cigarette smoker was gone, and Hargis would look for him again after taking the guard out.

He didn't have to check his watch with twenty seconds to go when he took a long breath, slowly exhaled half of it, and waited for his shot. He squeezed the trigger on the CheyTac exactly at 0400 and saw the guard's chest take the round. The man slid down inside the tower, dead.

As soon as he heard that shot, Kam let loose a short burst into the head of the sleeping guard in the other tower. Then he tossed a frag up there, ducked just in case, and knew that guard was also gone. He ran to the detonator for the Semtex now.

Closing his eyes so as not to ruin his night vision, he quickly ran over and jammed the handle down on the detonator and heard the explosion under the radio tower. The bright flash over, he opened his eyes and watched the tall metal structure crumble and fall to the earth.

As Kam's bullets were hitting the guard, Winkler started setting off the claymores as fast as he could. Their flashes lit the night up, and their sounds let everyone know the attack was truly on. Once those were set off, he and Kam ran down each side of the building dumping frags and stun grenades in through the now shattered windows. By the time the two invaders met, there wasn't a square inch of the interior that hadn't been affected.

Most of the sleeping guards in the room never got out of their bunks. Those not outright killed were seriously wounded. What the claymore steel balls and frag grenades hadn't bloodied, the stun grenades knocked senseless.

Somehow three men were up and stumbling around as Winkler and Kam burst through the door. Winkler, covering the right side, had one man coming at him. It was probably unintentional. The man's brain was most likely still in a stun-grenade-induced frenzy and he was just moving around. Winkler didn't care. He cut the man down with a solid burst through his chest.

The big Russian had two moving men on the left side. One of those had even managed to grab a pistol but couldn't see where to shoot. With his night-vision goggles, Kam could see what he needed to. He fired a short burst into one man, pivoted, and finished off the other one.

The rest of the wounded men were more than willing to let the two strangers who burst into the room move them outside by gunpoint. If they were too wounded to walk, their comrades grabbed them and took them out. By 0415 the barracks were empty of living men. Only eight steel- or lead-shredded bodies remained inside.

There were fourteen prisoners led outside. These were trussed up with plastic handcuffs, then made to sit on the ground in a line against the outside front wall. Winkler left six men uncuffed, four seriously wounded and two to tend to them. None of this group would cause any problem during the rest of the raid. It was Kam's job to watch over them and make sure they all stayed in place until the rest of the team called him over. If something went wrong, he was to shoot the uncuffed men and run over to assist the main assault.

Winkler headed to the main building to assist in the interior assault.

In front of the main building, Gat, his shotgun looking harmless hanging from his hand, had moved in to face the lone guard at the gate, slowly inching closer with each minute approaching 0400. When the explosions started, the shotgun was up and three rounds went into the guard before he could turn around—00 buckshot, slug, and 00 buckshot. The guard was ripped open. Gat ran over and made sure the man was dead before heading back toward the APC.

Custer started his attack with the MK-19 40mm grenade launcher. With a practical firing rate of sixty rounds per minute and a seeming endless supply of rounds being belt-fed, the wheelchair warrior sent round after round into the front of the building. Using the M-430 grenade, he had a five-meter kill zone and a fifteen-meter wound radius with each round. With the ability to penetrate up to two inches of steel on a direct hit, the 40mm rounds cut through the front of the structure.

The two main entrance guards died quickly.

Custer just kept sending rounds in through the front windows and door after he had blown it open. Custer watched as the right side of the front of the building collapsed under the assault.

One of the sleeping guards inside the front area never woke up again. The second had a few more minutes to live.

Van Zandt had also been waiting for the first explosions. As soon as they started, he began throwing frag and stun grenades through the back windows of Kramer's building. Again, by the time he had moved up front and added more through the front windows, no section of the inside was unaffected.

When Van Zandt entered the structure, he found the only person in that building wounded and deaf. It was Major Hataway. Van Zandt flipped him over, plastic-handcuffed his ankles and feet to each other, and left him trussed up like a pig waiting for slaughter.

Then Van Zandt headed for the main building.

Hargis moved his scope all over the camp. His vigilance paid off when one man came running toward the front of the prison to see what was happening. Hargis led him and fired right as he was reaching the front corner. The man fell onto his back. Hargis put two more rounds into the already dead body just to make sure.

When he found no new targets of opportunity, he knew that it all seemed to be going by their plan. Still he kept watching until it was time for him to roll the APC onto the prison grounds.

Hickey started his assault by moving into the kitchen through the back door. No one was in there. The staff didn't start cooking until 0500. He waited until he heard that Custer's grenades had ceased before moving into the front area of the building.

As he carefully opened the door and peered in, he saw two guards standing in the long hall starting toward the front of the building. They were jabbering at each other asking the same questions. Hickey opened the door, stepped through, carefully aimed, and swept the hall with a full clip. Both men went down fast and dead. He reloaded.

Next Hickey checked the generator and storage rooms. Both were empty. He began walking up the hall toward the front of the building. He saw no one to oppose him. He saw only the locked cell doors with prisoners behind them.

Those men were awake now, and some were demanding to know what the noise was. Hickey blocked those voices out.

Then he heard new sounds. Men were running up the stairs from the downstairs area, their heavy footfalls announcing them. Hickey was standing behind that stairwell entrance as Kong and Omar came up from underground, their backs to him. Hickey saw their uniforms and knew they were guards. He didn't hesitate.

Hickey emptied another clip into the backs of both men as they approached the top of the stairs. They never knew what hit them. As he reloaded again, he stared down and saw no movement save their blood flowing down the stair steps. He went and made sure they were dead before he continued toward the front of the building.

He checked each cell on the way up front, making sure they were locked and no threats could emerge from inside them. They were only filled with prisoners anyway.

As he approached the back side of the door that led to the former front guard room—the door slightly askew from Custer's grenades—the smoke grew thicker. The upper floor was cleared. Hickey went back toward the stairs going down and waited to see if any more guards came up before the other team members joined him.

The other sleeping guard somehow escaped instant death from the 40 mm grenades. He was wounded, but somehow he managed to grab an AK-47 and stumble out of the front door of the main building. His clothes were in tatters, his face blackened, and he was bleeding from wounds.

Custer didn't think, he just fired a long burst from the M-60 into the man as he came out the door. The guard flopped and fell down for his final rest.

There was no other enemy not killed or incapacitated on the ground-level area. Custer's men had taken them all out as planned.

After the deafening roar of battle, the fields of fire grew suddenly silent. The main assault was over. Every man was still tense and alert, adrenaline pumping, fingers on deadly triggers, each man moving in toward the main complex.

Winkler and Gat moved to the front of the building, and Van Zandt to the rear, where he was to hook up with Hickey. Custer stayed perched in his APC on the M-60 waiting to handle any covering fire if needed. Hargis got down and carefully stored his rifle before driving the second APC into the camp.

Van Zandt made it to the kitchen and started moving through to find Hickey. As he opened the door leading into the main prison section, he saw Hickey pointing his rifle at him. Hickey saw him, too, and they raised their weapons to safety.

"Hall is clear," Hickey flatly stated.

Winkler and Gat had let most of the smoke clear out before they opened the front door of the main building. It didn't take much effort. Once pulled, the door just fell off onto the ground. The room they entered was in shambles. They saw the body of the one guard but no other bodies. They located the keys to the cells before opening the door that led into the main top-floor area.

They were met by the sight of Hickey and Van Zandt pointing their rifles at them. Again, once they recognized each other, all brought their weapons to port and gathered at the top of the stairwell leading down.

"The hall is clear," Hickey said. "Anyone hurt?"

"A hundred percent here," Winkler replied.

"Good," Gat responded.

"I'm fine," said Van Zandt.

"And outside?" Hickey asked.

"As planned," Van Zandt stated.

"Then let's find Simpson," Hickey said.

Each man took two stun grenades and pulled the pins before tossing them down the stairs. When those had gone off, they rushed down the stairs. As the smoke cleared, they saw a well-lit hall with a few cell doors and the bright-white-lit room at the end where Kramer and Simpson were. Again, they checked the few cell doors down there to make sure no surprises would pop out.

They were walking single file, Van Zandt in the lead, when Kramer came rushing out of the room, a Beretta 9mm pistol gripped in both hands. Kramer was no military man, but he knew how to fire a pistol. In his rage he just centered at the first man he saw.

They all watched as Van Zandt took the bullets for the team. He actually stood there and made sure he could be the only target. By force of will he stood rocklike absorbing the attack until Kramer's gun clicked empty. Then Van Zandt collapsed.

Hickey rushed past the fallen man and slammed the butt of his rifle into Kramer's nose, breaking it and sending the torturer down and out. He kicked the pistol out of Kramer's hand and away before turning toward the open door before them.

Winkler went to the wounded man's side, checking the damage.

"How bad?" Hickey asked.

"Bad enough," Winkler responded. "He took at least four directly in the chest."

"Do what you can," Hickey ordered. Winkler was the team's best medical man. "Gat, follow me."

The African didn't waste words. He just followed.

Hickey threw another stun grenade into the room before rushing in, Gat behind him. As the smoke cleared, he saw Jim Simpson strapped to the machine. They quickly recovered from seeing the naked, bruised, and bleeding man and unstrapped him.

Jim Simpson slid to the floor once released. Hickey quickly got the rubber mouthpiece out. He gave Simpson a little water from his canteen, which was happily swallowed.

"Jim Simpson," Hickey told him, "we're here to free you. Your father sent us."

Simpson looked up through his tired eyes. "I know, and thank God," he replied in a croak.

"Medic!" Hickey screamed down the hall. "Winkler, get in here now. Wounded man."

Simpson was the purpose of the operation. Simpson was the reason they were there. Hickey cradled Simpson until Winkler rushed in to examine the wounded man.

"How's Van Zandt?" Hickey asked.

"Still breathing. Barely," Winkler said. "Don't ask me how, but he is. Nothing else I can do for him now."

"How's he?" Hickey asked, looking at Simpson.

"Not bad," Winkler replied. "Looks worse than he is, I suspect. He won't die of bruises and a few open cuts."

"Let's get them upstairs," Hickey ordered. "Kam, you take Van Zandt."

The Russian rushed off, and Hickey and Winkler lifted Simpson up and helped him walk out of the room. Away from the machine.

As they got into the hall, Simpson saw Kramer lying there. He dragged himself to a halt.

"He dead?" Simpson weakly asked.

"Not yet," Hickey replied. "I knocked him out."

"Good." Jim Simpson truly smiled for the first time in a long time. "Let me go."

"We've got to get—" Hickey started.

"Let me go!" Simpson commanded, suddenly standing with renewed energy.

They released him. Jim Simpson calmly walked over to where Kramer was and bent down and slapped him. There was no reaction.

"Get him in there." Simpson pointed to the final room.

"Look, Simpson," Hickey pleaded, "we are here to free you. We did that. We have to get going. Now!"

Jim Simpson paused a moment before answering. His bearing became beyond firm. He straightened himself up and faced Hickey. Even naked, bleeding and bruised, he spoke with authority.

"You can try to stop me," the former prisoner said. "You'll have to kill me before I leave here without taking care of him," Simpson said with disgust.

Now Hickey thought.

"Come on, Winkler," he finally said, "let's get this done and done fast."

The two men dragged Kramer back into the room, and under Simpson's instructions they strapped him onto the machine. Simpson connected the electric leads and turned them to make sure they worked. He saw Kramer's body move involuntarily. He turned and faced Winkler.

"You have any ammonia?" he asked Winkler.

Winkler dug a little glass vial out of his field medic pack and handed it over. Jim Simpson slapped Kramer's face back and forth a couple of times, then broke the ammonia vial under the torturer's nose. Simpson slapped some more until Kramer came to.

"Hello, asshole." Simpson smiled at the torturer.

"Who are you people?" Kramer asked, looking over to Hickey.

"Friends of Jim Simpson," Hickey responded.

"Forget them," Simpson told Kramer. "Think about me now. First I'm going to tell you what you wanted to know."

Simpson bent over and whispered into Kramer's ear so that only he could hear. Kramer's eyes grew wide with surprise.

"No!" Kramer exclaimed.

"Yes." Simpson smiled. "That's my secret to the money."

Simpson let it sink in for a few seconds.

"Now good-bye," Simpson said as he turned the knobs up as high as they went. He walked with a new energy now, a new life force.

They left the torturer on his own hell-machine as they walked out of the room. Manuel Kramer's body twitched and jumped under the restraints. His flesh absorbed far higher levels of electricity then any human body can withstand.

Jim Simpson didn't look back as he left the room. Kramer's screams lasted almost until they were at the staircase leading to the upper floor.

CHAPTER 33

Each PW has the right to exercise his religious duties,

to engage in educational and recreational pursuits,

and to take physical exercise.

—FM 21-78 Prisoner-of-War Resistance, December 1981

THEY GOT SIMPSON OUTSIDE AND INTO the back of Custer's APC. Van Zandt was already lying inside the vehicle. Gat was sent in to find Simpson some clothes. Winkler hopped in and began examining Simpson. Custer lowered the pneumatic seat and turned to face the man they had been sent to free.

"Jim, how are you?" Custer asked.

Simpson looked up and smiled. "Fred . . . Fred . . . I'm sorry, I cannot remember your last name."

"Custer," he was told. "It's OK. No problem. Your dad sent us. How are you feeling?"

"Thanks for coming," Simpson said. "I'm feeling better every minute. And what's not is nothing some of my mom's homemade chicken soup can't cure."

"Winkler, what do you say?" Custer asked.

"He's good for travel. Not that we have any choice," Winkler said. "I'll do what I can. Pump that plasma we brought into him. He could use a bag or two of blood, I suspect. A real doctor looking over him. But he's good to go." Winkler looked over to Van Zandt. "Now let me look at him."

"No." Custer was suddenly forceful. "He'll be all right. Trust me."

Hickey, Winkler, and Hargis just looked at their team leader, not believing what they were hearing. The man had taken four or five to the chest.

"Trust me." Custer was firm but reassuring. "Now, let's finish up and get the hell away from here."

Not understanding but knowing orders when they were given, the team members did as told.

They had discussed different possibilities before the operation. Now that they had taken the enemy out, Custer decided on what to do. They had Simpson and the team all together. That was their main objective. With total control of the camp, they could worry about the other prisoners now.

Gat returned with the clothes.

"Gat, go help Kam get those guards over here against the front-gate wire," Custer commanded. "Winkler, patch their wounded as you can. If there's no hope there's no hope. We're not the Red Cross. Hickey and Hargis, go get the other prisoners out of their cells and assembled up here. I want to be out of here in thirty minutes."

The men ran off. Custer looked over at Van Zandt.

"You back yet?" he asked the should-have-been-dead man. No response. "Not yet."

He turned and faced Simpson.

"Jim," he explained, "we're going to bug out of here as quick as we can. There should be no reaction force to interfere with us. If all goes well, we head to the coast, get picked up, and get you to a real hospital."

"And if something goes wrong?" Simpson asked as he slowly worked his way into the clothes.

"That we play by ear," Custer said, "but we're packing enough hardware to take on anything we should meet."

"Can we contact my wife? My son and parents?" Simpson asked.

"Soon," Custer replied.

Kam and Gat had the captured guards over by the front fence now.

"Gat," Custer yelled, "go help them with the inmates. I imagine some of them don't speak English."

The African ran off into the building. Winkler did what he could for the wounded guards. Some might make it, but a couple of them probably wouldn't.

Soon the prisoners of the Death Factory were filing out onto the main area. In ones or twos they came out, following Hickey's or Gat's orders, until they were all gathered in front of Custer's APC. There were twenty-seven of them. Custer sent his chair back up through the open hatch again and faced these men.

What he saw was horrible. Some could barely walk. Most were malnourished and carried the scars and bruises of their treatment here. Custer wanted to see them all to safety, but he knew he couldn't.

"Who speaks English?" he asked. "Raise your hands."

Seven arms rose into the air. Two Iraqis, three Afghans, and, to the surprise of all, two Americans. Custer addressed them first.

"You Americans," he said, "step forward."

The two men took a couple of steps toward Custer.

"What are your names?" Custer asked them.

"Mike Sumbera," the thin one in glasses answered.

"I'm Dwight Brown," the stocky other man replied.

"What are you two doing here?" Hickey asked.

"We were part of a human rights watch group in Afghanistan," Sumbera answered for the pair. "A village elder sold us to the CIA as helping the Taliban. He didn't like what we were reporting back."

"Are you Taliban supporters?" Custer asked.

"No, sir," Brown answered. "We were there to do a job. An important job. But we feel the same way about the enemies of the United States as anyone else back home."

"These people," Hickey asked, "and the CIA didn't check you out? They just bought the story?"

"They never asked," Sumbera replied. "They just sent us here, and here we got the rod first without any questions."

"Hargis, hand me my backpack," Custer ordered.

Hargis found it and handed it up to Custer. He began digging through it. First, he tossed them a pad and pen.

"Give me the names and phone numbers of anyone you want called back home," he said. "We'll call them when we can, tell them you are alive and moving toward Cairo. We can't take you with us. We need to travel fast. But we can give you a chance. Come around to the back of the APC here."

Both newly freed men did as ordered. Custer lowered the seat again and turned and faced them through the back door of the APC. He dug into the backpack some more. He handed a couple of fat rolls of cash to them. They wrote what they needed to on the pad and handed it back.

"I'm putting you two in charge," Custer told them. "If you think you can handle it."

The two men looked at each other.

"To get out of here," Sumbera said, "we'll handle it."

"Good." Custer smiled. "One of those rolls is American dollars. The other is euros. There's about five thousand dollars in each roll.

Use it carefully. Don't let the others know you have it. There's a big truck in the back of the building. Find someone in your gang that can drive it or figure out how yourselves."

The two Americans stood listening, absorbing it all.

"There's a map in the truck," Custer continued. "Take Gat to the truck and he'll show you your best chances on driving out of here. We'll take you as far as the main highway north. There's a couple of rifles in the truck. Try not to use them unless you have to. Find one of the other English speakers who also speaks Arabic and make him your right-hand man."

The pair took in what they were told but still felt as if they were waking from living the nightmare of the Death Factory.

"There's food and plenty of water in the truck," Custer went on. "Sorry, guys, I can't help you more, but that's what I can do for you."

"That's more than enough," Dwight Brown said. He put his hand out. "Your name?"

"Custer." He bent forward to shake the hand. "Fred Custer. Vero Beach, Florida. You call me up when you get out of here and are safe. I'm in the book. If I don't hear from you within thirty days I'll do what I can. For the whole bunch."

"We can't thank you enough," Brown said, shaking and shaking Custer's hand.

"Just get back to the land of milk and honey and I'll be happy," Custer said. "Gat!" he yelled.

The African soldier was there in a flash.

"Tell the ones who speak Arabic or any other language you know that these two are in charge," Custer ordered. "Find any ex-military men and give the best-qualified ones the rifles in the deuce. Tell them what's going on and wish them luck. But do it fast and get back here. We're almost ready to roll."

"Yes, sir." Gat saluted before taking off.

With that covered as best as he could, Custer concentrated on the guards and the Death Factory itself. It was almost 0600 now, and he knew their time was limited. He wanted to be gone as quickly as possible. He thought that no one from the prison had gotten a message out, but one never knows such things. Custer wanted to get out and get going.

"Kam, Winkler," he called.

The two men soon appeared.

"How quick can you two get the rest of our Semtex set to blow?" he asked.

The two looked at each other.

"Pretty quick, chief," Winkler replied.

"Good." Custer smiled. "Spread it around and set it to go off at oh eight hundred. I want this place leveled. Do we have enough?"

"We'll do what we can," Winkler replied.

"Enough to do a lot of damage," Kam added.

"If I had the salt and the time, I would make these guards plow salt into the ground," Custer added. "OK, get going. You have thirty minutes."

"Hargis, Hickey," he barked. "Get our prisoners outside the fence and safely away from the blast area. Uncuff whoever you need to carry their wounded, then recuff them. As we're leaving give them a pair of wire cutters. They'll eventually free themselves, but we'll be long gone. And we'll leave them some water but nothing else. Someone will eventually be around and find them."

Hickey looked over at the Egyptian guards. "One almost just wants to kill them for what they did," he said.

"Yeah," Custer agreed. "But we never were that type of soldiers, were we, Hickey?"

"No, sir," Hickey said. "No, sir, we aren't that type." Hickey and Hargis went to get the prisoners moving.

Gat and the two Americans came around the main building in the M-35, and the victims of the Death Factory started falling in and loading onto the truck. Like the two Americans, they would do what was needed to get away.

"You know, there probably are some real al Qaeda or Taliban

in that bunch," Fred Custer thought aloud, looking at the group. "But that's no way to treat them."

Hickey and Hargis were quickly back. Kam and Winkler took a few minutes longer, but they were both done under their thirty-minute limit. Winkler brought their final unresolved problem with him.

"Look what I found." Smiling, he dragged Major Hataway along to Custer's APC. They all recognized the major from a PIS Web site photo they had looked at while building their intel.

"Major Hataway," Custer said pleasantly, "how nice of you to join us."

"Who the hell are you?" Hataway demanded to know.

"People you wish you had never met," Hickey told him.

"Load him in an APC," Custer said. "We're taking him with us."

Custer looked around, making sure he had done everything he wanted to. He could think of nothing else. It was time to move. He slammed his open palm atop the APC again.

"Mount up, boys!" he yelled. "Mount up! We're Oscar Mike!"

Hickey looked up at his commander.

"So you watched that *Generation Kill* show," he stated.

"Oh yeah." Custer smiled. "Damn good stuff."

The team quickly piled in and turned the APCs around, heading away from the Death Factory. They had told the newly freed men to follow them as far as the main highway, then to cut north. That was their best chance. Get back to Cairo, dump the truck, and get out of Egypt by hook or by crook. They even told them about Tee and said to look him up and tell him who sent them.

As they rolled away Winkler jumped out, ran to the cuffed Egyptians, and threw a pair of wire cutters at one of them.

"More than you deserve," he told them, not caring if they understood. He ran and jumped up through the open back door of an APC, then slammed it shut.

Dawn was breaking as they drove away. They were well back

to the main highway when all of the Semtex went off, bringing the Death Factory down upon itself. Kramer was buried under his own sins.

Through their satellites, the NSA definitely noticed the large black cloud of smoke rising from deep within the Egyptian desert. It was still night back in their Virginia headquarters, but they were a 24/7 operation.

Within an hour they knew exactly what was burning. Within two hours the higher-ups were being woken early with the news. Starred generals, striped admirals, and the top intelligence men who wore suits all across D.C. and Virginia were rushing in to see what had happened. Even the president would hear the news in his morning intelligence briefing.

Inquiries were made. Field men were sent out, but the Americans had let much of their field intelligence abilities go soft over the previous thirty years. In time, they would ask the Israelis if they knew anything.

The Israelis would put together a pretty good guess as to who had done it. They thought they knew. They at least had pictures of the men. But they didn't share that intel. Not yet. The time wasn't right. No one knew when a fruit of intelligence was ripe and how to best pick and sell it better than the Israelis.

ONCE ON THE MAIN HIGHWAY and with the deuce and a half running north, Custer and his team moved quickly away from the vicinity of the Death Factory.

As they drove they hooked up one of their satellite phones and handed it to Gat. The African called his fellow Nuer tribesmen. They confirmed that all was in place.

For a little more money the Nuer were more than willing to send a boat out and rendezvous with Custer's team at a remote spot on the Egyptian coast. All the team had to do was get to the coast by night. There, Zodiac boats would ferry the team out to the sixty-foot fishing boat the Nuer were using for the operation. On board were a doctor and a nurse with more than what they needed to treat Simpson.

From Egypt the boat would take them across the Red Sea to the busy port of Jeddah, Saudi Arabia. With their military garb dumped into the ocean, in civilian clothes with Canadian passports they should have no problem getting from there to anywhere they wanted.

The Nuer boat had to ship out of Kenya, as there was no friendly coastline closer, but they had left three days before they needed to be on-site.

The team tended to Simpson as best they could. He was getting stronger with each minute. He demanded to call his wife, son, and parents. Geri and the women and boy were located via their cell phone and woken up half a world away. They were happy to be awakened by the call. The good news was spread.

When he talked to his mother and father, Jim Simpson heard the tears in the man's voice. He had never seen his father cry. He understood, though, as his tears began to flow.

Everyone made their arrangements. They would all meet Jim Simpson at a private Swiss clinic where he would be fully checked out.

"Won't the general miss you?" Jim asked his father about his boss.

"Son," Charles Simpson replied, "I'll resign if I have to."

The two-APC convoy rolled across southern Egypt with no problems. They were waiting on the coast at midnight when they saw a flashlight beam flicker across the water. They answered it with three flashes. As the Zodiac boats came to get them, the Americans said their good-byes to Gat and Kam.

The odd black-and-white pair wouldn't be going to Saudi Arabia. Part of the Nuers' payment was the two APCs and any arms and ammo left over. Other tribesmen coming in from the fishing ship would join Gat and Kam to drive the vehicles back to Southern Sudan. Such top-grade military hardware was what the mostly Christian Southern Sudanese needed to keep the militant northern Muslims in check. With the APCs and the cash the tribe was getting, they could well improve their defenses in their fight for survival.

The only weapon the Nuer wouldn't keep was the CheyTac rifle.

"Now you be sure to get that back to me," Hargis told Gat. "You have my address. I like that rifle. I'll pay what it takes."

"No problem." Gat laughed.

They all shook hands and thanked one another as they parted. Custer promised to wire their final payments to Gat's and Kam's bank accounts as soon as he could. He would make sure both men knew how to get in touch with him if they needed to.

"I know you will." The big African smiled as he bent down, wrapped his arms around Custer, and hugged him. "I know you will, my friends."

"He calls few friend," Kam noted.

"How can I get in touch with you two if I need to?" Custer asked them.

"Wherever the lead is flying hot." The Russian smiled.

"Or through our bankers," Gat answered more practically.

After everyone was loaded onto the Zodiacs, the Americans gave a final wave to the Russian and Gat as they slipped away on the water. As they hit one wave, Van Zandt was heard groaning. Custer looked over.

"Told you he would be OK," he said.

Once they were safely on the fishing boat and out of Egyptian territorial waters, Hargis looked back.

"Damn," he said.

"What's wrong?" Hickey asked.

"I left my hookah on that deuce and a half," the Texan noted.

* * *

WITHIN A WEEK JIM SIMPSON was in that private clinic in Switzerland under the name on a fake Canadian passport. He was well into recovering physically when his wife, son, father, and mother arrived to see him. There were tears and hugs and love in his room. He would rely on that love to deal with the mental scars. Time would heal those, save a rare nightmare.

Custer and his team members stayed away, letting the family greet each other. They waited a day before they sat down with Jim's family for a long dinner in a good, family-run restaurant. They had a private room to celebrate in.

The next day Custer and his men would return to the USA, leaving the Simpson family to celebrate as they wished. The mysterious Van Zandt had fully recovered as if he had never been hit by bullets. He was missing from the dinner. He hadn't left with the team from Saudi Arabia. He was on a final mission for the team.

"I can't thank you enough," Charles Simpson told Custer after he wheeled him outside where the two men could smoke their cigars.

"Wait till you see my bill," Custer joked, flicking his old 82nd Airborne lighter to life. He lit his cigar. "Seriously, Charles, I am glad it worked out."

"So am I, Fred," Charles returned. "So am I."

"So now what will you do?" Custer asked.

"I think I've spent enough time in uniform," Charles answered. "Nora has more than hinted that I should retire. She's right, I think. I see that now. We'll spend more time out west with Jim and his family."

"Good place to be, Charles," Custer noted.

"And at some point Nora and I will get to Vero Beach," Simpson stated.

"Yep, we couldn't last without the women." Custer smiled. "You and Nora are welcome anytime."

The two old warriors lapsed into silence, smoking their cigars and staring into the night. Just as they had done when this had all begun.

Two old dragons seeing if they still had a fiery breath.

CHAPTER 34

A hostile and antagonistic source is most difficult to interrogate.

—FM 34-52 Intelligence Interrogation, May 1987

JIM SIMPSON ROSE EARLY. HIS SLEEPING habits had changed since being held captive. Careful not to wake his wife, he sat up and paused, feeling a twinge of pain in his knee. Taking his walking cane in hand, he stood and turned, looking back at the bed. In the morning light he stared down at his wife, thinking how lucky a man he was.

He hobbled his way through the expensive double business suite at the expensive Swissotel Zurich where his banker had placed him and his family. He hadn't asked for such luxury. In fact, when he saw the lavish rooms he had called the man, stating that such a room was not necessary. Simpson wasn't used to hotel suites that cost eight hundred dollars a night. Even though the banker had insisted on paying the bill, Simpson was hesitant.

Herr Gasser, his bank officer, demurred, overcoming any objections by Simpson. In fact, the suite he would have usually booked was already taken for the days of his client's business stay. Clients with over $330 million on account are not to be treated lightly nor without manners. The cost of the luxury hotel room for his clients was not even a consideration to the bank officer.

Simpson limped down the hall and opened the door, checking on his son, Alex. Sound asleep the boy looked comfortable enough. When they woke up, his wife and son could explore Zurich as they wished while Jim handled his business with the bank. The hotel had access to the excellent Swiss public transportation systems at its doors. From there Jan and Alex Simpson could explore the famous Bahnhofstrasse, museums, art galleries, or even a medieval Old Town close to the center of world banking.

Simpson found the coffeepot and brought it to life. The fresh scent of good coffee filled his nose as he opened the packet and poured it into the machine and waited for it to brew. While the strong aroma filled the room, he went over and opened the curtains on the large windows giving him a view of the city and hills surrounding it as it slowly woke up.

Coffee in hand, he headed into the large bathroom. His knee still twitching—he would never recover full use of it—he decided on a long, hot bath as opposed to the showers he was used to taking. After drawing the bath, he stripped and sank into the warm water and relaxed as he finished his coffee. Contented, he fell into a light nap.

It was Jan who woke him up after she rose. Laughingly, she chased him out of the bathroom so that she could prepare herself for the day. The bathwater had gone cold anyway. They kissed as Jim left the tub and departed the bathroom, leaving Jan to her morning routine.

Slowly Simpson dressed in his only good suit, surprised at the time it took him to do so. It was a combination of his recovering from the long torture sessions, being out of danger, and being in such a luxurious room with his family that made him take his time. He just didn't feel in a hurry.

By the time he had finished, Jan was out of the bathroom and getting dressed. She and Alex would have breakfast later before exploring the city. They all decided to meet back at the hotel at noon, when they would head ten kilometers south of Zurich to the tiny hamlet of Küsnacht. In that small town was the famous Peter Mann's Kunststuben, and it was only open for lunch from noon until 2:00 P.M.

Downstairs Simpson had a light breakfast—he was never much of a breakfast man—of a croissant and another cup of wonderful coffee before he headed off to the bank. Waving away the doorman's offer to call him a taxi, Simpson decided to walk the short distance to the bank. He had gotten directions the night before. Cane in one hand, a small leather portfolio in the other, Jim Simpson set off in the warm Zurich morning.

Even though the bank was close to the hotel, Simpson almost didn't find it. He walked past it twice, once passing it, then again after turning around on the small street, which was off of the main thoroughfares of Zurich. Only after finding an address on the door next to the bank did he know he was close.

He walked up the three stone steps leading to the bank's thick oak door and found the bank name on a gold metal plate mounted into the stone around the door. That gold plate was no larger than a credit card. The bank was discreet, to say the least. There was a small button under the plate. Simpson pressed it. He didn't see the small camera lens mounted above his head. He was viewed and buzzed in, hearing the electronic sound of the lock clicking open after being released from inside.

Simpson opened the door and entered the bank. A conservative and very expensive interior welcomed him. Sitting behind an oak desk, dating back over two hundred years to the bank's founding, was a young woman who asked if she could help him. Jim Simpson announced himself, and the secretary smiled.

"Ah, Mr. Simpson, Herr Gasser is expecting you." She pointed to an expensive-looking lounge chair in the small lobby. "If you'll have a seat I'll notify him of your arrival."

Simpson sat while she announced the bank's very rich client to Gasser. After setting the phone down she again smiled, looking up at Simpson.

"Can I get you anything while you wait, Mr. Simpson? Coffee?"

"No, thank you." Simpson smiled back. "Maybe later, but thank you."

Gasser arrived downstairs ten minutes later. Clients with $330 million are not to be ignored. He warmly welcomed Simpson, and they shook hands. Gasser quickly ushered him upstairs into his private office. Both men sat down, the banker behind his desk and Simpson in one of the two thick Queen Anne leather chairs before the banker's desk.

"It is a pleasure to finally meet you, Mr. Simpson." The banker settled back in his leather chair, intertwining his fingers.

"The same here," Simpson replied.

"Coffee? Tea?" Courtesy demanded the offer.

"Nothing right now, but thank you," Simpson replied.

There was a brief silence between the men.

"So what may I do for you today, Mr. Simpson?" the banker asked.

"Please, it's Jim. Just call me Jim," Simpson replied.

"And I am Franz," the banker said. "Now, Jim, how may I be of assistance to you and your account?"

Jim pulled his portfolio onto his lap and unzipped the top. He rifled through the papers within and pulled a single sheet out and handed it over to the banker.

The banker's smile waned as he read the piece of paper. He leaned back into his chair and carefully reread the document, making sure that he understood the instructions completely.

It was a short, simple set of instructions. Herr Franz Gasser had never seen anything like it in his twenty-plus years of banking. He was quite sure that his father or even his grandfather, with eighty-four years of banking experience between them, had never seen such a document.

He read the document a third time before looking up at Jim Simpson.

"Mr. Simpson, are you sure about this?" Gasser asked.

"Quite positive, Herr Gasser," Simpson's voice came back with a firm, iron resolve in it. "I expect these instructions to be carried out before I leave Zurich."

Another pause settled between the men. The banker broke it.

"Mr. Simpson . . . Jim." He smiled, but not quite as sincerely as before. "We have never met, and the account associated with this document"—Gasser pointed to the now seemingly radioactive piece of paper—"has security protocols associated with it."

"Of course," Simpson replied. "I set them up myself."

"Yes." The banker seemed to be stalling, hoping for a way out. "Then you understand that I must request those protocols now. I must insist, actually. Not that I doubt you, but anyone could claim to be the Jim Simpson who opened this account."

In fact, the banker had zero doubt that the man before him was the rightful owner, thus controller, of the account sitting in his bank. The account with over $330 million dollars in it. Swiss bankers are not foolish people generally, and Herr Gasser certainly was not. After Simpson had sent the money to the little Swiss bank, the banker has hired the best private detective agency in Zurich to investigate him. He had seen Jim Simpson's photograph.

Within two weeks Gasser not only had photographs of Jim Simpson but every detail of his life which could be found, bought, or bribed on his newest client. All of this was professionally presented to the banker in a nice Moroccan leather binder. It was that binder that Gasser had reviewed before going to greet Simpson downstairs.

Gasser knew that the man sitting in his office was really Jim Simpson, but he was hoping for some way out of the instructions before him, which would send over $330 million out of his bank, out of his control. He had plans for that money while it was in his care. In fact, some of it was already invested elsewhere, and Gasser would have to pull those monies back, costing him investments and possibly even some penalties.

No, the instructions before him did not please the banker.

"I understand," Simpson replied.

He reached into his inside jacket pocket and removed his passport and handed it to the banker.

"I believe this is the first proof," Simpson stated before digging out his wallet. From that he produced a thin, flimsy card, well worn and even Scotch-taped along the edges. He handed that over to the banker. "And this is the second proof."

Gasser examined the passport and card. He had never seen one of the cards. Few on the planet had. He did not even know what one was until the detective agency report had come in. The card before him did indeed have everything the second proof of identity required.

The card dated back over twenty years. It was a membership card for the fan club of *Mystery Science Theater 3000,* an obscure American cable television show of the late 1980s and 1990s. While it did have a cult following, including Jim and his wife, Jan, few ever bothered to join the fan club, much less retain such an obscure piece of twentieth-century American pop culture memorabilia.

When Jim Simpson had set up the account with the Swiss bank, his instructions on proof of identify and thus the ability to access the account were quite clear. A passport and an *MST3K* fan club membership card were the first two steps. While the first could be gotten by forgery by anyone wishing to defraud the bank, the latter was virtually unknown and a very obscure reference.

"As proof I instructed that either myself or my wife present our passport and our membership card to the *Mystery Science Theater 3000* fan club," Simpson noted.

"Indeed you did, sir. Indeed you did," the banker replied. "And your complete set of instructions also included a third proof. Mr. Simpson, I need that third proof now." The informal "Jim" was gone.

"Certainly." Jim Simpson smiled. He sat up a bit straighter in the chair before beginning the third and final proof. He spoke in a clear, strong voice.

"Our Father, who art in heaven,
Hallowed be thy name.
Thy kingdom come,
Thy will be done,
On earth as it is in heaven.
Give us this day our daily bread.
And forgive us our trespasses,
As we forgive those who trespass against us.
And lead us not into temptation,
But deliver us from evil.
For thine is the kingdom, the power, and the glory,
forever and ever.
Amen."

Kramer had broken Jim Simpson. Twice under torture Simpson had revealed what the torturer had wanted to know. That was what Simpson had whispered into his torturer's ears that final night in the Death Factory.

Gasser, with all of his plans for using the $330-million-plus dollars in Jim Simpson's account, had all of the proofs required for full access to that account. He didn't like the instructions on the piece of paper that he had been handed, but being a good Swiss banker, he would carry them out. He would carry them out to the letter.

It would take time, he explained to Simpson, possibly as long as two business days. Simpson said that he understood and that when all the documents and the certified checks were prepared the banker could contact him at the hotel.

The banker affirmed this and smiled, now quite insincerely, as he led his client back to the bank's front door and watched him walk away. Herr Gasser thought about the $330 million that would soon leave his bank. His plans for the money had now gone up in smoke.

"I should have put him in the Hotel Montana," he mumbled to himself as he closed the oak door. The secretary heard more of his mumbles. "I should have put him in a youth hostel." Not even looking at her, the banker commanded, "Mrs. Schmidt, bring me a schnapps," as he headed back upstairs. "In fact, bring the bottle."

And it wasn't even noon yet.

CHAPTER 35

Make him understand his actions as a PW have as much international political impact as his performance in battle.

—FM 21-78 Prisoner-of-War Resistance, December 1981

TWO WEEKS LATER A BONDED COURIER walked through the halls of the Cannon House Office Building in Washington, D.C. He carried a metal briefcase, which was chained to his wrist. He was very well dressed. As well dressed as any top Washington lobbyist.

His suits were custom tailored in Zurich and cut of the finest cloth. He had flown from Zurich the day before. Not your usual courier, the man handled large bank transfers when they had to be done by hand. In his career he had handled the movement of billions of dollars in cash, gold, bearer bonds, and any other form in which money is transferred.

He had proven his honesty and integrity numerous times. He had never stolen anything in his life. Not even a piece of candy as a child. The man could be trusted. Because of all that, he demanded and got very high wages for his services.

Two not so expensively dressed men walked behind the man. They were from the D.C. area. Both were former Special Forces—one a SEAL and one a Delta Force—and both carried pistols in quick-draw holsters under their jackets. Both men knew how to use those pistols quite well. The weapons were as familiar to the pair as a baby's every sound is to its mother.

Their credentials got them through the security checkpoint still carrying their weapons. They were very good men at what they did. They were the best private security armed escorts to be found in D.C. They were there to protect the Swiss courier.

The three men went through the front office door of U.S. Representative Ron Paul of Texas.

A true Libertarian maverick in the usual D.C. political scene, Ron Paul was very tough on any matter dealing with the United States of America's money. No one was tougher or more honest than Ron Paul.

The courier walked up to the congressman's aide at the desk. The two armed men stood back and positioned themselves for any situation. An energetic Houstonian named Dan Workman looked up at the visitor and smiled.

"May I help you?" he asked.

"I am here to see Congressman Ron Paul," the courier said in his thickly accented English.

"Do you have an appointment?" Workman asked. Among his jobs was keeping those without appointments from stealing the precious time of his boss.

"I have an introductory letter," the courier stated, handing over his business card as well as a thick sheet of vellum paper on which Simpson's banker had written in his precise Swiss hand. "I believe the congressman will want to see me."

Workman sighed and started reading the letter. His eyes popped out. He looked up at the visitor.

"Are you serious?" Workman asked.

"I am always serious, young man," the courier stated.

"Can you wait a moment?" Workman asked, standing up from behind his desk. "I have to show this to Mr. Paul's personal assistant."

"I am prepared to wait for as long as is necessary," the courier said before turning and finding a chair. He sat, spine as erect as a steel rod, and rested the briefcase upon his lap.

He knew he wouldn't be waiting long. Not with what he carried and with what the letter said.

Dan Workman rushed to find Ron Paul's personal assistant, Harriet Seltzer.

It took less than three minutes for Seltzer and Workman to return to the front office. Harriet Seltzer reread the letter in front of the courier and checked his business card again before she spoke. She was precise and to the point.

"May I see inside that suitcase?" she asked.

"Certainly," the courier said. He took a key out and unlocked the steel case and opened the top, turning the case for the woman to see.

Harriet Seltzer thought she had seen it all in D.C. Now she knew she had.

"Mr. Paul is not in the office right now," she said.

"But he is in Washington?" the courier asked.

"Yes," came her reply. "He is over in a meeting at the Dirksen Building. It will take me a few moments to contact him."

"I will wait," came the cold Swiss reply. He knew the woman would also call his employer, Herr Gasser, before calling the congressman.

The courier and his guards had to wait less than an hour before being ushered into a back office conference room. Representative Ron Paul was waiting as they entered the room. He was going over the letter a third time. He had personally called the small Swiss banker Jim Simpson had chosen and confirmed what was going on.

Ron Paul loosened his tie and sat down.

"Well, gentlemen," the congressman intoned in his soft Texas drawl, "you are certainly the most interesting group I'll meet up with this year. Hell, this life!"

The courier remained stonelike.

"Come on," Paul continued, "sit down and let's see what you have there. You want a drink or anything? I'm not much of a drinking man these days, but you sure have me tempted."

The courier sat down and unlocked the handcuff that secured the briefcase to his wrist.

"Maybe some water?" he asked. "And if they want anything, please."

"Water it is." Paul slapped his palms down on the conference table. He looked up at the two guards. "Anything for you boys?"

"Water for us will be fine," the ex-SEAL said.

"Water it is, then." Paul looked up at Seltzer. "Harriet, think you can wrestle us up four waters?"

"Yes, sir," Harriet Seltzer said, leaving the room.

Ron Paul watched as the courier unlocked the briefcase again, opened the top, turned the case toward the congressman, and slid it across the table.

Ron Paul carefully pulled one of the slips of paper out and examined it as if he were holding unstable dynamite.

"Looks real enough," he said.

"They are quite genuine," the courier stated.

"As are their brothers and sisters," Paul added. "Do you realize the shit storm this will cause?"

The courier paused before answering.

"That is not my job, sir," he said. "I only make the deliveries. Now if you would please sign here." The courier pulled out three folded pieces of paper, opened them flat, and slid them toward the congressman. They were identical documents. One for the congressman, one for the banker, and one for the courier's private records.

Ron Paul thought for a moment before signing—before he took responsibility for the briefcase full of paper.

"Why not?" he finally said, grabbing his pen and scribbling his name across the bottom of each piece of paper. "In for a penny, in for a pound. Or should I say in for three hundred and thirty million."

The courier then took the three sheets, countersigned them, and returned one to the congressman.

"Thank you, sir." He rose. He bent forward, laying the briefcase keys on the table, and extended his hand.

Ron Paul stood and shook the man's hand.

"It has been a pleasure, sir," the courier stated. "You may keep the briefcase. Now if you'll excuse me, I can still make an early flight back to Zurich if I hurry."

"Enjoy the trip," Paul said. "And keep reading the funny papers, because this will sure be in them."

"These gentlemen are paid through at least tomorrow to protect those." The courier pointed at the contents of the briefcase. "They are at your full disposal."

The courier bowed and exited the room as Harriet Seltzer returned with the water.

"Well, get comfortable, boys," Paul told the two guards. "Because none of us are going anywhere until the Treasury boys get here."

What the courier had brought to Ron Paul was a briefcase full of certified bank checks. Three hundred and thirty of them each made out to the United States Treasury in the amount of one million dollars each.

When Jim Simpson had hatched his plan, he had never intended to keep a penny of the money. Not one red cent. He wanted it returned to those PIS had stolen it from, the United States government.

Ron Paul was the most honest congressman he could think of.

He hated burdening the man with the money, but he knew Ron Paul was the best shot he had. He had been correct in thinking that.

Paul would get the money back into the U.S. Treasury no matter what it took. He would see plenty of headline ink and TV time over this. Ron Paul would use the opportunity to advance his Libertarian ideas to a wider audience. Yes, Paul would use the money to get that exposure, but only after first making sure it went back where it belonged.

Jim Simpson almost sent back every penny in the account. But after his ordeal and the Death Factory he had changed his mind. The money he had transferred from PIS had acquired almost three million in interest in the time it sat in the Swiss bank. Simpson decided to keep that for services rendered.

He first insisted on repaying Custer every penny the operation to free him had cost. Custer, having a bank account well able to fund such an operation many times over, of course refused at first. But Simpson was more than insistent, and finally Custer allowed the young soldier to pay for everything.

Even after those expenses Simpson had over $1.8 million left in the Swiss bank. He would keep it there and let Herr Gasser massage it daily and sweep up the little pieces of interest off of the floor. The little pieces that only bankers know how to massage out and sweep up.

With the money Jim would keep his prison promises. He would never spend more than a night away from his wife or son again. He and Jan opened their little coffee shop and bookstore. It took almost three years before that business showed a profit.

Jim Simpson didn't mind. He didn't mind at all.

THE SAME DAY THAT RON Paul was signing for the money, Van Zandt was half a world away.

He had to utilize some dark contacts he knew within the CIA and elsewhere to do what he did. Van Zandt was one who understood dark and light. He knew that sometimes one could twist the darkness for the good, make it hurt itself.

It had taken him a lot of time to travel from Saudi Arabia to Afghanistan with his unwilling companion. They had been forced to use numerous nontraditional forms of travel to get where they were. But then, there are always men willing to do things for the right price. Van Zandt had the money, the connections, and the knowledge of how to bring them all together.

He was glad to finally be rid of his unwilling companion. The man just begged and cried and pleaded wherever they went. Most of their traveling was done through men who didn't speak English. In fact, most of that traveling was done through men who hated Americans.

But they liked Van Zandt. He wasn't American. There was something universal about the man. That and he paid well and didn't try to barter. Plus he spoke their languages.

So Van Zandt had no problem getting himself and his unwilling companion into Pakistan and across the Afghan border. He talked village Pashto to the elders. Most of the trip, his unwilling companion didn't understand a word being spoken. He didn't realize that Van Zandt was paying the Afghan village elder $5,000 in gold. Whatever the Americans would pay for the prisoner the elder could have also.

The unwilling companion didn't even realize where he was until he was turned over to CIA operatives in the remote hills between Pakistan and Afghanistan.

When he heard English again he was relieved. He thought he could explain what was happening to him, the injustice of it all, and get free. But everyone he tried talking to ignored him.

They ignored him even as he was led into a U.S.-run airbase. The two men, dressed completely in black with ski masks covering their faces, ignored him as they prepared him for his flight, as he was gagged and drugged.

He was well under the drugs' influence as he was loaded onto the Gulfstream jet with tail number N379P.

When he came out from under the effects of the drugs inside the walls of a CIA-run prison, no one there listened to his pleas either. Not even when he screamed from the torture.

Major Hataway screamed and protested the injustice until the end.